THE UNMAN / KOVRIGIN'S CHRONICLES

VADIM SHEFNER

THE UNMAN

*Translated from the Russian by Alice Stone Nakhimovsky
and Alexander Nakhimovsky*

KOVRIGIN'S CHRONICLES

Translated from the Russian by Antonina W. Bouis

Introduction by THEODORE STURGEON

Macmillan Publishing Co., Inc.
NEW YORK

Collier Macmillan Publishers
LONDON

Macmillan Publishing Co., Inc.
866 Third Avenue, New York, N.Y. 10022
Collier Macmillan Canada, Ltd.

Library of Congress Cataloging in Publication Data

Shefner, Vadim Sergeevich, 1915-
The unman / Vadim Shefner; [translated from the
Russian by Alice Stone Nakhimovsky and Alexander Na-
khimovsky]. Kovrigin's chronicles / Vadim Shefner;
[translated from the Russian by Antonina E. Bouis].

Translation of Chelovek s piat iu "ne" and Devush-
ka u obryva.
I. Shefner, Vadim Sergeevich, 1915-   Devushka
u obryva.   English.   1980.   II. Title.
PZ3.S54275Un   1980   [PG3476.S466]   891.73'42
ISBN 0-02-610060-6   79-27576

10 9 8 7 6 5 4 3 2 1

Designed by Jack Meserole

Printed in the United States of America

INTRODUCTION

He is unskillful, unintelligent, unoutstanding, unlucky, and unhandsome. He knows this because early in his life his father told him so. He believes everything that anyone tells him; apparently no one told him that his father was a pathological liar, and he just didn't pick up on the evidence. In naiveté he is Billy Budd multiplied by twelve, and the improbability of his adventures would fill the good soldier Schweik with disbelief. He calls himself Steve, and what, above all, will keep you reading his astonishing adventures is that very improbability. What on earth will he get into next?

This is a very funny story indeed, but it is a good deal more than a sequence of hilarities. A deft caricaturist, Shefner presents us time after time with people we all know, with their more abrasive qualities enlarged just enough to be joyful rather than irritating. There are the brother (a very archetype of pomposity), the purblind parents, the delightfully mad scientist who can cure all ills by having his patients drink an elixir (one drop per storey) and then jump out of skyscrapers. And there's the wonderful old lady chemist, with her stash of bottles treated with mysterious powders—bottles which, when filled with water and set in the sun, produce endless quantities of wine. And—but let Shefner amaze you.

The point has often been made that lasting literature and living literature—that which grows as the reader grows—is fable. Gulliver on the beach, tied down with ropes like threads by little people, is a great yarn for kids. Read it later, and it's a political cartoon of great poignancy. Still later, it becomes a multileveled explication of human foibles and foolishness, courage and resourcefulness. Shefner's marvelous story of his simpleton has few pretensions at being great literature, but it is unquestionably fable. It is the delightfully satisfying account of an impeccably honest man who is ridiculed, robbed, cheated, and mistreated, most of the time utterly unaware that evil is being done to him—and yet he wins out and lives to see all his dreams come true.

Kovrigin's Chronicles is quite something else. Its foreword, written by the publisher in the year 2301, describes the work as the "338th Jubilee Edition," a chronicle written by one Matvei Kovrigin (2102–2231), a literary historian who "was not a Writer by profession . . . [and] had no pretensions to literary fame." His subject is the biography and achievements of his lifelong friend Andrei Svetochev, ultimately honored as the greatest scientist in the history of mankind. "The book's style is archaic," says the foreword, "certainly not contemporary. As a specialist in 20th-century literature, the Author, unable to find his own creative style, imitates 20th-century writers, and not the first-class ones at that." This whole approach, which might seem purely an effort to fend off potential critics, is, I'm sure, an example of Shefner's irrepressible puckishness. He does indeed try to tell a dramatic tale, and to do it seriously; but, at the same time he skillfully delineates Kovrigin's limitations in Kovrigin's own words. Kovrigin's assiduous delving for 20th-century cusswords (awfully hard to come by, apparently, in the polite 22nd) and his amusing use of acronyms (explained in footnotes) are joyful examples of Shefner's love of language. All honors to the translator, who must have had a horrendous time wrestling out English equivalents to these acronymic monstrosities.

Shefner's prognistications are interesting indeed. The return of sailboats and horses into a 22nd-century high-technology culture is intriguing; and nowhere can one find a more ardent example of the Soviet worship, verging on idolatrous, of Science. There's a nice passage describing the day that money is abolished, and there's one image that quite took this reader's breath away. On a passenger dirigible is a swimming pool with a transparent dome and a transparent floor. Standing under the clouds, one may dive into the landscape thousands of feet below. . . .

Theodore Sturgeon

THE UNMAN

Introduction **1**

Let me pull myself together, literary-wise, and tell you, dear readers, the true story of my life. Certain facts of my biography may strike you as unbelievable, since even in this age of cosmonautics, electronics, and psychotherapy, they border on the fantastic. But to believe me or not is your problem. My problem is a different one: to relate what happened to me without embellishment and without evasion.

I will describe everything as it actually was, concealing only the last names of the dramatis personae so that some of them won't take on airs and others won't get offended. I will be silent about my own last name as well. My superiors and co-workers respect me now, and I am afraid that my life, which took off such a short time ago, will fall to pieces if they recognize me in the hero of this tale. Certain populated areas that come up in these recollections will also be renamed, as I don't want the inhabitants to bear a grudge.

I have no intention of concealing my first name. I am called Stefan, which in translation from the ancient Greek means "wreath," or "crowned with a wreath." In fact, however, I'm Stefan only in my passport. In real life everybody calls me Steve.

Homelife **2**

In calling me Stefan (i.e., wreath) they had in mind my future consolation. The reasoning went like this. When my older brother was born in the peaceful year of 1913, his healthy exterior and loud voice prompted my father to call him Victor, in other words, conqueror. My parents believed that he would go far and become a famous scientist, in which they were not mistaken. The signs at my own birth were a lot less auspicious: I entered the world at the height of World War I, in the leap year 1916. My parents quickly realized that nothing much would come of me. My father had been saving up the name Leonid, in other words, lionlike, but at birth no particular resemblance to a lion, neither moral nor physical, could be detected in me. I spent my time whining and being sick, and it wasn't at all certain that I would make it. For that reason my father decided to christen me Stefan. And so it was, although they had to bribe the priest over the letter *f*, since Stefan was a foreign name. My father's reasoning showed his great concern for me. If his younger son should die in infancy, he would not be departing as an ordinary person, but as one already crowned with a wreath. And if I did make it, then the name would comfort me in life's maelstroms and misfortunes. And at my funeral there would be no need to spend money on a wreath, since I would be one myself.

You may well ask yourselves how it was that during the First World War, when all the men were mobilized, my father sat in the rear and occupied himself with thinking up names for his son. The answer is that although he was physically and mentally in excellent condition, he had been born with a finger missing on his right hand. So they never called him up.

This minor defect did not prevent my father from working an abacus and giving out exact change. He served as a cashier in various small businesses—in our town, there weren't any big ones. Incidentally, I will give our town the following name: Greetica-Leaveittown—in token of the fact that it was here I first greeted life, and here that I hope to take my leave of it.

After the revolution, my father retained his profession, only now he worked for government enterprises and handled Soviet denominations instead of tsarist ones. For a while he worked in the accounting department of a curtain factory. Then he worked for a brewery, then he was unemployed for a while, and finally he set himself up at a flour mill. Alas, he could never stay anywhere for long, although he didn't drink, knew his business, and was scrupulously honest.

His problem was that he loved to talk about things that never were and never could be and got terribly angry when he was doubted. His specialty was hunting tales in which he played the main role, although everyone in Greetica-Leaveit-town knew that he had never held a shotgun, the more so as he was missing the very finger needed to pull the trigger. Father tormented his co-workers with his stories, making sceptics into personal enemies. He'd stop talking to them, look for errors in their work, and even complained to his superiors about them. The result was that the given department would soon be the scene of a many-sided scandal, the epicenter of which was Father himself. In the end, they would cease to have a need for his services. But they always gave him good references, since, I repeat, he was a fine worker.

Father liked to tell his hunting stories at home too. Mother, being totally under his influence, never made critical comments, and Victor always humored him with polite inquiries about what happened next. That's why Father adored Victor, and Mother, as usual, shared his opinion. Toward me Father was rather cold. He was offended because I didn't show any promise, and also because I loved truth.

One day I remember finding a copy of a prerevolutionary journal in the attic. By that time I already knew how to read, and I brought it down to my room. I was fascinated by the huge drawing, the size of a whole page, of a snowy field and a bear that had just been killed. Near the beast stood a few important-looking gentlemen in elaborate hunting gear. One of them was standing with his back to the viewers, looking, no doubt, at the bearskin and judging its quality. Beneath the picture was a title: "His Highness Prince Nicholas and his retinue at a bear hunt."

"Papa, how come everyone is looking at us except this one man?" I asked my father.

Father looked at the drawing and said softly:

"How fortunate I am that the artist drew the hunter that way. If he had drawn his face, then everyone would have recognized him, and he would have been arrested for his connection with the imperial family. Know, then: I was that man. And I was the one who killed the bear."

"You mean you killed the bear yourself?" I was astonished.

"I did indeed. I remember it well. The great prince himself invited me to the hunt, and I made the kill. Of course the prince got credit for it, but they called me to the Winter Palace, elected me to the Presidium, and gave me some material for a winter coat."

"Is it scary to hunt for bears?" I asked.

"No, I wasn't in the least bit frightened. I had my method. I would wait for a heavy snow and go to the lair on skis. Bravely, I'd poke my ski pole into the lair and wake the bear up. The bear would be too sleepy to figure out what was happening. He'd come out—and at that very moment my dog would jump him, so as to divert his attention from me. While that was going on I'd shoot. One well-aimed shot and the beast would fall, vanquished by the bullet of a brave hunter."

"But how did the dog walk in the snow? You were on skis, but the dog . . ."

"The dog had skis too. He got around perfectly in them."

"How many skis do you need for a dog, two or four?"

"Two," said Father. "Two are quite sufficient."

I had no doubts about the bear or the invitation to the palace, but the dog on skis put me on guard—and not right away either, but about two days later, when I had immersed myself in the problem. The worm of doubt had stolen into my childish consciousness, and in order to destroy it I decided to carry out an experiment on the family dog Rover. I tried to tie my skis to his paws. But Rover, who never barked at anyone and was very gentle, got so furious that he bit me. And when I told father about this experiment, he got mad.

"Bellyacher!" he shouted. "Skeptic! How dare you not believe me. Today you'll go without dessert."

Another time Father told us his method for hunting lynx. A lynx, as everyone knows, always throws itself on the victim's neck. Father would protect his neck with a towel, and above the towel he'd place some fine fishnet. Instead of a rifle he'd take a pistol. Then he'd go for a walk in the woods and stop under a tree. The lynx, seeing an unarmed man, an easy prey, would attack, catching its claws in the net. Then Father would take his pistol out of his pocket and hold it to the temple of the enraged beast. One shot, and the lynx would be no more.

He also had his way of hunting wolves. As soon as he'd hear that there was a wolf pack around, Father would set off with a rifle and a ladder. When he found the pack he would entice it out of the forest. The pack would run after him, expecting to tear him to pieces and devour him, but he would run out onto a field, quickly open the ladder, and climb up to the top. The wolves would crowd around the bottom and try to reach him, but he'd beat them back one by one until the whole pack was felled by the fatal bullet.

At first I would believe these stories, but two or three days later I would begin to doubt. And a few days after that I would understand that it was a lie. Then I would tell Father, and he would get mad. And Mother would get mad at me for getting Father mad. She always made an example out of Victor, who never contradicted his parents.

In general, all hopes were focused on Victor, and I—as Father put it one day—was a boy with five uns. To prove his point he took a piece of paper, making it a matter of record that I was

$$un \left\{ \begin{array}{l} \text{skillful} \\ \text{intelligent} \\ \text{outstanding} \\ \text{lucky} \\ \text{handsome} \end{array} \right.$$

The saddest part was that all five uns were quite fitting, and I understood that for me there was no chance for great success and achievement in life. I didn't try to become a scientist, like Victor, and I didn't make any big plans. I tried to study well so as not to hurt my parents, and in general I managed. Despite all my negative attributes, I had a good memory.

A good memory was in fact the only thing I had in common with Victor, given all his positive characteristics. He could also memorize things very quickly. Thus, in order to speed his progress in his chosen career, he took scientific works out of the library and memorized serious words. He soon began to use these words at home, which eased his life and gladdened his parents.

For example, when Mother told us, "Children, go chop some wood," Victor would answer, "Polygamous anthromorphism and epidemic geocentrism on the level of the present day arouse within me a thermodynamic demonism and electrostatic duality, which renders the chopping of wood impossible."

Father and Mother would exchange proud glances, taking joy in Victor's scientific grounding, and I would get to chop the wood. I performed my domestic duties carefully, so as to somehow make up for my five uns.

And in the meantime, the sad news that I was a boy with five uns had spread throughout Greetica-Leaveittown: despite all his virtues, Victor could not keep his mouth shut. The neighbors looked at me with pity, and in school a few children came right out and teased me with those same five uns, so that at times I had to get into fights. The girls also behaved miserably and played all sorts of dirty tricks. For example, my deskmate Tosya once invited me to a rendezvous in the city park under the fourth linden to the right of the entrance. But when I arrived at the precisely indicated time, there wasn't any Tosya. However, her younger brother, with whom she had made an agreement, was hidden in the tree, and he greeted me with a mixture of liquid glue and ink, employing for the purpose a rubber enema bag. When I clutched at my head, almost all the boys and girls of our class came running out of the pavilion and collectively laughed at me.

At home I didn't have an easy time of it either, especially when I expressed my disbelief in Father's stories. But at home, as they say, even the walls help. And I had, in the full sense of the word, helpful walls.

In those years, you couldn't buy wallpaper, and when our prerevolutionary wallpaper had gotten completely dried out and worn down, Father somewhere got hold of numerous rolls of advertisements left over from the tsarist regime. And we papered the walls with them. The room I shared with Victor took up a good quantity of uncut rolls, each of which contained around sixteen ads. And on each ad was a beautiful girl smiling tenderly at the viewer, that is to say, at me. With one hand she was stroking her loose blonde hair, and with the other she was holding a vial. Under the picture was an inscription in big bold letters: CARESS ME. Following this was a legend in small print:

Of all eau de colognes
   ladies young and old
      prefer one
         Caress Me
The tender and long-lasting fragrance,
   like the scent of a flowery meadow,
the elegant package, and inexpensive price
   make our cologne the only choice.
      Wherever you buy, the only cologne you
      should ask for is
         Caress Me!
Blanchard and Sons
Suppliers to H.R.H.

I never paid much attention to the text, but I often stopped to look at the girl, and she always made me feel better. She looked down at me from all four walls. Each of her portraits was the size of a streetcar ad, and I calculated that all in all our room held 848 images of her. Looking at "Caress me!," I would wonder whether such beautiful girls existed in real life, and if they did, then who they married. For a girl like that I would gladly throw myself into fire or water—her choice.

Further Developments 3

In those days the schools had nine grades. Victor finished eight of them, and decided not to bother with the ninth, the quicker to plunge into science. Our parents completely approved of this and bundled him off to Leningrad, fitting him out with clothes and handing over all their cash. Soon we got a letter from him. It looked like this:

DECLARATION

Dear Sir or Madam:

With the present letter I declare and certify my respect for my honored parents, with the additional purpose of communicating my intention to successfully attain a position as Senior Laboratory Assistant in Energetics at the Institute for Physiology and Philology, where I intend to climb steeply up the academic ladder and where my participation will in great measure further the cause of science.

In part two of this declaration I would like to declare that hybridization and synchronization under conditions of urbanization and polymerization require amoralizing and melioration, in connection with which I request you to respond with the immediate forwarding of 50 (fifty) rubles to the 86th postal district *poste restante*.

Your talented son,
Victor

With difficulty, my parents collected the required sum and sent it to Victor. As a whole, the letter made them happy.

Mother gladly read it to the neighbors, and they praised my brother for his erudition, looking at me with pity and reproach.

Soon there arrived another declaration, and then still others. We started to have a hard time with money. To rid themselves of one more mouth to feed and to help, ever so slightly, fill the family coffers, my parents found me a temporary job.

Although it was just for a while, in the depths of my soul I knew that it would be some time before I returned to my parents' home. Leaving my room, I cast my last glance at a portrait of the charming stranger whose beauty adorned my walls in an edition of 848 copies. "Caress Me!" I read with sadness beneath her image, thinking, *Anybody would caress someone like you, but who will caress me, a boy with five uns?* With these unspoken words I bowed to her and with tears in my eyes left the room.

I must confess that in taking leave of my parents I did not experience the requisite grief. Mother's reproaches and Father's continual lies had hurt me terribly. But as I left my prevaricating father, little did I know that I was about to be submerged in a flood of events so strange that by relating them I risk being called an even bigger liar.

Aunt Limpy 4

Greetica-Leaveittown is on the Uvaga River. If you go about five miles downstream, you come to the estate of the former landowner Zavadko-Bomet. At the time of the revolution, the landowner cleared out. His land was given to the peasants, and the big manor house on its picturesque hill was given to the local board of education. There was a proposal to turn the site into a museum-park on the domestic life of the bygone nobility. But in the meantime, the board of education had no funds to pay for guides or operation costs, and the building fell to a certain Olympia, an old woman who guarded it for a modest salary. Around town and in the surrounding villages she was known as Aunt Limpy.

Aunt Limpy was a product of the old regime and even knew French, but despite this, she was not a counterrevolutionary. On the contrary, before the revolution she worked for Zavadko-Bomet as family governess, and in some way suffered from the despotism peculiar to his class. This was no doubt the origin of her eccentricities.

One summer day, mother brought me to Aunt Limpy. They agreed that I would help with domestic chores, in return for which I would get my meals and, in addition, ten rubles a month. The money would be handed directly to Mother, without my outside interference. Having concluded this oral agreement, Mother left. In parting, she advised me to behave myself and, to the best of my ability, keep my five uns under control.

"Do you see visions?" asked Aunt Limpy in a businesslike manner when my mother had disappeared beyond the gate.

"What visions?" I said.

"Well, the usual kind," explained Aunt Limpy. "Say you're walking along, and there's some saint coming towards you, or a dragon—you never know what."

"No, I don't see visions," I confessed honestly. "Is that bad?"

"It's bad. I could use a helper with visions, so we could see them together, share our impressions. . . . Well, maybe you'll learn."

But I never did learn, although Aunt Limpy saw them practically every day. With some of them she spoke French for practice, so as not to forget how. At first when she'd suddenly start looking over my head and start talking to nobody in particular, I felt funny, but then I got used to it.

In general, Aunt Limpy was kind. She never yelled at me, and on Sundays gave me twenty kopecks for a movie (over and above the sum she entrusted to my mother). I'd get a ride into town on somebody's cart and there I'd see pictures with

Mary Pickford, Harry Peal, and Monty Banks. Aunt Limpy herself never went to the movies, because her visions made it unnecessary.

She didn't overwhelm me with work. My duties were to help her feed the hens, separate the roosters, make sure the cats didn't steal the chicks, the dogs didn't chase the cats, and in general ensure a peaceful balance of power among chickens, cats, and dogs.

Aunt Limpy loved animals, in particular dogs and cats. She took them in from all over our district, furnished meals three times a day, and provided them with shelter—which, thanks to the size of the old manor house, proved sufficient. Her protégés had sonorous appellations in place of names, and she demanded that I address each cat and dog properly. The bitches were Melody, Rhapsody, Elegy, Prelude, and Dream; the males were Diamond and Topaz, Accord, and Record. Names like this are nowadays given to radios and televisions, but then, there being no radio technology, Aunt Limpy could peacefully bestow them on her dogs.

The cats had artistic names as well: Margarita, Josephina, Cleopatra, Magdalene, Demimondaine, and Melancholy. Nor were the toms forgotten. There was a Valentine and a Constantine, a Prosecuting Attorney, a District Attorney, a Free Mason, and a Fall Season. I could never keep abreast of all their names, since her dogs numbered twenty persons (her expression) and a head count of cats revealed over forty.

No doubt you're curious as to how Aunt Limpy, this poor old lady living by herself, could support such a menagerie? On what dough? But as I already mentioned, she had a lot of hens. She kept her chickens in the former coach house, and bought her feed from the neighboring peasants. The eggs and hens she sold in Greetica-Leaveittown, and kept her pets on the proceeds. They didn't make her pay taxes, since she was considered a white-collar invalid, due to her suffering under the landowner's yoke.

My life at Aunt Limpy's went smoothly; I filled out and got

stronger. I handled the conflicts that arose occasionally between the dogs and cats by peaceful means, never resorting to
blows and not even raising my voice. I have great respect for
animals, and they respond to me in kind.

The dogs and cats all had distinct personalities, each with
its own virtues and weaknesses. Among the canine staff, the
little terrier Abracadabra stands out particularly. Abracadabra
was a good-hearted and creative sort. The cats had all gone
lazy from good food, but Abracadabra daily made the rounds
of the manor house, looking for rats. He did this purely as
a preventive measure, not expecting any quarry, since the
overabundance of cats had caused the rats to leave a long time
ago. Abracadabra believed in obtaining his food through some
risk, so as not to forfeit his hunting instincts. To this end, he
sometimes stole meat from the cats, and sometimes, when
Aunt Limpy wasn't around, made off with the dog food warm-
ing on top of the stove. Before jumping onto the hot stove, he
would go down to the water and dip his paws in the wet clay
of the riverbank. Then he would lie on his back with his paws
in the air to let the clay dry. In this way he provided himself
with fireproof boots. So armed, he would get onto the stove,
push the cover off the pot, deftly remove the meat, and replace
the cover as though it had never been touched. I am describing the small dog Abracadabra in such detail because he
served as a sort of detonator for the explosion of events that
follows.

The peaceful flow of my summer was interrupted by a
single incident.

One day, when Aunt Limpy was out, a gypsy walked into
the yard of the former estate.

"What's your name, young man?" she said, and I told her
my name.

She brightened. "Then you're the one I'm looking for. I
just spoke to your mistress, and she told me, 'Go to Stevie
and tell him to give you two hens: one black one, and one
speckled one. My present to you for telling me a good fortune.' "

I had never seen this gypsy before, but I immediately believed her. After all, Aunt Limpy wasn't giving her any old hens, but had pointed out precisely which ones she had in mind: a speckled one and a black one. So I helped the gypsy catch the hens, and she put them in her sack.

Then the gypsy said: "And now I'll tell your fortune for free. Put out your left hand."

At which point she told me the following:

"I can see by these lines that you are very trusting, and have more than once suffered for it, as you may, in fact, suffer later on today. But the future has far greater disappointments in store for you, up to the very worst. In the end, however, your trustfulness will aid you. On the day you start believing in something that no normal man would believe in, and take the most foolish possible step, on that very day, your misfortunes will come to an end and you will find happiness with the Queen of Diamonds."

Upon making this announcement the gypsy disappeared as if she had never been, and for a moment I even thought it was a dream. But on the other hand, it couldn't have been a dream, because there were two hens missing.

When Aunt Limpy returned and I told her that I had precisely fulfilled her orders regarding the hens, she flared up and told me I'd fallen for a trick like some dimwit. For the first time since I started to live with her, she made me stand in a corner for an hour and contemplate the existence of swindlers and cheats. Instead, I stood in the corner and thought about the gypsy. She may indeed have deceived me, but she was basically right: I was too trusting and got my just reward —for after all, she had predicted it. In addition, it occurred to me that if her predictions had worked out for today, it was possible that her long-term forecasts might be equally accurate.

When winter came, my parents didn't take me home. They kept me working at Aunt Limpy's, and had me transferred from the city school to the village one. As soon as I'd get home from school, I'd start in on my duties. I fed the chickens, helped to feed the dogs and cats, and in my free time, accompanied by the dog Abracadabra, I wandered through the cold rooms of the huge manor house and looked at the portraits hanging on the walls. Among them were a lot of beautiful girls, but not one could bear comparison with the wallpaper of my old room. Sometimes I would look into the huge mirrors that lined the walls and, seeing my unprepossessing reflection, would think sadly that no girl would fall in love with a boy with five uns, and when I grew up, no woman would love me either. And when I die, then, if there is a hell and I am burning in it, not a single lady devil will fall in love with me, and if there is a heaven and I am sent there, then I won't attract a single lady angel.

And then it was spring.

One Sunday morning I was awakened by the sound of the river. It was the ice breaking. I ate quickly, ran down the gently sloping bank, and started to watch the ice flow.

Suddenly, from around the manor house came the furious shriek of a cat and a dog's barking. I turned around and saw Abracadabra running to the river with a hunk of meat in his mouth, followed swiftly by Prelude, Elegy, Melody, and Accord, as well as by the cats Constantine, Fall Season, and Prosecuting Attorney. Two more cats, Josephina and Melancholy, brought up the rear. I knew that things were in a bad way if the cats and dogs had united against Abracadabra.

There was no time for peacekeeping measures. The terrified Abracadabra leapt off the shore onto a floating chunk of ice, from that piece of ice to another, and from that one to a third. The dogs and cats calmed down and went home.

When I saw the dog floating downstream, I knew that he would perish if I didn't extend some comradely help. I hurried towards him, jumping along the ice floes. In one spot I didn't jump far enough and fell into the icy water, but I managed to clamber onto the next chunk of ice and soon found myself next to Abracadabra, who was still holding on to his meat. Only when I picked him up did he drop it onto the ice and start to howl piteously.

Looking around, I saw that the manor house had already disappeared beyond the bend of the river. There was nothing but ice floes around us, and we were being carried to an unknown destination.

Further Developments **5**

It was only in the evening that we were rescued, as we sailed by a village that I will tentatively refer to as Rescueville-Hospitaltown. The journey had so thoroughly chilled and frightened me that I couldn't think straight. I barely had had time to tell my rescuers Aunt Limpy's address and my address at home when I lost consciousness. I was put in the local hospital. When, about two weeks later, I came out of it, the nurse told me that while I was in a coma, the dog Abracadabra was constantly by my side. Aunt Limpy had to come and remove him by force.

It turned out that my father had been to visit me as well. He told the patients a few hunting stories, after which their temperatures shot up so high that the doctors had to ask him to shorten his visit. He left greatly offended.

Hearing this news threw me back into a coma, where I stayed about two months. To make the long story short, I was sick all spring and summer, and then all winter. It was a miracle that I remained among the living. I think that if I'd had only one disease, I certainly would have kicked off. But I had no less than three: meningitis, radiculosis, and double pleuritis. While these disputed among themselves about which of them would dispatch me to the other world, I went ahead and, in my inconspicuous way, recovered.

In the spring, the head doctor had a visitor: his brother Andrew. Andrew arrived from the Crimea, where he ran a children's colony. The head doctor was fond of me, and so he asked his brother to take me with him to the Crimea, where I

could get back into shape and fully recover. Andrew had a talk
with me. When he had heard out my life story he invited me
to come along. I jumped at the opportunity, though honesty
compelled me to tell him about my five uns. But he said that
this was insignificant, maintaining that there were boys in the
colony with up to fifty uns, and they were managing just fine.

Shortly thereafter I took my leave of Rescueville-Hospitaltown and found myself in the Crimea.

Vasya the Martian 6

The children's colony was housed in the former palace of
a count. The palace was on the seashore, on the outskirts of a
small city which I shall call Vasya-by-the-Sea. In the beginning, I did nothing but lie on the beach and swim, and when
autumn came they enrolled me in the colony school. I was
placed temporarily in the class for slow learners—that is, for
the feebleminded. But I ended up there only because I had
missed a school year during my illness and also because they
had a slot to fill. There were all sorts of kids in it. Some were
my age, and some were a lot older—the ones who had
knocked around on their own for a long time. We got along
fine, and nobody insulted me or reproached me for my five
uns. I studied hard and even got to be first in my class in
behavior as well as scholastics, and I was made an example
for the others.

One day, a boy of about my age was brought into the colony. He had come from somewhere in the surrounding hills
and was found, half-starving, in the bazaar. There he had
walked up to a pie vendor, grabbed a pie from her cart, and
started to eat it without paying. All the vendors wanted to beat
him up, but a policeman intruded and took him to the center
for lost children. From there he was sent to us. In the colony,

because he seemed like an underachiever, he got placed in our class. They sat him next to me, and asked me to supervise him and go over our lessons, since he didn't know a word of Russian. Instead he spoke some language no one could understand. When we all told him our names, poking ourselves in the chest to make the point clear, he also poked himself in the chest and pronounced something on the order of Vaosaouuuoso, so we called him Vasya.

Vasya proved to be unusually gifted and after only two weeks was speaking fluent Russian. Since I wasn't the only one teaching him Russian, and among his other instructors were a good quantity of runaways and former juvenile delinquents, he managed to pick up underworld slang at the same time. Instead of "car," he said "wheels"; instead of "house," "pad"; instead of girl he said "chick," and so on. In another two weeks he had mastered reading. He began to go through several books a day, for the most part dictionaries and encyclopedias. I should also note that when he had learned to speak and write, it became immediately obvious that he had an excellent knowledge of mathematics, physics, and chemistry. Soon he became first in our class, leaving me in second place. But I didn't envy him at all, since we had become very friendly. Vasya turned out to be a good kid, "one of the guys," as we used to say.

The only thing Vasya didn't know was geography, and we were all astonished that such a well-rounded student should be behind in a subject like that. Once the geography teacher brought a big atlas to school and started to call us up to his desk. Everyone was supposed to point out the place where he was born. I found my own Greetica-Leaveittown immediately, and the others were also more or less able to find their places of birth. But when it got to be Vasya's turn, he stared at the map of the Soviet Union, hemmed and hawed a little, and finally said that he wasn't born there.

"So you're a foreigner," smiled the teacher and began showing him pictures of Africa, Australia, and America. But

Vasya still insisted that he hadn't been born in any of those places. "You must have been born in a place so far away it isn't even on the map," the teacher joked.

"He fell from the moon," came from one of the desks.

"He flew in from Venus," said someone else.

"From Mars!" said a third.

There were no further suggestions, since these were the only heavenly bodies we knew.

The teacher, hearing these voices from the desks, opened the book to a page with a map of the stars.

"Perhaps you were really born on some other planet," he asked Vasya as a joke.

Vasya poked his finger somewhere in the starry sky and said, "Right around here."

The teacher approved of Vasya's witty reply, but nevertheless gave him an "unsatisfactory" and asked the best geography student, Crooked Kolya, to take care of him. This Kolya had been a runaway for a long time and had a good practical knowledge of geography which he'd acquired circling the country on train roofs.

Starting on that day, they began to call my friend Vasya the Martian. It was all the more appropriate as he was the fourth Vasya in our class. In addition to him, we had Vasya the Nut, Vasya the Chicken, and Vasya the Horse. Because of these nicknames, it was impossible to confuse any of them. My friend was not ashamed of his nickname and answered to it willingly.

From the colony I wrote several letters to my parents, telling them the details of my new life, but I never got an answer. Finally I got an angry note from my father. He was indignant because I was in a class for slow learners, together with runaways and delinquents, and because at the same time as my brother Victor was showing great promise, I was dishonoring the family. "Don't dare come back to your parents' house until you get over your uns," the letter concluded.

My father had enclosed the last letter from Victor to make

me feel the lowliness of my own moral and intellectual level in comparison to that of my brother:

DECLARATION

Respected parents!

With the present document, certified by my own signature, I announce to you that my future ascent into scientific spheres continues with great success. In the Institute of Terminology and Equilibristics, now entrusted to me, a broad scientific idea will be concentrated and shelved on a massive scale, as a result of which the graph of my authority will unhesitatingly move upward.

I also inform you by way of confidentiality and consultability, that erotization of granulated integrals and the pasteurization of consolidated metamorphoses called forth a high molecular atavism and asynchronic separatism, which may lead to adulterated anabiosis and even to an invariant epithelial amphibrach. In order to forestall the latter, I request you to immediately forward 15 (fifteen) rubles to postal district 24, *poste restante*.

Your talented son,
Victor

My father's severity hurt me a great deal, and I walked as though doused with cold water. When Vasya the Martian asked what was going on, I showed him both letters. To my astonishment, my friend had no reaction to my father's letter, and in regard to Victor said something unprintable. Because of this I almost got into a fight, but then I realized that Vasya had simply said the wrong thing because of his still imperfect knowledge of earth language.

Since I was moping so much, my friend said that he would show me my parents' house. To this end, he took me to the colony's Turkish bath, which on that day wasn't being used.

We walked into the empty steam room. Vasya the Martian took a basin and filled it with cold water from the tap. Then he reached into his jacket pocket and took out a tiny bottle. A light blue pill about the size of a pea rolled out of the bottle and onto his palm. He threw it into the basin with the cold water. The water clouded up, then began to look like jelly, then became smooth and shiny like metal.

"Think about whatever you want to see," said Vasya.

And suddenly in the basin there appeared my room, and in it my father and mother. Father was standing on the stepladder, and Mother was handing him pieces of wallpaper dripping with glue. My parents were repapering the room, and 90 percent of the 848 reproductions of "Caress Me!" had already been buried under the cheap green cover. There remained but a single narrow strip whose portraits still looked down on me. It seemed as though "Caress Me" was looking at me personally, asking me not to forget her. Then Father stuck the last piece of paper onto the wall, smoothed it down with a rag, and it was all over.

"Just like new," he said to Mother in a satisfied voice, climbing off the stepladder. "Now we'll be able to rent it out and send the money to Victor, our pride and joy. May he boldly advance along his scientific path."

The papering over of the beautiful "Caress Me" upset me to such an extent that Vasya began to fear for my health.

"My old earth pal," he said to me one day, "can't I find some way of comforting you? Maybe you're tired of living in the colony?"

"Alas," I said, "there's no cure for my sorrow. And the colony isn't half bad, there are good kids here. The only thing that upsets me is that some of them like to lie. You know how at night all the tutor has to do is leave the room, and they start telling the sort of true-life adventures that make my whole body start to blush for them. Since my childhood I haven't been able to tolerate lies."

"I'll see what I can do," said Vasya the Martian.

At this very time, we were whitewashing the ceilings in the colony. When it was time to do our room, and the bucket was full of white paint, Vasya took a small, flat box out of his pocket. In the box was an envelope with some sort of powder in it. He explained that where he came from they used the powder when they made paper, but I never did understand why. Vasya emptied the powder into the paint bucket.

No sooner had we whitewashed the ceiling than an interesting fact emerged: now, whenever someone telling his adventures would begin to lie, the white ceiling instantly turned red. And the worse the lie, the stronger the red, right up to a deep carmine. Then, when the narrator returned to the truth, the ceiling once again turned white. As a result of this undertaking, the boys become a lot more truthful.

I never made the ceiling blush.

Vasya the Martian slept in the cot next to mine. One day I noticed that he was hiding a portion of rusks under his mattress. He should have been eating them for breakfast. When I asked him what he needed them for, he said that he was going to go home, and needed provisions for the trip. After all, he would have to eat during his journey.

Then I began saving my own share for him, and soon he had a good supply.

And then one day early in the morning Vasya quietly awakened me and said that it was time for his flight home. I took my pillowcase off my pillow, and we stuffed it with rusks. Then we noiselessly crawled out the window and into the park. Soon we had climbed up into the hills, descended into a deserted valley, and again climbed up a hill grown over with bushes. Here Vasya found a cave that was completely hidden from the outside, pushed aside the bushes, and went in.

In the depths of the cave I caught sight of a large, metallic object. In form it was like a milk can, only a very big one.

"Help me roll out this means of transportation," said Vasya. "This is what I'm going to fly in."

I put my shoulder under it, but it didn't budge. It must have weighed several tons.

"Oh, shoot, I almost forgot," said Vasya and loudly pronounced some word in an incomprehensible tongue. The cylinder suddenly lightened, and we easily rolled it out of the cave.

Then Vasya the Martian said a different word, and a door

opened on the side of the cylinder. Vasya walked in, shook out the rusks into a drawer, and gave back the government issue pillowcase. Inside the cylinder was a maze of buttons. I also noticed an armchair, something like a dentist's. Then we walked out to a platform on the very edge of the cliff. Vasya said:

"When I get inside my means of transportation and close the hatch, rock me over toward the cliff and throw me off. Be bold: this is essential for takeoff. Don't be afraid, nothing is going to happen to me. And just so nobody thinks I've perished, I prepared this document; you give it to the people in the colony." And he handed me a piece of paper, on which was written:

CERTIFICATE

I ask that no one be held responsible for my takeoff. I depart in full health, both mental and physical. Accept my heartfelt thanks for your hospitality. One of your guys,

Vasya the Martian

"Vasya," I shouted nervously. "Now that we're saying good-bye, tell me exactly where you came from and where you're going."

"I won't tell you for your own good," answered my friend. "If you believed me you could go crazy."

"You're not an angel, I hope," I said. "Because if you're an angel, then I might have a religious seizure."

"You can bet your sweet ass I'm not," shouted my friend in runaway slang. "Set your mind at rest—there aren't any angels, and none are foreseen."

To conclude our conversation, Vasya asked if I had any declarations or desires. In answer, I made the following wish:

"May my talented brother Victor stand firmly on the path of science! May he gladden the hearts of my parents and myself personally with his achievements! May my parents and I never be disappointed in the talented Victor!"

Upon hearing this request, my friend Vasya, for some reason, frowned. But then he said:

"Oh, well, he's not the first and he won't be the last, as you say on Earth. . . . All right, I promise you that your brother will have his scientific career. Are there any more requests?"

I turned to Vasya with a series of requests:

"May my parents never get sick and live long lives! May our house stand for a long time, and not get struck by lightning, war, or faulty stoves, so that the beautiful 'Caress Me!' existing beneath the wallpaper, in an edition of 848, should not suffer to the end of my days and even longer!"

"It shall be done," said Vasya. "Let's have the next request."

"My last request is as follows," I said. "If somewhere, sometime, someone should come to me with a request and if I ask you to help me with it, then let this request be fulfilled."

"Done," said Vasya. "I know what kind of request this will be, and I will be happy to fulfill it."

"How can you know what kind of request it will be when I don't even know myself?" I said. "I'm asking you just in case, on the off chance."

"But I know," Vasya the Martian repeated. "And it will be my pleasure."

"How do I get in touch with you?" I asked.

"Very simple," said my friend. "Go to the telephone, pick up the receiver—"

"And what do I tell the telephone lady?" I interrupted him.

"By that time there won't be any telephone ladies. We'll have direct dialing. Just dial eleven ones and five fives—I have a very simple number, it's easy to remember it. . . . But now it's time for us to say good-bye."

We shook hands. Vasya crawled into his cylinder, and the doors shut behind him.

I rocked the cylinder over to the cliff and threw it off, down to where the Black Sea was rolling. At first the cylinder fell like a stone. But then, just as it reached the water, it slowed down. For a brief second it froze in the air, and then it shot off into the sky. It disappeared so quickly that I didn't even get a chance to wave to it.

When I got back to the colony and passed around Vasya's note, nobody believed that he had flown off. Everyone decided that he wrote his certificate as a joke, while he himself, with my knowledge, had left the colony and hit the road. I demanded that all the doubters follow me into the bedroom and hear me out there. When I had once again run through my account, and the ceiling failed to blush, the majority believed me. But some of them believed me only up to the point where I threw our friend's vessel into the sea. They decided that Vasya had gone nuts and that I shouldn't have pushed him, since it was clear that he had drowned. In vain did I insist that he hadn't drowned, but taken off; those of little faith could not believe this. So they began to call me a dirty liar and almost branded me a murderer.

The boys' attitudes toward me changed drastically. They started to do all sorts of nasty things to me. Sometimes, when I'd go to bed, I'd find a dead mouse under my pillow. Other times, putting on my shoes in the morning, I'd find goat turds in them. My life became unbearable. It wasn't the dirty tricks that upset me so much as the fact that I, a person who hated lies, was taken for a liar.

It ended in my going to see Andrei and, without naming my tormentors, announcing that I could no longer live in the colony.

The good man heard me out and said that I had rotten luck. To comfort me, he told me the story of an ancient Greek by the name of Policrates who, from his earliest youth, seemed to have it made, but when he got old he had such bad luck that they skinned him alive. With all his heart, Andrei wished me the opposite.

After this, Andrei asked me what I would like to be. I said

that as far as a profession was concerned, I would like to follow my father's footsteps, that is to say, to be a bookkeeper. Then my mentor told me that the colony had the right to send its charges to a vocational school, where they would ease the entrance requirements and provide space in the dormitory. Only first I would have to finish seventh grade in the colony and make a temporary peace with my moral adversities. I said I was ready.

And the day finally came when, armed with documents and money for the road, I set off for Leningrad. In my pocket was a paid trip to the Leningrad Four-Year Finance and Accounting School.

I will not try to describe my impressions of that remarkable city in which I found myself for the first time. Our classical writers, and even some contemporary ones, have done a much better job. As for me, I was painlessly enrolled as a first-year student. The entrance exam was easy because there weren't many applicants. Everything worked out in the dormitory, where they found me a place to sleep.

As I took up my studies, I wrote my father about the change in my life. He sent me a quick answer, in which he approved my choice. He advised me to study hard, so that by good grades I might somehow vanquish my five uns. Further on he hinted that although I now had the happiness of living in the same city as Victor, it was not my place to visit my brother, as this might lower his estimation in the eyes of others. Father enclosed Victor's latest declaration, so that I might delight in his achievements.

Honored Parents!

With the present document I declare that my creative searches have brought me complete success. I invite you to join in my exaltation and sing with me a song of triumphant love. Not so long ago I took the action of entering into an actual marriage with a person who fell head over heels in love with me, by the name of Perspectiva, daughter of the well-known professor of anthropophagy and chairman of the department of Animalistical Linguistics and Choreography of the Institite of Melancholy and Taste-Therapy, the which marriage being actual, morganatic, and, for greater stability, solemnized by myself and Perspectiva in the said marriage bureau, and the Russian Orthodox and Catholic churches, as well as in a mosque, synagogue, and Buddhist temple.

Knocked out by the exaltating facts, the professor provided me with living space for my creative takeoff, and guaranteed help in my progress through science, so that the husband of his daughter would be worthy of her father.

P.S. In consideration of the fact that pyrotechnical geoinclines and idiosyncratic trypanosomes have a tendency toward myocardiac inflation, as well as taking into account that convergent incunabula and psychomotor constants require a tri-phase varicose turbulentness, I am forwarding to you 50 (fifty) rubles for your personal expenditures and entertainment.

Your talented Victor

I must confess that I didn't understand everything in my talented brother's letter, but the most important point was clear: he had stepped firmly onto the path of science, and I no longer had to worry about him. Vasya the Martian had kept his word.

For three years I didn't miss a single lecture and, advancing carefully from one class to the next, earned the reputation of a hard worker. My life flowed smoothly, and there were no more strange events. In my free time I read science fiction, and sometimes went to the movies with a certain Sima, a girl student who had noticed me. Sometimes she would invite me over to her house, and we would dance to the record player. Her parents were sympathetic to our relationship, and looked upon me as a suitor.

One day a letter arrived from my father with the joyous news that my brother would permit me to pay him a visit. Father tactfully provided me with some friendly precepts concerning my behavior at Victor's. I was not to linger more than an hour, and I was not to ask scientific questions, since I wouldn't understand the answers. I was not to blow my nose loudly, I was not to throw myself on the food and wine, and I was to refrain from visiting the bathroom. There followed yet another series of instructions, all of which I took into account.

Having forewarned my brother by telephone, I appeared at his door at the indicated time. The door was opened by an imposing housemaid, who led me into the solidly furnished study. On the walls were portraits of Stephenson, Pasteur, Lomonosov, and numerous other famous scholars and inventors. Among them was a large waist-length portrait of my talented brother. Victor himself was seated at a big desk. With a gold feather pen and glossy red paper, he was making notations from the huge scientific tomes which lay before him.

Absorbed as he was in the process of scientific creation, Victor did not notice me immediately. As soon as he did, he gave a responsible smile, asked a few leading questions about my life, and expressed his approval of my modest achievements.

After that, the maid led me into the immaculate kitchen, where a bottle of Benedictine liqueur and a plate of hors d'oeuvres were already waiting. I drank down a glass of liqueur and nibbled at her delicious marinated mushrooms, after which she led me into the living room. Here my brother made his appearance and once again asked a few tactful questions on nonscientific subjects. His wife Perspectiva was also in the living room. Dressed in beautiful blue pajamas, she reclined on the couch in an exotic European pose. She didn't participate in the conversation, as she had been born a deaf-mute, but she was able to laugh, and from time to time enlivened our discussion with a delicate titter. Then she stood up, went to the piano, and played a few resounding chords.

Soon my time ran out. In parting, my brother wished me further modest success and said that I could visit him quarterly. I left, charmed by his noncommunal apartment with its scientific atmosphere, and impatiently awaited my next visit.

But, alas, this pleasant period of my life was soon destroyed by unexpected events.

The Honorable Wool Man   7

At my Four-Year Finance and Accounting School I was considered a hard worker and noncutter, and so, after my junior year, I was given a free trip to a general purpose resort a hundred and twenty miles from Leningrad. At the resort they rented out bicycles, and I soon learned how to ride. Taking advantage of the good weather, I often rode off on my own.

During one of these pleasant trips, I turned off the main route and rode for quite a while along an unfamiliar forest path, finally turning onto a trail. I soon found myself in a field. In the middle of the field there was a hut, and surrounding the hut was a vegetable garden. Since the day had been extremely hot and I had been thirsty for a long time, I walked over to the hut and knocked on the door.

"The owner isn't home," said a man's voice from behind the door.

"It makes no difference," I said. "I'd like something to drink."

I could hear footsteps, and soon the door opened a crack. Through the opening there extended a hand holding a glass of water. But what a hand! It was the hand of a human being, but completely covered with thick, green wool. I felt funny, but so as not to offend anyone, I drank what had been given to me. As I was returning the glass, however, I made an awkward movement, and the door opened wide.

Before me stood a being with a middle-aged human face. But the rest of him was totally grown over with thick wool. He didn't have any clothes on, but considering the thickness of his woolly coat, he didn't need any. I started thinking about elves, then recoiled and almost fell off the porch.

"Don't be afraid of me," said the being. "I'm the same as you are. Come inside, and I will outline the story of my life for you."

With some trepidation I followed him into the hut. I thought it was all a dream. But the being took a seat in the normal way and announced that his name was Valentine.

Whereupon Valentine proceeded to tell me his life story. Since his youth he had worked as a pharmacist, and he was always upset that he could do nothing for bald men, who came to him for medicine to restore their hair. The patent medicines that were advertised from time to time in magazines were sheer frauds, of no use for anything. There was no real means of restoring hair. Although he himself possessed a fine head of hair, Valentine was a compassionate sort. He felt deep sympathy for bald men and took it as a personal affront that the medical establishment had done nothing to alleviate the problem. After long thought, Valentine decided, by dint of his own intelligence, to invent some means of combating hairlessness. He began to work on this scientific problem at night and in complete secrecy, so he wouldn't get laughed at if he failed. Many years passed, and he himself went bald from the mental strain, but the great day finally came when a true and precise medicinal formula for hair-growing had been found. On the basis of this formula, he put together a powder to be taken internally. He called it Progress-Behaired.

Although the accuracy of the formula was beyond question, Progress-Behaired still needed testing. It was only natural that Valentine decided to try it on himself first. Thus, as soon as his vacation rolled around, he asked for an extra month without pay and set off for the secluded forester's hut. He counted on returning to the pharmacy with a full head of hair and telling everyone about his significant medical achievement. He felt in advance the joy of all bald men who, by means of his discovery, would be restored to their former good looks.

Valentine swallowed the powder and began to await results. They began on the third day, when the subject lost the remainder of his old hair. Immediately after this, new hair began to grow. However, it grew not only on his head, but equally over all parts of his body. In addition, for some unknown reason the hair was greenish. To put it more precisely, it was not hair at all, but wool, and the texture was soft and silky. A few days later, the growth had become so thick and long that Valentine discovered that he no longer needed clothes. He started to go around without them, and thanks to the isolation of the spot and the absence of visitors, nobody but the forester took fright. The forester was a drunkard, and when he saw the pharmacist in his new aspect he decided that it was an alcoholic mirage. In the spirit of self-criticism he went to the regional hospital to free himself from booze and was promptly hospitalized.

At first the strange action of Progress-Behaired brought Valentine to despair. He thought that his life's dream had gone up in smoke. But he comforted himself with the thought that the powder lasted only for two months, after which the hair would fall out. So, even if he hadn't presented mankind with the gift of a new preparation, his failure would remain secret and he would return to the city without having lost anything. His despair was replaced by a lyrical melancholy. In this state, quietly waiting for the effects to wear off, he passed a few days wandering through the forest and gathering mushrooms and berries.

Soon he noticed that his fleece was more comfortable than clothing, because it didn't cramp his movements and was good against the heat. At the same time he established that it was equally good against the cold. And one day, caught in a downpour, Valentine stayed completely dry, because the rain streamed along the wool and never reached his body. When the downpour had stopped, Valentine shook himself off, and not a drop of water remained.

And then one day, like a bolt of lightning, the thought hit him: what he considered to be a failure was in fact a great discovery. He compared himself to a prospector who, in search of gold nuggets, had come across a huge deposit of platinum.

He understood that a new era of civilization had begun. Thanks to him, Valentine, people would no longer need clothing. All a person would have to do would be to take Progress-Behaired once every two months, and he could go around in his own fur, needing neither underwear nor anything else. With their personal, hygienic, fleecy coats, people would be protected from heat and cold. Their expenses would diminish tremendously. Instead of wasting their money on clothing, people could use it for their cultural needs. There would be a revolution in agriculture, since it would no longer be necessary to grow cotton or linen. The fields where these once grew would be given over to the cultivation of wheat and other cereals, so that humanity would be forever supplied with grain. The textile industry would become obsolete, and the industrial space could be used more expediently, resulting in an industrial boom. Hunters and trappers, released from their heavy labors, would stop killing animals. Who would want fox or beaver if each person could be his own fur coat?

I listened to Valentine attentively, and before me shone the bright picture of a future when humanity would be dressed in its own personal fur. But I was a little put out by the thought that since clothing makes it possible for individuals to express their personal taste, people covered with their own wool would all look alike. I shared these doubts with my new acquaintance.

Valentine answered that he had also thought about this. In the future, he would be working on hormonal additions to Progress-Behaired so that each person could grow wool of any color. Wool of orange, pink, or sky blue would look good on young girls, and a rich array of colors—from yellow and lilac to electric blue, in a herringbone—would be available for the ladies. Men would be fully satisfied with modest grays, dark blues, and browns. Every two months, a wool-wearer could change the color of his fleece according to fashion or personal taste. Furthermore, with time Valentine would perhaps succeed in providing every wool-wearer with the possibility of sporting a motley coat, combining colored spots in accordance with individual taste. In addition, it must be kept in mind that wool can be curled easily, thus providing women with a wide-open field for creative competition and individual expression. It is true that the number of hairdressers and beauty parlors would increase by a factor of ten, since the expansion in the surface area to be curled would result in much more time being spent on each client.

For a short time Valentine fell silent, and then brought forth some further advantages to wool-wearing. He said that it was necessary to look at the moral and ethical side of the matter. Once all women began to wear their own wool, they would stop envying one another's clothing, since clothing as such would not exist. This pleasant change of circumstances would first be evident in wives. Now some of them are ready to ruin their husbands in the race for fashionable togs. The wool-wearing woman would be the ideal wife.

"Yes, I see now that you've made a great discovery," I told my new acquaintance. "It's hard to believe in a miracle like that!"

"But this miracle exists," said Valentine with dignity. "To convince yourself of it, you may stroke my back. Don't be afraid, do it. You will be convinced of the value of my wool."

With some trepidation I stroked his back. Indeed, it was high-quality wool, soft and fluffy. "What fine wool!" I exclaimed. "You have made a valuable gift to mankind."

"Alas, the gift has not yet been made," answered Valentine with sadness in his voice. "I've only tried it out on myself, and it's possible that no one will believe me, they'll take me for a charlatan. I need people who would agree to repeat the experiment on themselves and corroborate my discovery.

Then the whole world will believe in Progress-Behaired and the new era will begin."

My friend looked me straight in the eye and announced that from the first glance he had discerned in me a conscientious, brave, and progressive man and that people like me were just what he was looking for. He asked me to take a dose of Progress-Behaired and test its action on myself. When I heard his proposal I got a bit unnerved, since I could foresee a few difficulties.

"Perhaps you are worried about your looks?" said my friend tactfully. "But I can tell you honestly that you're not very handsome now, and the wool will make you look original. This green attire will adorn you like Mother Nature's own gift. Just think: aristocrats used to have blue blood and now you, a mere student, will have your own green wool! And all for the sake of science!"

I became ashamed of my indecisiveness. It occurred to me that my talented brother had completely dedicated himself to science while I, a person with five uns, had yet done nothing for it.

"I agree," I said to Valentine.

He immediately gave me the powder, which I took with water. Then I hurried back to the resort, but before I left I agreed that I would make regular visits to my friend in his isolated hut, so that he could observe the changes going on in me (or rather, on me). In parting he shook my hand in a friendly way and said that the population of the earth would be grateful to me and give me the title of Honorable Wool Man.

I returned to the resort, and life flowed in its accustomed course. A day later it even seemed to me that my meeting with Valentine was nothing more than a pleasant dream, for how could a person with five uns become a participant in great events?

But a day after that, the hair on my head started falling out on an intensive basis. My roommates expressed their sympathy, not understanding that it was joy that was called for. A few days later, the first woolly strands made their appearance. To make the long story short, within a week my entire body was covered with long, high-quality green wool. It was so thick and abundant that I could no longer get into my clothes, but indeed, I no longer needed them. My woolen fleece not only protected me from cold and heat, but did an excellent job covering what had to be covered. However, out of politeness I went around in underwear. So dressed, I went to visit Valentine; he was very glad that the experiment had proved successful.

Unfortunately, in the resort my transformation did not meet with the expected response. It is always difficult to accept what is new, and the advantages of wool-wearing left everyone cold. The doctors thought that I had come down with something strange and stuffed me full of medicines, while certain resort guests refused to sit at the same table with me. The less intelligent among them even pulled at my wool to see if it was real, since they were unable to believe in this achievement of scientific thought. But the worst part was that, for everyone, my appearance called forth peals of inappropriate laughter. A huge audience followed me everywhere, as a result of which the status of the resort entertainer fell considerably. It was the entertainer who gave the director the idea that they had better get rid of me. And indeed the director called me to his office. Pointing out that my appearance was not consonant with regulations, he asked me to depart as soon as possible from the resort entrusted to his care.

I put my stuff together and went to see Valentine, whom I discovered all packed and ready to go. He was about to go back to the city and was waiting for a cart to take him to the station. He was in clothes and out of wool. The latter had fallen off, since two months had passed since his last dose of Progress-Behaired.

I told Valentine about my misfortunes and he began to comfort me, reminding me that I was serving science and science demands sacrifice. Further on he hinted that when they erected a monument to him, my own small statue might possibly be placed nearby. I would be depicted in wool and with the torch of knowledge in my hand.

When the cart rolled up, the horse was for some reason very frightened of me, and even tried to rear. The driver had a hard time calming her down in order to give Valentine a chance to get in the cart and load his things. He permitted me to put my suitcase in the cart, but asked me to follow them on foot so as not to disturb the uncomprehending horse.

When we arrived at the station and got into the train, the passengers became noticeably discontent. Even though I was wearing sandals, underwear, and a cap—clearly indicating that I was a human being—a certain lady whose child had gotten scared and burst into tears demanded that I leave. Valentine took my ticket and went to the ticket office. When he got back he handed me a receipt and returned a portion of my money.

"You see, the advantages of your position have already begun to take effect," he said. "You'll be traveling on a baggage ticket, as a domestic animal, which makes your trip a lot cheaper than mine."

It was no fun riding in the baggage compartment, since, in addition to myself and various pieces of luggage, the compartment was occupied by two dogs. They didn't particularly trust me, barked continuously, and did their best to sink their claws into my wool. I had to barricade myself with suitcases and trunks.

When I reached Leningrad, a whole series of misfortunes began. I will not attempt to describe all of them. Sima, the girl student who had been somewhat fond of me, called me a gorilla and said that she had been mistaken in me. When I appeared in class, instead of listening to the instructor, everyone stared at me. So as not to disturb the lessons, I was forced to refrain temporarily from visiting the institute and to wait for my wool to fall out.

Seeking psychological support, I went to see Victor. But when he saw my fleece, my brother reacted coldly. He said that my internal animal nature was revealing itself, and asked me not to present myself to him in such an antisocial form. He then expressed the desire that in private conversations and dossiers I not mention our relationship, so as not to cast a permanent moral shadow on him. I left feeling deeply guilty for having troubled my talented brother with my visit.

Finally, I made up my mind to take an unpardonable step, and ask Valentine for some drug to release me from wool-wearing ahead of its time. But, alas, the inventor of Progress-Behaired confessed that there was no such thing.

During this visit I noticed that Valentine was again in wool, but that he looked sad. I asked him why he wasn't happy. After all, now that the infallible action of Progress-Behaired had been proven experimentally, he should be joyful for himself personally and for all of mankind. But in answer he gave a mournful smile and, in a nervous whisper, told me about his wife's intrigues.

Apparently the inventor's wife, having found out about the wonderful qualities of Progress-Behaired, decided to reap some personal profit from it. She made Valentine quit his job and devote himself exclusively to growing wool, which she harvested systematically with the help of sheep shears. With this wool, she learned to knit sweaters, pullovers, and cardigans, which she sold at markets and in specialty shops. In such a way was the great scientific discovery debased and compromised. From that time on, I heard nothing more from Valentine or his Progress-Behaired.

Indeed, Progress-Behaired didn't make me happy either. When, after two months, my wool fell out, the normal covering of hair returned, and I once again began to go to classes, it turned out that I was so far behind that there was no sense in continuing my studies. I left school with a certificate that I had completed three years, and went to work as a cashier in a Turkish bath in the Petrograd district. My pay wasn't very good, but the job came with a room at the bathhouse. The room was only seven by ten feet, but it was warm, and the only thing that kept me from complete satisfaction was the absence of a portrait of "Caress Me!"—even a single one of the 848 reposing under their layer of wallpaper in my parents' home.

Soon the war broke out, and I enlisted as a private. I had two light wounds, but there were no strange adventures of the type I have described. Therefore I will not discuss this period of my life, turning right away to the postwar years.

The Big Bottle **8**

After I was demobilized I returned to Leningrad and took up my job as a cashier in the Turkish baths. My old room was occupied, but they found me some space in an apartment, also in the Petrograd district. My new apartment consisted of two rooms. My room was ten by six feet and the other one, about twenty by twelve feet, was inhabited by a delightful married couple. The husband, whose name was George, was a quality controller at some plant; he was already past forty. His wife Marina worked in a library; she was in her thirties. My neighbors lived happily together, and were very pleasant to me, so that when I was around them I forgot that I was a man with five uns. On red-letter days they even invited me to share in their festivities.

I especially liked their respect for one another. They never had fights, and I never saw them drunk, or even a little tipsy. On holidays, there would be a bottle of sacramental wine— the one alcoholic beverage they would accept, since it was good for the digestion. But in a whole evening they never drank more than a glass each, although they constantly pressed me to have more. But since I wasn't a big drinker either, I also never had more than a single glass. And so we lived in friendly harmony for four years.

But, alas, there came a day when I, against my will, brought such discord and confusion to this friendly family that I was forced to move out, tainted by scandal and slightly maimed.

I will tell it all in order.

In the Turkish baths where I worked, a certain old woman of prepension age earned her honest wages as a bathhouse attendant. Her name was Antonia. She worked in the First Class Women's Steam Room, where her duties consisted of keeping the dressing room tidy, taking tickets, and showing the visitors where to put their clothes. She was considered a very conscientious worker and always fulfilled her politeness quota.

One day Antonia didn't come to work. She informed our supervisors that she had come down with a heavy cold and had gone on sick leave. Since it was known that she lived by herself, it was decided to display some comradely feeling, that is, to write a collective letter expressing our wishes for a speedy recovery and bring her an edible gift. The task of presenting her with the gift and letter fell to me. Social tasks involving people's private lives were usually given to me, because I was a bachelor and had more free time than the others.

On my next day off, I made an early morning trip to the grocery store, where I picked up a small cake, a box of Red Poppy candies, and a couple of oranges. Then I set off for the address shown on the envelope.

Antonia opened the door herself. When I explained the reason for my visit, she was touched by our concern for another human being and invited me to have a glass of tea in her company. She lived in a separate apartment, consisting of a bedroom, entrance hall, and kitchen. This was a part of an older apartment that had been divided in half or even into thirds and rebuilt.

Over tea, I told Antonia the latest bathhouse news and gave her, in addition to the letter, the personal greetings of our mutual acquaintances. As I talked, I could not help glancing around the room. It had a molded ceiling, on which you could make out flying cherubim and swans. The furnishings hardly corresponded to the modest earnings of the owner; there were several armchairs upholstered in natural leather, and numerous bookcases with books in rich bindings. Last but not least, there was a piano in the corner.

At tea, Antonia showed an interest in my life, so I gave her a brief autobiographical sketch. The latter, apparently, made a good impression on her, although I did not hide the fact that I was a man with five uns.

"Your simple face and sincere speech inspire me with trust," said Antonia suddenly. "And since I am in my declining years, I would like to tell you a secret that must not die with me. But first I would like to ask you a personal question: do you drink?"

I answered frankly that I didn't. In my mind I decided that I had made a slip by not bringing a bottle of port or vermouth with the rest. Therefore I added that if Antonia felt like a drink, I could run around the corner and treat her to a bottle of wine.

My hostess, however, answered that she never drank anything alcoholic and that she merely wanted to know whether I would like something myself, since she had a fairly good assortment of wines.

I answered that out of respect for her I was always ready to drink a glass to her health.

"Go over to that wall, take the painting down, open the hidden cabinet, and take any bottle you like," said Antonia, pointing to the wall at our left.

I walked up to the painting, a portrait of a young man with an Eastern moustache wearing a white turban, took it off the wall, and found a copper doorknob at about the level of my head.

"Press down four times," ordered Antonia.

I did as she said, and with a sudden crack the wallpaper split open. A vertical line appeared along the wall, a heavy metal door opened, and I beheld the hidden cabinet. Rows of bottles stood on its mahogany shelves. Attached to each bottle was a neat piece of paper indicating the sort, and what sorts they were! But, alas, all the bottles were empty, a fact which I communicated to Antonia.

"That doesn't mean anything," she said. "Choose the bottle with the right label and then do as I say."

I chose a bottle with the label "sacramental wine," since I knew that it helped the digestion.

"Now go into the kitchen and fill the bottle with tap water," said my hostess.

This surprised me, but so as not to offend an old woman, I set off for the kitchen. There, wiping the dust from the bottle, I discovered that it was made of ordinary glass. Inside you could see a reddish sediment, which did not disappear when I rinsed the bottle and filled it with water.

"What should I do now?" I asked Antonia as I entered the sitting room.

"Put the bottle on the window sill, and let it stand there seventeen minutes zero seconds," answered my hostess, glancing at her tiny watch. "In the meantime I will tell you about my life and my unique scientific discovery."

And she told me the following. She was born in Petersburg to a rich aristocratic family and studied at a private gymnasium. She was gifted in all the sciences, chemistry in particular. After graduation from the gymnasium, the unusually talented girl was sent abroad by her parents. There she graduated from two universities, with honors. Upon her return to Petersburg, Antonia plunged into scientific research. While her highly placed girlfriends enjoyed themselves at balls and fashionable dressmakers, she devoted her days and nights to productive labor in her chemistry laboratory, which had been set up in her parents' town house. Although she was very pretty, she categorically refused the offers of hand and heart made by brilliant officers, landed aristocrats, and captains of industry. Several of them, unable to withstand the blow that fate had dealt them, committed suicide.

In her early childhood, during a lesson on the Gospels the young Antonia had noted that at the marriage at Cana in Galilee, Jesus Christ was able to turn ordinary water into wine and serve everyone present. This legendary fact took firm root in her childish soul, and when she grew up, she decided to re-create the ancient legend with the help of science. She wanted to provide people with the opportunity to drink healthful and delicious wines in place of vodka, which, as is well known, leads to no good.

Day in and day out for several years, Antonia searched for the formula that would allow her to fulfill her dream. And then one day, in the wee hours of the morning, my hostess succeeded in synthesizing a universal compound that would transform ordinary H_2O into wine. By the addition of some microadditives, it was possible to vary the taste, color, and alcoholic content of the wine.

Then Antonia told me that to get an "endless" bottle, it was essential to dissolve the synthetic compound in a special solution and pour it into an ordinary bottle. The bottle should then be put in an oven and the temperature gradually raised in order to evaporate the water in the solution and allow the sediment to settle permanently on the walls and bottom of the bottle. In that way you got an endless bottle. Later, if you filled it with water and placed it in the light, the water would react immediately with the compound, and in seventeen minutes the bottle would be full of wine. You could drink it right away, or keep it in a dark place.

"Allow me to ask one question," I said to my hostess. "How many times can you use the same bottle?"

"Approximately fifteen thousand," answered Antonia.

"Antonia, you have made a great discovery," I exclaimed. "Why have you kept it a secret up till now? Why don't you get it into production, so that the broad masses of drinkers could move from vodka to a harmless bottle of wine that would cost practically nothing?"

"Hear out the story of my life and activities, and you will see why I have kept the secret of the magic bottles to myself," answered Antonia with sadness in her voice. "Alas, my discovery did not bring me happiness."

My hostess went on to tell me that instead of rejoicing at the news, her father, a prominent landowner and aristocrat, got furious at her. He said that the invention would result in a tremendous loss for him, since he owned vineyards and wineries in the south. Furthermore, if people stopped drinking vodka, it would ruin the state liquor monopoly. Then he called for a priest, who had a talk with Antonia to the effect that she was committing a great sin by wishing to repeat a miracle performed personally by Jesus Christ. The priest threatened her with excommunication and promised her eternal residence in hell if she failed to keep the formula a secret. Being a believer, she swore that for fifty years she would not tell a soul and then she would entrust the secret only to an honest and trustful person.

Only once over all that time did she break her oath, and it brought her a fateful misfortune. After her talks with her father and the priest, Antonia put an end to her scientific activities and started to appear in society. At a high society reception at the Argentine ambassador's she danced the tango with a young Persian prince. It was love at first sight and till death do us part. She went off with him to Persia and there, having converted to Islam, got lawfully wed and became a Persian princess. The prince was fantastically wealthy. He dressed her like a doll, gave her diamond necklaces, chains, and diadems, and was always irreproachably sober, since he was a staunch supporter of Islamic law which forbade the faithful to drink not only vodka and cognac, but all other drinks having an alcoholic content. One day he drank—and destroyed himself.

The way it happened was this. In partial violation of her oath, Antonia brought one of her magic bottles to Persia. One day, when the young princess and her husband were summering at a luxurious, one-of-a-kind villa on the shores of the Caspian Sea, she got the idea of giving the prince some wine, to keep his spirits up in the heat. The prince took one goblet from her hands, then another, and, feeling a rush of new strength, decided to go swimming. When he was sixty yards away from the shore, he gave a shout, and was no more. Toward evening, the waves brought in his body. At the autopsy it was discovered that the alcohol, taken by the prince for the first time in his life, had done its fateful work, as a result of which the prince suffered a heart attack with mortal consequence.

The young widow returned to Petersburg, where she applied to a convent in the hopes of becoming a nun. But since she had become a follower of Islam, they wouldn't accept her. While she was doing the paperwork for returning to Christianity, the First World War broke out, followed by the revolution, and she changed her mind. Then she decided to work in the Turkish baths, the more so as the warm air of the dressing room reminded her of the torrid shores of the Caspian Sea, where she had found her first happiness and then lost it to the fateful bottle. And now, many years later, looking forward to her pension and, eventually, removal to the other world, she wanted to publish her formula gratuitously. But she was afraid that her discovery would only bring harm to people.

"I am giving you this bottle as an experiment," she said in conclusion. "You may use it yourself, or you can give it to some worthy person. If, over the space of a year, this vessel brings no one any harm, I will publish my formula. Incidentally, the wine is ready now."

Glancing at the bottle on the windowsill, I convinced myself that it was full of a dark red wine. I poured myself a glass and tried it. The wine was thick and sweet, with a natural taste and aroma. It was a typical, high-quality sacramental wine.

Soon I thanked my hostess, neatly put the cork back in the bottle, wrapped it in a newspaper, and went home.

A few days later, I was invited to my neighbors' to celebrate George's birthday. It was clear that I couldn't find a better gift, and so I presented it to the man of the hour, first explaining how I had received the wine. The couple was overjoyed with such an interesting gift, but Marina immediately announced that they wouldn't be using the bottle often, since, thank God, they were nondrinkers. Toward the end of our modest party, however, George made a pronouncement that somewhat disturbed me.

"It looks like we won't be paying for our wine anymore," he announced, turning to his wife. "In the store you have to fork out two rubles twenty for wine like this, and here we can drink to our hearts' content."

"Strange logic," laughed Marina. "What a joker you are."

But the next day, it became apparent that George had not been joking. When I returned from work and saw my neighbor in the kitchen, I had to confess to myself that he was under the influence. His eyes were red, and he was slurring his words a little.

"Today I saved two rubles twenty," he announced to me. "By drinking two bottles a day, you can save four rubles forty! That's one hundred and thirty-two rubles a month! A wonderful invention!"

Soon he had trained himself to drink two bottles a day, and then moved on to three. When his wife said that it wasn't good for him, he explained that the harm wasn't significant, since every day he saved six rubles sixty. You don't find money like that on the street!

One morning, getting ready for work, I noticed that my neighbor wasn't leaving for his plant.

"I want to save eight rubles eighty today," he said, winking at me. "But in order to beat my record, I'll have to stay home for a day."

Soon George stopped going to work altogether. Marina, hurt by his behavior, had to spend a month in a health resort in order to calm her nerves.

Taking advantage of his wife's absence, my neighbor became completely unglued. Now he went through five bottles a day. He started to pick up alcoholic pals and even good-time girls. The bottle was constantly at work. Every seventeen minutes someone would weave into the kitchen and fill the bottle with tap water. The drinkers were limited by the fact that the process required daylight, but soon one of George's buddies dragged a powerful neon lamp from somewhere or other, and they started putting the bottles under it at night. Thus, the bottle started to work around the clock. In addition to all this, my neighbor's pals came up with the idea of pouring the wine into ordinary bottles and selling them on the market. With the money they earned they started to buy vodka, which made things even worse. Day and night the visitors shouted, sang rousing lyric songs, stamped through Western European dances, and proposed continuous toasts to the wise possessor of the Big Bottle. When I knocked politely on the wall and asked for quiet, they made fun of me and even threatened to have it out physically.

Soon Marina's time at the health resort ran out, and she returned home. When she came upon the sad scene in her own living quarters, her cure dissolved in thin air. In her overwrought state she tore the endless bottle out of her husband's hands and ran into my room.

"You're the scoundrel who thrust this cursed bottle upon my husband!" she shouted. "You're the monster who pushed my husband to drink!" And with these words, she flung the Big Bottle at me. It shattered against my head, and I fell down, spurting blood.

When she saw her error, Marina burst into tears, threw herself on me, and started to give me first aid. But the wound from the bottle was serious enough to require the attention of a specialist, and so I wrapped my head in a Turkish towel and went to the neighborhood clinic. There they bandaged me.

When the doctor began taking the case history, he asked me to describe the circumstances surrounding my head wound. So as not to put my neighbor on the spot, I said that I was attacked by some members of a street gang, who then ran off unharmed. The doctor believed me completely, since we have our share of street gangs.

Antonia, the inventor of the Big Bottle, saw me at work with my bandaged head. She asked me what had happened, and I told her the whole sad story.

"Alas, now I see that my unique discovery can only bring harm to people!" she said sadly. "It's too soon for people to switch to free wine."

Soon I left the baths, went to work in another place, and never saw Antonia again. Not long ago I learned that she had died. And since there hasn't been any mention of the Big Bottle anywhere, it is clear that the inventor took her secret to the grave.

As for my neighbors, after the bottle was broken, George stopped drinking, returned to work, and made up for his enforced absence with honest labor. Peace returned to the couple, but I was no longer invited to family celebrations. I felt myself responsible for the misfortune that had come down on this friendly family, and decided to move away so as not to remind them by my presence of the sad events connected with the Big Bottle. I exchanged my room for another one in a crowded communal apartment in another building on another street.

But I keep talking about myself, and you, dear reader, are probably interest in my most talented brother Victor.

After I appeared at my brother's covered with wool, thus provoking his just wrath, I stopped visiting him so as not to interrupt his scientific activity. But I continued a regular correspondence with my father and from time to time sent him small sums of money from my modest wages. In his instructional letters Father always informed me about Victor's advancements and his family life.

During the war, my talented brother, as a leading light of science, was evacuated to the rear, together with his wife. There, with no unnecessary fear for his safety, he could bravely move science forward. After the war he got a promotion and returned to Leningrad. Soon my father informed me that Perspectiva had presented Victor with a pair of strapping twins, a boy and a girl. Victor personally registered their births, giving them soundly based names. The boy's name was Oak!; the girl's was Pine! The names were intended to inform all present of the high intelligence of the father and, in the future, to help the children strengthen their authority in their studies and their daily lives.

I was very happy for my brother—now he had worthy descendants—and wrote him a congratulatory card. It's true that I was somewhat surprised by the arboreal names my talented brother had conferred on my niece and nephew. The exclamation points documentally attached to each name particularly disturbed me. I shared these thoughts in a letter to my father, and he soon sent me an answer that dispelled my doubts. Father gently chided me for not having reversed my five uns, in particular "unintelligent," and then simply and understandably explained the essence of the matter. The name Oak! did not mean simply "oak," but was a shortened form of "Only A-1 Koncrete!" The name Pine! was not just any old pine growing wild in the forest, but another exhortation: "Phase In the Newest Ecotechnology!" Thus, my young relatives Oak! and Pine!, if taken separately, represented industry (he) and agriculture (she). And together they represented the union of city and country.

At the end of his letter, my father called on me to quickly get rid of my five uns and multiply my modest achievements, so that my brother would not have to be ashamed of me.

The Music Man 9

When I moved into my new apartment, I hoped that under new conditions my life would flow without all sorts of upheavals and perturbations. My new job was as an assistant warehouse worker for defective silicone products; it was peaceful and without much responsibility. My apartment, despite the number of people in it, was distinguished by its comparative quiet, and on the whole the inhabitants got along with one another. Thus I was now able to rest from my recent misadventures. However, fate was to provide my ship with new sandbars and rocky shores. The warehouse was unexpectedly closed for repairs, I was given a long vacation, and I set myself up with a temporary job on a geological expedition.

Our expedition worked in the Caucasus, and we based ourselves in a small mountain village. My job included doing the cooking and assisting in various ways. I was assigned a local helper, a fellow by the name of Orfis. He was a capable and conscientious worker and, in addition, spoke good Russian.

Ond day there was a thunderstorm with a heavy downpour. It went on for the whole day. One of our research teams, consisting of three persons, did not return to the base on time, and there was no word from them. The group had been working in a distant canyon, and we began to fear that something had happened.

Since on the day the thunder started the group was supposed to be returning to base, nobody could pinpoint their exact location. It was therefore decided to send two rescue crews in different directions. The primary crew was made up of three qualified geologists, headed by an experienced guide. Less hope was placed on the second group, consisting of myself and Orfis, who knew his native mountains very well.

When I volunteered to take part in the search, I was afraid that they wouldn't let me go because of the nature of my work, but in fact they were rather willing. Among those who stayed there could be heard rude hints concerning the quality of my cooking and statements to the effect that now they could get some rest from my concoctions.

Orfis and I picked up our knapsacks filled with canned foods and medicines, and set off toward the northwest. For a long time we kept to the valley, but then my leader made a steep turn to the left and we started to climb the mountain. Towards evening we found ourselves in a green meadow nestled among the high hills. There was such a silence all around that you could feel it in your teeth, which ached as though splashed with cold water.

Soon, on the side of the mountain I saw a lot of yellow-gray boulders resembling sheep. A man was walking among them and waving something like a stick or knout.

"What's that man doing?" I asked Orfis.

"That's my great-great-grandfather," says Orfis. "He's herding stones."

"Poor old man," I said. "If he's gone off his rocker, then he should have medical help."

"He's not crazy," said my companion, offended. "He's as healthy as you and me, he's just very old. His whole life he herded real sheep, but his legs aren't what they used to be, so he herds stones. He can't live without work."

"Why didn't he move to the valley?"

"He's used to heights, and doesn't want to. My relatives tried to get him to go a thousand times. Many years ago they got a room ready for him, the best in the house, covered with carpets, and he hasn't been in it once. He lives all year 'round in a straw hut and sleeps on sheepskins."

"Maybe they offended him somehow?" I said.

"Impossible! Everyone is full of respect for him, and he loves his family. But he likes to live here."

We walked up to the stone herder and greeted him respect-

fully. He was very, very old, but hardly a walking ruin. He
was lively and affable, and quickly went to his hut to get some
wine. The three of us sat down on the grass. We nibbled at a
delicious stringy cheese and took turns drinking the dry wine
from a leather pouch. The old man didn't know much Russian,
but Orfis served as our interpreter. Taking advantage of this, I
told the respected old man my life story. He listened with
interest and sympathy. Then he asked Orfis to tell me that
everything bad is for the best, and that soon I would find that
person whom I was destined for and who was personally destined for me. Before that, however, I would jump into an
abyss, but at the moment of falling I would sprout wings.

As we drank and talked, the old man did not forget his
duties. From time to time he got up, took his knout, and hurried over to one of the surrounding boulders. He clucked his
tongue, shouted something stern, and waved the knout at the
stone. He did this all seriously, but there was an element of
play in it too.

"What did he tell the stone?" I asked Orfis during one of
these moments.

"He said, 'You sneaky sheep, do you want to stray from the
herd?' " explained Orfis.

When we had eaten our fill, I stretched out on the grass
and dozed, and my companion and the old man had a long
talk. Then Orfis told me that it was time to go out on the
search. The old man advised him to go towards the mountain
shining blue in the distance.

"But it's going to be night soon," I objected. "We could
get lost."

"I know these hills," my guide said calmly.

We said good-bye to the hospitable old man herding his
stones, and set off. Soon we reached a mountain hollow and
started picking our way among the huge stones. It had gotten
dark.

"We won't lose each other," my companion said suddenly,
guessing my thoughts. With these words, he got out a small

bar of a waxlike substance. Then suddenly he began to rub his forehead with it.

"What's that?" I said.

"You'll see," he answered.

Suddenly we heard some soft but rather pleasant music, like the sounds of a shepherd's horn. You'd almost think that my companion had a transistor radio in his pocket. But I knew he didn't.

"Where is the music coming from?" I asked.

"From me," said Orfis. "I'm making it. I rubbed my forehead with a secret paste, and here I am making music. It will go on for eight hours without stopping. In order to start it up again, all I have to do is rub my forehead."

Then he explained to me that each person has his own life music, and everyone lives in harmony with this music, although nobody can hear his own and other people can't distinguish it either. The secret paste transforms a person into something like a musical instrument, translating his internal rhythm into a melody. Every person has his own melody, the partial expression of his personality. No two people have the same melody, just as no two people have the same fingerprints. In ancient times shepherds used the secret paste so as not to get lost in the mountains. Moreover, the music maker is safe from predators, and if he falls asleep on the grass, then not a single snake will crawl up to him.

"But that's a tremendous discovery!" I exclaimed. "Why isn't anything written on it?"

"The paste is the secret of our ancestral clan," said Orfis quietly. "The method of preparing it has been known from time immemorial and is transmitted from old man to old man. The present bearer of the secret is the man who was herding the stones. He will tell it to his son when his son reaches a hundred and twenty. Know that not only the secret of preparation but the secret paste itself has never been given, sold, or presented to any outsider." Orfis paused and then continued: "But the old man who was herding stones took a great liking to you, your constant misfortunes touched his heart, and he is giving you a bar of this paste for eternal personal use, with the right to lend it to blood relatives only."

With these words, my companion took a second bar, wrapped in clean paper, out of his pocket and handed it to me.

I was terribly excited by my valuable present, but I was somehow scared to try it on myself. *A man with five uns might just put out the sort of music that would make the saints squirm*, I thought.

But I overcame my fear, carefully began rubbing my forehead with the bar, and then I began to sound! To my spiritual relief, the melody that issued forth was, if not particularly artistic, then at least not unpleasant. It was something like a foxtrot or a rhumba and, to give the truth its due, it was rather easy to walk to. My companion's sounds were more melodic, but softer than mine, and his rhythm was slower.

Thanks to the secret paste and the forehead music, we walked a long way in the pitch darkness without losing one another from earshot (I can't say "from view," since we couldn't see anything), and soon entered a deep canyon. Suddenly, we could hear someone's astonished cry: "What idiot came here with a transistor radio?"

Thus we found the lost group of geologists. The hungry travelers threw themselves joyfully on our provisions, not waiting for the dinner I was ready to prepare for them.

When we got back to the base, I was distressed to learn that the camp supplier had used the time to hire a new cook from the local population. I was demoted to the rank of kitchen helper, without the right to prepare food. Offended at the injustice, I asked for my pay, which was given to me without much resistance. When I got the money that was due me, I left for the nearest resort town, which I will tentatively call Vacation-Deceptionville. The city had an airport, and I intended to fly from there to Leningrad.

While I was at the airport waiting in line for plane tickets, a pleasant-looking vacationer, all in tears, walked up to me.

She motioned me over to a side and confided that she had been cruelly robbed and left without the ten rubles she needed for a ticket to Vladivostok, where her small daughter, who had been run over by a car, lay in the hospital. I was touched by her understandable grief and decided to help out by giving her the missing ten rubles. I had in my hands a hundred and nine rubles, but the hundred was a single bill, so I told the unfortunate lady that I would run to the restaurant to change the bill, after which I would give her the necessary sum.

"Oh, don't trouble yourself, my savior!" exclaimed the pleasant-looking lady. "I'll do it for you myself, and bring you the change right away."

The lady took the bill and went to change it. She didn't appear again, and I soon understood that under her pleasant exterior there was concealed a speculator and deceiver.

I simply didn't know what to do. I didn't feel right about sending a telegram to my Leningrad acquaintances asking for help. I didn't want to turn to my brother, since now that his family contained an Oak! and a Pine!, his expenses had naturally grown; and anyway it would not be tactful to tear my talented brother from his scientific thought with such a mundane request. So I made up my mind to borrow some money from my father, the more so as I had given him material support whenever possible. Thus, I sent a telegram to Greetica-Leaveittown with the following message: LOST MONEY REQUEST FIFTY ON LOAN POSTE RESTANTE.

I spent the night in the Vacation-Deceptionville city park. In the morning I appeared at the post office and, taking out my passport, asked if there were any money for me.

"Nothing," said the girl behind the window, sympathizing with me. "But we did receive a strange telegram. I've been asking everyone if it isn't theirs. It's addressed to a 'man with five uns.' "

The text of the telegram was as follows: FIND IT WHERE YOU LOST IT YOUR FATHER.

My father's severe but just response to my tactless request stunned me and threw me into a quandary. Spending my last funds on food, I passed the day wandering the streets of Vacation-Deceptionville in a pitiful state. When it got dark, I went to the back yard of a rest home. I meant to spend the night on a bench and decided to wait for the vacationers to stop strolling around and enjoying themselves and go inside to sleep. But in the meantime it was very crowded in the garden, particularly around a platform that had been set up for dancing. However, there was no music to be heard. This surprised me.

Suddenly the administrator of the rest home appeared on stage with the announcement that the staff accordionist Comrade Ukhomorov had been taken ill unexpectedly, so the dance would have to be put off. There were rumblings of discontent. There were even some direct threats in the direction of the administrator, promising to beat him up for his poor management of cultural affairs.

At that moment, I understood the hidden wisdom of Father's telegram. Making my way through the crowd, I walked up the five steps to the stage, went over to the administrator, and offered my services. I told him honestly that I couldn't play fashionable dances like rock and roll or the twist, but that for an undemanding public my music would be quite sufficient.

"God Himself must have sent you to me," exclaimed the administrator joyfully. "What are your conditions?"

"I will play five concerts, for which you will give me a room and your best meals for five days, followed by a plane ticket to Leningrad." That's how I put it.

"Agreed, my friend! Agreed! Let's get started! Where is your instrument?"

"I am my own instrument," I answered and, taking the secret paste out of my pocket, began to rub my forehead.

I sounded off, and the couples began to dance. My music pleased everybody, and the dance lasted until late at night. It

would have gone on even longer, but the administrator politely led me off the stage, since it was time for the vacationers
to get some sleep. I was given a full meal and was settled for
the night in my own little house, which they used as an infir-
mary. This was done so that I wouldn't keep the vacationers
up with my music. After all, the secret paste worked for eight
hours, and I was still making music.

The news about the musical man spread swiftly among the
vacationers, and when I appeared on the dance platform on
the next day, there was a huge crowd. A day later, the entire
garden was packed with lovers of music and dance, who had
come from all over Vacation-Deceptionville. No matter where
I went over the next three days, I was followed by a troop of
hummers and dancers. The vacationers had managed to develop a conditioned reflex, so that even when I wasn't making
any music they thought I was, and as soon as I came into view
they would start singing and dancing and having a good time.

My popularity attained such heights that a certain cultivated vacationer by the name of Musya even fell in love with
me. She wasn't opposed to the idea of marriage, either, at least
until I told her the story of my life. After that she didn't bring
it up again. Alas, I never had any luck with women—nor,
indeed, with anything else. But in my heart I stayed true to
my ideal, the beautiful "Caress Me!" who had once adorned
the walls of my room in an edition of 848.

When the five days had passed, the administrator handed
me my plane ticket to Leningrad, adding three rubles for a
taxi and other expenses. As a token of his thankfulness, he
gave me, gratis, an album with pictures of Vacation-Deceptionville, which he inscribed on the first page in his own hand.

Further Developments 10

When I returned to Leningrad, joyous news awaited me. My multitalented brother had sent me a letter. It began like this:

DISPATCH

I hereby announce and declare that on Saturday following due respect will be paid to my creative achievements in the areas of science and domestic life, and due joy taken in the aforementioned by our own father, who has been granted the honor of staying here at my expense for a period of 7 (seven) days.

You have been invited to appear at my residence that same Saturday at 19 hours and remain until 20 hours, adding your voice to the general exaltation and having on your person boots, trousers, a jacket, a shirt, and other such accoutrements of human dress . . .

The letter concluded with scientific phrases that I found incomprehensible, but the first part of the dispatch was clear: my brother had invited me to see him!

I prepared myself for the visit with great care, appearing at his door at precisely the indicated time. I shall not describe my joy upon seeing my father and brother, both of whom looked very young for their years. My niece and nephew, Pine! and Oak!, also made a very pleasant impression on me.

During my long absence, my brother's beautiful apartment had been adorned with more expensive furniture and so many carpets that in some places they were two layers thick. There were changes in his study as well: where once the portraits of illustrious scholars and inventors had surrounded a single portrait of Victor, there now hung many portraits of Victor, in multiple poses and variations. The others had been annulled. From this fact alone, I could see how my brother's role in science had grown.

Supper passed in a friendly, cultivated atmosphere. I tried to say as little as possible and pay close attention to Father and Victor, who gave me practical advice for ridding myself of my five uns. When, finally, I told about the secret paste, Victor expressed an interest in it and proposed that I demonstrate its action.

I took the paste out of my pocket, carefully rubbed some on my forehead, and sounded off. My father and brother cut off their conversation and started listening to me intently. Only the deaf-mute Perspectiva did not take part. She reclined on the sofa in a fetching pose.

"I want to make music too," said my brother suddenly. "Tomorrow I have to give a paper in front of the administration, and I would like music to flow from me as well as words. You've got some sort of tap dance going, but given my position, I should produce something more cultured. I expect no less than Bach and Beethoven."

I told my brother that unfortunately I didn't have the right to make him a present of the secret paste, but that I could lend it to him for a day.

Two days later I went to see him. Handing me the secret paste, he said in an angry tone:

"What kind of thing was that to palm off on me? So you felt like harming an important scientist! I should inform you-know-who!"

My infuriated brother proceeded to tell me what had happened at the institute. Before delivering his paper, he rubbed some of the paste on his forehead—and suddenly found himself producing such unharmonious sounds that he was forced to make a hasty exit from the department and take refuge in the toilet, where he spent eight hours without food or drink, until the noise stopped.

This unpleasant incident shocked me to the core. It dawned on me that the secret paste had one important drawback: it did not always call forth the music that was hidden within a person, and it could result in a misleading impression, as had happened with Victor. For that reason, I decided to get rid of the paste. I did not want anyone else to be victimized by it. I took the stone herder's present, wrapped it in some paper, and threw it into the Neva from the Palace Bridge. This just act did not bring me any joy, but I felt that I had done the right thing.

PMP **11**

I soon found a job as a buyer's helper. The salary wasn't much, but I had a lot of free time that I could devote to furthering my education, in other words, to reading science fiction. Our communal apartment was peaceful and orderly. True, one of the quietest inhabitants had left, and his room was now occupied by a young bachelor, a mathematics teacher. His name was Alex. He was also a calm sort; you couldn't even hear him. During the day he taught at some institute, and when he got home he sat in his room till the early hours of the morning, poring over books and papers and computing something.

One day I was short five rubles, and stopped by to ask him for a loan. It was then that I got a good look at the room. The room was strikingly modest, but everything was in perfect order and there were a lot of books. Next to the desk there was another table, which supported some sort of machine, like a typewriter, only much bigger. Alex explained to me that it was a computer, his own design. As for the walls of the room, Alex had covered them with white paper which he had then inscribed with endless rows of figures and multilayered formulas.

My new neighbor instantly fulfilled my request, and without further ado handed me the five-ruble bill. Then he asked me if I didn't need a larger sum than five rubles.

I answered that having endured a number of setbacks I would of course, in principle, like to have more money than I had at the present. However, I only borrowed exactly the amount that I knew I could give back. I took the opportunity to tell Alex my life story, which he heard out with the proper attention.

"Yes, you need help," he said thoughtfully.

"No, five rubles is enough," I repeated. "I won't accept charity."

"Please, don't be offended," said my new acquaintance in a comforting tone. "You can give me back the fiver, and I have no intention of engaging in private philanthropy. But all the same I'm going to help you. I've put you in line, come back to see me in twenty-seven days." Having said that, he wrote something down on a pad.

"But how can you help me if, as I see by your modest surroundings, you yourself are not rich," I asked, astonished.

"I could be very rich in a financial sense but, in the first place, I consider it dishonorable to use the resources at my disposal for my own enrichment, and, in the second place, money just doesn't interest me. What I have now is sufficient. The simpler my food, clothing, and furniture, the lighter I feel. My mind works more freely."

My neighbor's speech made me think that he was a bit out of it. How could somebody without money help somebody else get some?

However, hardly had a week passed when I was convinced that Alex had told me the absolute truth. Even more: it soon became clear that he was a brilliant mathematician and inventor and, above all, a wonderful person.

This is how it happened.

I already mentioned that the inhabitants of my communal apartment were, in the main, worthy people. But, alas, there is no barrel of honey that lacks its teaspoon of tar. In our apartment there lived a well-to-do woman who, it was said, had obtained her wealth in some underhanded way. She had a lot of money but she kept it a secret, doing her best to live modestly. Despite this she was very envious, and whenever somebody bought something new, she would be sick for a whole day, or for two days or sometimes even for a week, depending on its price and quality. She hated everybody, and behind her back the neighbors called her the Wicked Witch.

In our apartment there also lived a quiet old lady by the name of Varvara. Varvara lived with her son Valery, a student at the polytechnical institute. She had been a widow for twenty years, and had a clerical job in a construction firm. One day, having received a bonus at work, she bought her son a small desk for forty-six rubles and fifty kopecks. In order to make space for the desk, she took an old bureau out of the room and, with everyone's approval, put it in the hall.

When the Wicked Witch heard about the purchase, she got sick for two days, and upon her return to health started pestering Varvara with daily demands that she remove the bureau from the hall.

Varvara would have been glad to get rid of the bureau, and even hung up ads in an attempt to sell it. But things like that are no longer in fashion, and she was hardly inundated by buyers. In vain did she explain this to the Wicked Witch, and in vain did the other neighbors declare unanimously that the bureau in the hall did not disturb them. No, the Wicked Witch didn't want to hear a word, and even complained to the house committee.

Finally, one evening all the neighbors gathered in the hall, sent for Varvara, and asked her how much she wanted for her old bureau. She answered honestly that it wasn't worth more than twenty rubles.

Then the neighbors began taking up a collection. Some people gave two rubles, others gave three, and finally the bureau was paid for. Then they put an ax to it and, in a friendly way, hacked it into pieces, the easier to bring the wood down to the cellar.

The noise brought the Wicked Witch out of her room.

Standing apart from everyone, her arms folded, she observed the proceedings with a triumphant grin.

"I won," she said in a loud voice when the last pieces had been carried out.

Alex threw a withering look at the Wicked Witch, but said nothing. Turning to Varvara, he politely invited her to stop by his room. He asked me to come with them and serve as his assistant for three or four hours.

Alex offered Varvara a seat in his only armchair, and asked her a series of questions.

"What are you doing this for?" said Varvara, becoming curious.

"I want to help you," said Alex. "But I can only help people who won't do harm either to themselves or to others. Now that I am convinced that you are an honest and honorable person, I'm ready to help you. In the meantime, I ask you not to spend the twenty rubles you were given for the bureau."

When Varvara left, Alex turned on his computer, pushed some buttons, and asked me to take a seat and write down in three columns the numbers that would be appearing in the green, red, and light blue little windows. He himself laid out some tables and schemes on his desk, and started drawing all sorts of symbols, formulas, and graphs.

An hour and a half passed. I had gone through seventeen sheets of paper, when suddenly something sputtered in the machine. The green window turned yellow, the yellow window turned dark blue. Only the light blue window stayed the way it was, but in place of numbers there appeared an inscription: PROBABILITY IN SPACE USED UP.

"What do we do now?" I asked Alex.

"Start a new page with two columns," ordered the mathematician.

A half hour later, an inscription appeared in the green window: PROBABILITY IN TIME USED UP.

"Now start a new page with a single column," said Alex.

Twenty-three minutes later the machine turned itself off.

Alex offered me a cup of tea and told me something about himself. Chance events had interested him since childhood. While he was still in kindergarten, he wasn't interested in games, but in game theory. He spent all his free time throwing a five-kopeck coin to see if he could get tails five times in a row. Even then, young Alex had come to the conclusion that we are all swimmers in the ocean of chance events. We don't notice this because, in the same way as any object consists of atoms, so are our lives and everything surrounding us created out of chance events. A chance event seems chance to us only when it separates itself from the familiar series of chance events. If we put together 100,000,000,000 needles with their points up, we can walk along them barefoot and even dance on them without hurting our feet. But a single needle, separated from the 100,000,000,000, can give us a painful prick.

Then Alex explained that the ocean of chance events has its own currents, and if you study them, it is possible to swim far into the distance and discover new continents.

When we had finished our tea and talk, we again took up the task on hand, and worked another hour. Then my friend said that he would work on the problem by himself. He took the sheets of paper with my notations and began to look them over, underlining some figures in red, some in green, and others in blue. Then he got out from under the bed a huge and very accurate map of Leningrad and spread it out on a wide drawing board. On top of the map he placed a sheet of clean tracing paper, and he began to draw some complicated graphs with blue India ink. Then he took a second sheet of tracing paper and began to draw on it with red ink. Finally, he took a third sheet of tracing paper, placed it on top of the other two, and wrote on it with black ink. But these lines were already much simpler, and they all led to a single point.

"Now we've found the PGP," said Alex in a satisfied voice and pierced the point with a mapping pen. He removed the three sheets of tracing paper from the map of Leningrad, took a magnifying glass, and drew a tiny green circle around the puncture mark. "The PGP's here," he repeated. "In the Vyborg district."

"What's this PGP?" I said, curious.

"PGP is the Point of Greatest Probability," answered the mathematician.

And with these words, he wrote down on a piece of paper the street, the number of a house, and the time: 12:08. He gave this paper to me.

"Tomorrow, have Varvara appear at the indicated address at the indicated time. The address should belong to a savings bank. Let her buy a government lottery ticket whose serial number ends in a seven."

The next day, taking Alex's advice, Varvara went to the Vyborg district. She found the savings bank on the indicated street and, at precisely the indicated time, bought a lottery ticket whose serial number ended in a seven.

The drawing took place a week later, and when, a few days after that, the table of winners appeared, Varvara saw with her own eyes that she had won five thousand rubles. Naturally, her first act was to run and thank Alex.

"Don't mention it," said the young mathematician politely. "To the best of my abilities I try to correct the mistakes of fortune and direct the proceeds to those who truly need them."

With the money, Varvara bought, not counting the clothes for herself and her son, an electric floor polisher, a vacuum cleaner, a Volna television, a Riga 55 washing machine, a Melodia radio–record player, and an Astra-2 tape recorder. All the neighbors were pleased that this modest woman had won so much money, and the Wicked Witch got so ill from envy that she had to be taken to the hospital, where she passed away. Two persons were present at the funeral, the janitress and the girl from the passport registry, both because of their professional concern for people. And when they opened the room where she had lived, they found money and jewels in such quantity that they would have paid for a hundred televisions and a thousand washing machines.

As for myself, Alex helped me win one thousand rubles. Part of the money I sent to Father, and with the rest of it I got some clothes, bought an armchair that opened out into a bed, and healed almost all of my financial wounds. Alex promised to win me a motorcycle for the summer, and advised me to use the time I had left to take a course in driver's ed, which I did.

In the weeks and months that followed, Alex often consulted with me as to whether he should help some person or other, and almost always took my opinion into consideration. But when, one day, I brought the conversation around to Victor and talked, as well as I could, about his great role in science and also about the need for extra income caused by the appearance of Oak! and Pine!, Alex curtly refused to help my talented brother. I was terribly hurt.

One day I asked Alex how he had come to the idea of predicting winners. He answered that the idea was secondary, even tertiary in its significance. It arose in the process of his work on a more important problem. At this point he began to explain the nature of that problem, but I sat there like an oaf and didn't understand a thing. I confessed as much to him and asked a simpler question: could he predict things that had no relationship to numbers, or, to put it in a nutshell, could he make a forecast for my future life and give me the hope that my eternal failures and troubles would someday come to an end.

The young mathematician answered, slightly offended, that he was not a fortune-teller and worked only with figures. But then he got interested in my question, and asked me to draw up an account of the events in my life. I was to evaluate every unpleasant event on a scale of -1 to -5, and every joyous event on a scale of $+1$ to $+5$, depending on its degree of joyousness. I soon provided him with my report, and he put the data into his computer. A half hour later it gave out the results, which could be read as follows: $-1; -2; -1; -2; -3;$

$-4;\ -2;\ -3;\ (-5\ =\ \pm\ =\ +5)\ +5+5+5+5+5+5+5+5+5+$
$5+5;\ 0.$

"May the song of your computer rise up to heaven!" I exclaimed. "As far as I can see by these figures, after a lot of troubles, which I'm already used to, there awaits me a cloudless, happy life! But what do those fives in brackets mean?"

"I can't figure it out myself," said Alex. "It's possible that what's indicated here is an event of extremely short duration, in the course of which the five changes its sign. But I can't say anything precisely, and in general I ask you not to give too much significance to the forecast." With these words, he tore up the paper with the figures on it and turned the conversation to another subject. It seemed to me that something in the forecast had upset him.

Toward the beginning of summer, I successfully completed driver's ed. And then one day, not long before the next lottery drawing, Alex worked out my PGP for obtaining the lottery ticket. With this lottery ticket, I was to win the motorcycle.

When at 15:38 I appeared at the indicated address, on one of the streets near the Warsaw Station, I saw to my astonishment that the corner house, the number of which had been given to me by my benefactor, was not a savings bank at all. There wasn't even a store where I could have bought a lottery ticket.

Depressed by this breakdown in the system of the young mathematician, I hung my head and slowly made my way homewards. But hardly had I taken two steps, when somebody lightly tugged at my sleeve.

"Listen, pal, how would you like to buy a lottery ticket from me," said a hoarse voice. Turning around, I saw a middle-aged man whose eyes were bleary with drink.

"Buy the ticket, pal," the stranger addressed me again. "I need a glass of beer, my head is aching."

I realized at once that the PMP was right again, and that Alex's system didn't allow for breakdowns. Taking out a ruble,

I handed it over to the poor guy, so badly in need of a drink to cure his hangover. I didn't ask for anything in return, and told him in a friendly way that he shouldn't sell his ticket to anyone because he would win a motorcycle with it.

"Thank you, sir," exclaimed the stranger. "I'll follow your advice."

When I got home, I told Alex about this incident, and he drew up another PMP. The next day I bought a ticket and won a motorcycle with a sidecar.

I didn't really need the sidecar, since I was a bachelor and didn't have anyone to take for a drive. Somewhere faraway, under the wallpaper of my childhood room, the beautiful girl of "Caress Me!" hung in 848 copies. But I thought that, as a person with five uns, I was fated never to meet with my dream.

All the same, when I got a vacation and set off on a motorcycle trip to the south, I left the sidecar on.

EIRO **12**

I was trying to make it back to Leningrad on time. For two days I drove full speed, and slept in the bushes at the side of the road. By the third day I was so tired that, when I got to a city, I decided to take a rest. Since events of great significance for me took place there, I will call the city Hopes-Fulfilledsville.

I stopped my motorcycle on a main street and asked a passerby how to get to the hotel. The latter immediately pointed to a new eleven-story building that towered over everything and was the pride of the inhabitants of Hopes-Fulfilledsville.

Although I am writing an accurate account of my life, and not science fiction, and although I know that there are never any vacancies in hotels, still I took off for the building. Of course I wasn't counting on a bed, but I hoped to park my motorcycle in the hotel yard and take a snooze in the lobby. In that I was successful, and soon I was sleeping in a comfortable leatherette chair with my knapsack at my feet. All around me were vacationers awaiting rooms in the hotel. Then suddenly I felt someone touching my shoulder, and I woke up. In front of me stood a man of about thirty-five, with an intelligent and sympathetic face.

"Come into my room, there's an empty cot," he said.

"But I don't have a business-trip certificate," I said, unable to believe what was happening.

"It doesn't matter. They'll register you."

The stranger went with me to the administrator, and indeed I was registered without further ado. We took an elevator up to the eleventh floor, where his room was. On the way I asked him why he wanted to help me, a complete stranger.

"Because of the influx of tourists they're doubling everybody up, and they wanted to stick me with some guy with a noisy transistor on his hip. I can't stand those brainless organ-grinders. And since I have a single room, I have the right to choose who I'm going to be with. So I went down to the lobby and started to look over the guests. The expression on your face was so honest and simple that it decided me. I trust that your knapsack doesn't contain any transistor radios, tape recorders, or similar noisemakers."

"No," I said, "and I like quiet myself."

"Then I wasn't mistaken in you!" said the kind stranger with feeling. "And here's our room."

We walked into a small room, number 1155, and my guide pointed out the cot.

"Please excuse me if I sleep on the bed and not on this wretched folding cot," he said politely. "But there's nothing to get offended at, because I'm much older than you."

"You . . . you're older than me?" I was astonished. "But I'm forty-nine! And you can't be more than thirty-five."

"I'm sixty-three," said my new acquaintance calmly. "If you don't believe me, have a look at my passport."

I did, and saw with my own eyes that my new friend, whose name, according to his passport, was Anatoly, was really fourteen years older than me.

"But how come you look so young?" I asked. "Even on your passport picture you look much older."

"The passport picture is an old one. I had it taken three years ago," said my strange acquaintance. "In those three years I became younger."

"I don't understand anything!" I exclaimed. "Everybody gets older as the years go by, and you get younger!"

"My young and lively look, and the youthful clarity of my mind, are all the result of EIRO," he said.

"What's EIRO?" I asked.

"EIRO stands for Elixir for Instant Regeneration of the Organism," answered Anatoly in a weighty tone.

Since I was always running into inventors and discoverers of every sort, my experience suggested that before me stood the man responsible for EIRO. When I gave voice to my assumption, my new acquaintance answered in the affirmative. Then I gave him a brief account of my life from childhood to the present. He listened with interest and enthusiasm, and, by way of an answer, told me about himself, his discovery of EIRO, and EIRO's great significance.

Anatoly was born in a big city. At school he was first in his class in chemistry, botany, and biology, but in those days he didn't make any scientific plans for himself. But one day, when he was about to finish school, an event occurred that had a great effect on him. His younger brother, who had been playing on a windowsill without his parents' knowledge, fell out and crashed into the street from a height of seven stories. The young Anatoly was deeply disturbed and decided to invent something so that a person falling from a great height would not crash into the street, but would remain alive and well.

Anatoly well understood the difficulties and unusual char-

acter of his chosen task, and did not start working on it immediately. Having finished school, he went to the medical
institute, and when he graduated he took some courses at a
chemistry institute. After that he immersed himself in botany,
specializing in medicinal herbs.

He took part in numerous botanical expeditions. On one
such expedition in the Siberian taiga he heard that certain animals, if they were wounded, sought out a particular
unprepossessing-looking grass. Having eaten the grass, the
animal would get better very quickly, and the wound would
heal as if it had never occurred. With great difficulty, Anatoly
found the plant and started to cultivate it. He prepared an
extract from the seeds, and recommended its use in hospital
emergency rooms. The medicine fostered the quick healing of
wounds and broken bones, and had great success in the medical world. All the same, it was not precisely what the scientist
had been looking for. He needed a preparation that would
work instantly, at the very moment of trauma. He soon realized that to get such a preparation, he would have to synthe-
size it. He dedicated the remainder of his life to this project.
And then, three years ago, after a great number of experiments, he succeeded in finding what he had searched for since
his early youth. He was in his sixty-first year.

It was necessary, of course, to put EIRO to a practical test.
As an opponent of experimentation on innocent animals, Anatoly decided to carry out the first experiment on himself.
Since he was still living in the same apartment, he would
make the first leap from the same window that had witnessed
the death of his unfortunate younger brother so many years
ago.

Finally, during the summer when his family was away in
the country, he got up at two o'clock in the morning, dissolved
seven drops of EIRO in a glass of water, and drank it down.
The window was wide open. For a few seconds he stood on
the windowsill, overcoming his fear, and then he cast himself
to the winds from a height of seven stories.

In the moment of falling he thought that his heart was

about to give way. Then he felt a sharp, painful blow and for an instant he lost consciousness. A minute later he picked himself up from the stones. He was not only alive and well, but in a completely blissful state. It was as if he had bathed in curative waters. However, his suit had split its seams and lost its buttons, his shoes had lost their heels, and the key to his apartment had flown out of his pocket. He had to get down on all fours and look for it all over the dark yard.

Since the sound of his body falling against the stones was on the loud side, a lot of people who lived in the house woke up and rushed to look out their windows. When they made out some ragged type crawling around their yard in search of God knows what, they began to call the janitor. The janitor didn't recognize the respected scientist right away either, and was about to haul the crackpot off to the police station. But everything ended well, and, having found his key, Anatoly returned to his apartment.

In the course of the next two weeks, the self-propelling researcher withstood another eighteen leaps from the window, each one as successful as the first. So as not to spoil his suits, he designed a special jumping suit: a canvas jacket, canvas pants, and felt boots. The people who lived in his house gradually got used to the experiments and stopped calling the janitor. But soon Anatoly realized that his neighbors and acquaintances no longer recognized him when they met him on the street. He started to look into the mirror more frequently, and became convinced of a strange fact: after every jump he looked younger and younger. His wrinkles disappeared, along with his gray hair, and a youthful ruddiness appeared in his cheeks. Like many people of his age he used to be short of breath, but now that too had gone. He had begun to see and hear better, and his memory had become almost what it was in his student years.

When he went to see a doctor, the latter told him that, according to most indicators, he had the health of a man of thirty.

"Anatoly!" I exclaimed in delight when I had heard out this scientific pronouncement. "Anatoly! You have made a great discovery! Your EIRO has to be put into mass production immediately. There are a lot of people who need your elixir —steeplejacks, roofers, mountain climbers, and tightrope walkers, not to mention children and drunkards living in high buildings. Even housewives when they have to wash windows! And its rejuvenating side effects! That's nothing short of a miracle. Just think of it—"

"Alas, it's not as simple as you think," said the scientist, cutting off my burst of enthusiasm. "I have to tell you that, at the present time, EIRO works only when the fall occurs no later than three minutes after the medicine is administered. And steeplejacks can't exactly take EIRO every three minutes. Right now I'm working on lengthening its activity. Of course, even in its present state my elixir is necessary and worthy of mass production. But before we take that step, it's imperative to prove that it is universally effective. I myself still don't know whether instant restoration of the organism occurs in all individuals, since at the present time, the experiment has only been made on one, namely myself. I need volunteer subjects. For three years now I've been traveling all over the country looking for volunteers, and I haven't been able to find them. There are a lot of brave people in the world, but all I have to do is explain the conditions of the experiment—that is, to note that EIRO may not work at the moment of landing—and the bravest people for some reason refuse to go through with it. In fact, I came here on an agreement with a local parachutist, a very courageous guy. But despite the educational campaign I carried out with him, he's started vacillating and trying to get out of it. Tomorrow I'm going to try to convince him again. No, it's not that simple at all. Take yourself, for example; would you agree to leap from an eleventh-story window?"

"I'm afraid that a scientific feat like that is beyond me."

"Well, you see, and a moment ago you were saying, 'a great discovery!' " said my roommate in an offended tone.

For all my exhaustion, it took me a long time to get to sleep that night. I was disturbed by the misfortunes of this eminent scientist, who dreamed of presenting humanity with his miraculous elixir, only people themselves would not meet him halfway. I yearned to help him, but since childhood I had been afraid of heights, and I understood that it would be next to impossible for me to take that leap. In addition, I couldn't help recalling my previous contacts with dreamers, discoverers, and inventors. As a rule, they did not bring me any happiness. My experience with the wool-wearer was especially bitter, since it was because of him that I failed to complete my education. And here I was threatened with something far greater: loss of life.

With those thoughts I fell asleep, and when I awakened I discovered that my roommate had already left on his educational campaign. I went out and wandered around Hopes-Fulfilledsville, which turned out to be a very pleasant place. But the thought that EIRO might never reach mass production weighed on my heart like a stone and prevented me from observing the city sights with the proper attention.

When, in the evening, I returned to the hotel, Anatoly was already in the room. He was sitting in the armchair with an unhappy, dispirited expression. I thought I saw traces of tears on his cheeks.

"I didn't manage to convince the parachutist. He turned me down point-blank, saying something about his wife and two children," said the scholar in a trembling voice.

I felt ashamed of myself. I had no wife and no children, and nobody in particular would mourn my passing if something should go wrong. Only cowardice prevented me from agreeing to the experiment.

Mechanically I went into the bathroom and looked at myself in the mirror. Staring back at me was an old bachelor, whose face was marked by all five of his uns: unskillful, unintelligent, unoutstanding, unlucky, unhandsome.

To this litany could be added yet another un: unyoung.

Who needs a guy like this? I thought. *And this is who's refusing to risk himself for the sake of science, brazenly clinging to his bachelor life!*

With these unspoken words I left the bathroom and, returning to the room, told the scientist:

"I am ready to take EIRO and carry out a scientific leap from the window."

"My friend!" shouted Anatoly. "People will not forget you. What happiness, that I met you on my life's path! . . . When do you want to do the experiment?"

"Now, if you like," I answered.

"Right now is a bit early. Our window looks out on the street; we'll have to wait till nighttime, when there won't be anybody walking past. In the meantime, in any event, I advise you to make out your will. You already know that during the experiment your organism may not respond to EIRO in the expected way."

I sat down to write my will. This didn't take too long, since I possessed exactly 2 (two) valuable items: the armchair-bed and the motorcycle. I bequeathed the armchair-bed to my talented brother Victor, and I entrusted the motorcycle to Anatoly, with the understanding that he would sell it and send the money to my father.

Late that night, Anatoly gently reminded me that it was time for the experiment.

"So that nothing happens to your clothing, I'll lend you my own jumping suit," he added in an obliging way, and pulled out of his large suitcase a canvas jacket, canvas trousers, and thick, high-quality felt boots.

I arrayed myself in the jumping suit, and Anatoly took out a small vial of EIRO and poured eleven drops (the number of stories) of the greenish liquid into a glass of water. When I had drunk it down, the scholar shook my hand with feeling and silently pointed to the window. I clambered onto the windowsill and looked down. I got upset.

"I won't impose my presence on you, as I fully rely on

your integrity," said my roommate. "I'm going downstairs, where I expect to greet you. But I hope you will be down below before me."

I got even more upset. The words "down below" brought to mind not the street, but a far sadder place, that is to say, the cemetery. It occurred to me once more that all the projects and experiments I'd taken part in had never brought me any good. Even the motorcycle that I won through the good offices of PMP wasn't necessarily good, since my travels on that same motorcycle had brought me to this windowsill, preparing for my fatal jump. But like it or not, I had to keep my word. I thought about my brother, ever ready to sacrifice himself for science; my brother, the beacon that should light my journey. Many thoughts flashed through my head! But the three minutes were running out. I overcame my fear and, making a face, jumped off.

The speed of my flight caused me to lose consciousness for a moment. There followed a sharp and very painful blow, and then I picked myself up from the sidewalk. There was a dent in the asphalt.

"I see I wasn't mistaken," said Anatoly, walking over to me. "You did get here first. How do you feel?"

"I don't understand a thing," I said. "I feel some sort of lightness in my body, as if I'd just come from a steam room. And my spirits are high."

"It's the side effect," observed the scientist in a businesslike fashion. "There was a momentary restructuring of cells in the organism. You have grown younger. Another ten or twelve jumps, and not only will you be completely young, but you will possess physical and spiritual qualities such as you never had before. Incidentally, in continuing the experiment you will be a great help to science."

"I'm ready now!" I said.

"I'm afraid that multiple jumps from the hotel window might evoke the dissatisfaction of the administration," Anatoly pointed out. "But in the local park I noticed a tower for parachute jumping. Why don't we go there? If you have nothing against it, wait for me here, and I'll get the EIRO, a jug of water, and a glass."

In a few minutes he was back, and we set off for the park, walking along the dark, deserted streets. We got to the top of the tower without any difficulties, and the scientist gave me a glass with fourteen drops of EIRO. (The height of the tower was roughly equivalent to fourteen stories.) I jumped, then got back on the tower, then jumped again. Getting into it, I jumped once more, and then again and again and again. With each jump I grew less afraid, and after every landing I felt younger and livelier.

"Well, enough is enough," said the scientist after my fifteenth jump. "I also want to make a couple of jumps, to improve my physical, emotional, and intellectual condition. I haven't jumped for a long time."

The night was warm. We undressed and Anatoly put on the jumping suit. He made two jumps, and we got dressed and returned to the hotel. It was already getting light, and we passed by some early risers, who stared at my felt boots in astonishment. The doorman didn't want to let me into the hotel, but Anatoly sternly declared that I was a famous actor on my way back from a filming session. The floor supervisor, a kind woman of middle years, didn't recognize me, and my companion had to go to the room and get my passport. But when she saw the picture, she said that I didn't look like myself at all. The scientist explained that the lack of resemblance was a side effect of EIRO. This was followed by a brief discussion in the area of popular science, after which she expressed her desire to make a jump as soon as possible.

"It was a mistake to propagandize EIRO among men only," said the scientist, rubbing his hands gleefully, as we walked into our room. "It's been known for a long time that women possess as much courage as men, and sometimes even more. Of course, it seems to me personally that in this given instance the subject was attracted by EIRO's side effects rather than its underlying scientific basis, but for the experiment this is insignificant."

I went to the bathroom and looked in the mirror. I didn't recognize myself! Looking back at me was the intelligent face of a nice-looking man of thirty. Shocked by the miraculous transformation, I couldn't believe my eyes, so I closed them and made two turns on my heels. But when I once again looked in the mirror, I saw the same pleasant-looking, totally transfigured face.

I took a shower and fell fast asleep. When I woke up, it was already midday. I got some breakfast in the hotel cafe, and went for a walk along the delightful streets of Hopes-Fulfilledsville. As I passed a deserted garden, I saw a middle-aged woman sitting on a bench and crying. I went up to her. When she saw me, she shuddered and said:

"I have an important request to make of you. Help me find the thief who stole my pocketbook; it had all my money in it, and an address book with my son's address! I flew here from the Carpathian Mountains to see him, but I don't remember his address, and I don't have money for a return trip, since it was in my purse, which was in my shopping bag, and they stole my shopping bag in the streetcar when I was riding to the city from the airport."

Then she burst into tears with renewed vigor.

"A difficult situation," I said and started to think of how I could help her. And suddenly I remembered that when my friend Vasya the Martian was leaving the earth, he gave me his simple telephone number and promised to fulfill any request.

"I'll be back in five minutes," I told the crying lady. "I hope to give your affairs a positive turn."

I ran to the nearest telephone booth and dialed eleven zeroes and five fives.

"So it's you, my best friend for ever and ever, cross my heart and hope to die! So you finally thought about me!" It was Vasya's voice. "Well, how are things on the earthly pad?"

"Everything's fine, no snafus," I answered. "Last night I made a scientific leap, as a result of which—"

"I know, I know," Vasya interrupted me. "I knew about it when I took off from Earth. Only don't blow it!"

"Vasya, I have an urgent request for you. You promised, remember?"

"Sure I remember. The shopping bag with the purse and the address book was not stolen, it simply got lost in the street-car crush. Seven minutes ago it was turned in at the Lost and Found, which is at No. 9 Drovyanaya Street. When you leave the garden where the lady is crying, turn left, go two blocks, then turn right. You want the fourth house. And prepare yourself for an important event."

"What event?"

"The more you know, the older you'll grow," said Vasya the Martian cryptically.

"Vasya, my other-planetary pal, aren't you going to come and see us?"

"No, things are different now," said Vasya thoughtfully. "But you'll see me at your wedding. And now get going. Bye!"

I took his words about my wedding as a joke, that is, to mean that I would see my friend when hell freezes over. I hurried to the square.

"Your shopping bag with the purse in it has turned up. It's at the Lost and Found," I said.

"Oh, I don't believe it," said the weeping lady. "You're only saying that to comfort me."

I had to take her to the Lost and Found myself.

The aforementioned lady and I soon found ourselves at the entrance to No. 9 Drovyanaya Street. The Lost and Found was rather large. There was a sort of counter, behind which sat the head clerk, and in back of her were a lot of numbered lockers. The weeping lady described her loss, and the clerk, looking into a record book, said that the found object would be returned at once to its rightful owner.

"Cressy!" she shouted, turning towards the lockers. "Cressy, could you get me found item five hundred fifty five?"

"Right away," said a lovely voice from somewhere in the back.

And then, between the rows of lockers there appeared a young woman of about twenty-five, carrying a large yellow shopping bag. I took a look at her, and my heart pounded even faster than when I was standing on the windowsill getting ready to jump from the eleventh floor. In front of me was the living, original likeness of my dream! It was as if one of the 848 portraits from my childhood room had come alive and taken up residence at the Lost and Found. The beautiful young woman handed the shopping bag to the weeping lady, who then began to thank her, switching from tears of grief to tears of joy. And I stood off to the side, unable to tear my eyes away from her.

"Caress me!" I cried out involuntarily. She threw a glance in my direction, turned pale, and clutched at her heart.

"What's the matter?" I asked nervously.

"You are the one I've been waiting for so long!" she said softly.

The head clerk, seeing this unexpected scene, advised us sympathetically to go behind the lockers where we could conclude our private talk without witnesses.

And there, among the lockers with their lost objects, I told Cressy the story of my life, beginning with my childhood and ending with the most recent events. In answer, she told me that her grandmother had been a winner in a beauty contest, and that the artist who had done her portrait for a perfume ad had so fallen in love with her that he asked her to be his wife, to which she agreed. When Cressy was ten years old, and her grandfather artist was already advanced in years, he jokingly drew her the portrait of her supposed fiancé. This imaginary man pleased her to such an extent that when she had grown up and become a beauty in her own right, she didn't want to look at any other man. Many people, among them men with responsible positions, offered her lawful wedlock with a solid

material footing, and even sent letters to the higher authorities
complaining about her intractability. But she was cold and
unapproachable, like the golden fish of the fable. But now her
destiny had arrived, and she was ready to follow him right to
the Wedding Palace.

We embraced and kissed and agreed that we would set up
our household not just anywhere, but in Greetica-Leaveittown, in that very house where I had first seen "Caress Me!"
in an edition of 848.

Then Cressy took me to her house. I moved in with her
temporarily, and she took care of the paperwork involved in
quitting her job. On the walls of Cressy's room hung my portrait, painted by her grandfather and placed by her own hands
in an elegant plastic frame.

Five days later, Cressy took her seat in the sidecar of my
motorcycle and together we left Hopes-Fulfilledsville on our
joint path to a happy future.

Before leaving Hopes-Fulfilledsville, I went to say good-
bye to Anatoly and thank him for EIRO's side effects. When I
was still fairly far from the hotel, I saw a huge line winding
around an entire block.

"What's the line for?" I asked an elegantly dressed lady.

"It's the jumping line," she said merrily.

Only then did I notice that the line was composed almost
entirely of women. A few men, with hangdog looks and poi-
sonous expressions, were sprinkled here and there; these
were husbands, brought by their wives and morosely awaiting
their turn to jump. I was surprised to see among the women of
various ages more than a few girls of eighteen or twenty; they,
of all people, had no use for EIRO's side effects. Apparently
they had been seized by the whirlwind of fashion.

Following along the line, I arrived at the hotel entrance. A
police squad had been stationed there to keep order. Part of
the street had been cordoned off by police barricades, and
everywhere were signs prohibiting vehicular entry. Every few
minutes another volunteer would come flying out of the scientist's window, land with a resonant boom, and then, with

torn clothing, ruined shoes, and a radiant expression, walk off. Some of them would run right back to the end of the line. The part of the sidewalk and road that had borne the brunt of multiple landings was so torn up that it looked as though a column of heavy tanks had gone through.

When I had finally made my way to Room 1155, and congratulated the scientist on his success, I was struck by his sullen and tired look.

"Ever since the night our floor supervisor made her first jump and told her girlfriends about it, and they, in turn, told their friends, I've had so many clients I can't get rid of them," said Anatoly joylessly. "It's true that EIRO's universality has been firmly established, since there hasn't been a single accident, but I'm so tired from all this fuss that I feel like a sixty-year-old again. I don't even have time to take a jump myself!"

I told the scientist about the sharp, positive turn in my fate. In answer, he shook my hand warmly and wished me happiness in my family life. Then I bid a hasty retreat, since the people at the head of the line had begun to bang down the door.

Alas, EIRO has not yet been put into mass production. The inventor suffered an early death and thus was unable to bring his labors to fruition. As I found out later, he had spent the next two weeks attending to the needs of his clientele, who were at him day and night without pause. Finally, in an attempt to improve his physical, emotional, and intellectual condition, he jumped out the window. But recent events had so unnerved him that he forgot to take his own elixir.

Happy Endings **13**

We arrived safe and sound in Leningrad, after which Cressy insisted on selling the motorcycle right away and using the money to buy a television. I hit the books and in a short time had passed exams in the technical college's correspondence courses. When I got my diploma I called my talented brother, who congratulated me and invited me to see him, together with my young wife. At first Victor didn't recognize me. When I told him about EIRO, he said that, personally, he would never submit to such an experiment because the side effects of the elixir would lower his level of venerableness and might even provoke the displeasure of the institute administration. He was favorably impressed by Cressy and approved my choice. Cressy was also much taken by my brother and the intelligent atmosphere that prevailed in his noncommunal apartment.

Soon Cressy and I made our final move to Greetica-Leaveittown, where my parents gave us two rooms. With great caution I removed the layers of wallpaper that had accumulated over the years in my childhood room, covering the 848 images of "Caress Me!" and restored the walls to their historic state. But now, the 848 portraits had been joined by the girl whom I had once dreamed of meeting when, as a child, I gazed at the portraits on the wall.

We had our official wedding in that very room. In addition to my parents, a lot of neighbors came, and they were all satisfied with both the cooking and the beauty of the bride. To crown the festivities, my brother sent a congratulatory telegram, which I read to my parents and guests. The telegram proclaimed:

CONGRATULATIONS ON ENTERING HOLY PATRIMONY COMMA WISH FUTURE SUCCESSES PERIOD PARAGRAPH SINCE THE IRRATIONALITY OF METABOLIC ALGORITHMS AND SINUSOIDOSITY OF PHYSIOTHERA-PEUTIC DIELECTRICS REQUIRE LOCALIZATION OF ISOTHERMS COMMA AM SENDING ONE HUNDRED RUBLES WEDDING EXPENSES PERIOD YOUR HIGHLY EDUCATED BROTHER

After the reading of the telegram, my father stood up and, with tears of joy in his eyes, pronounced a toast in honor of the newlyweds. He warmly congratulated me on losing my five uns and becoming a worthy member of the family, which had given my parents great joy.

But the events of this great day did not end here! When the guests had all danced to the record player and left for home, the screen of the new television, which hadn't even been plugged in yet, suddenly lit up. On the screen appeared the face of Vasya the Martian. It hurt me to see that my friend had aged noticeably over the years.

"Hi, bum!" said Vasya. "Well, how are things on the wedding front?"

"Everything's fine, strings and twine," I said gaily. "My dreams have come true!"

"I see, I see," said my other-planetary friend. "Congratulations and best wishes for more of the same!"

"Thank you, Vasya," I said with emotion.

"Don't mention it, my friend."

"Vasya, when are you going to show yourself again?" I asked.

"Never again now," he answered and, waving a hand in farewell, quietly disappeared from the screen.

My life in Greetica-Leaveittown is going nicely. I have a fairly responsible position, and everybody is completely satisfied with my work. My father has stopped telling his hunting stories: when I gave him a detailed account of my life, the true events made such an impression on him that he stopped lying.

Now nobody thinks of me as a man with five uns, and my resourcefulness and efficiency are held up as an example to others. Cressy and I live peacefully and happily, and haven't had a single fight yet.

Once in a while, in the middle of the night, when everyone else is sleeping, my slow-witted past comes back to me and I give way to foolish grief. Without turning on the light, I slip out of bed and sit in front of the television. But nothing appears on the screen.

KOVRIGIN'S CHRONICLES

Foreword to the
338th Jubilee Edition

Seventy years ago, in 2231, this slim volume was first published. Since then it has been reprinted 337 times in Russian alone. When it was published it was translated into all the languages of the world, and now it is known to all the Inhabitants of our United Planet as well as to our countrymen living on Mars and Venus. Over these seventy years so many articles, papers, and dissertations have been written about *Kovrigin's Chronicles* that just listing them takes up nine thick volumes.

In publishing this anniversary edition, we would like to give the reader a brief history of *Kovrigin's Chronicles* and to explain why every new generation reads this book with unflagging interest.

It must be said that the reason for the everlasting popularity of *Kovrigin's Chronicles* is certainly not found in the book's literary merits. Don't look for universal ideas or broad visions of an epoch. Anything that falls outside the author's narrow theme simply does not interest him. And he would not have been able to handle such an undertaking anyway: he was not a Writer by profession. The author, Matvei Kovrigin (2102–2231), while working on this book, had no pretensions to literary fame. A Literary Historian by education, who researched the 20th century, he expected glory, at at least fame, to come for his historical literary compilations, which he published in great number and which were not popular even in his lifetime and are now completely forgotten. But this small book, published after his death, brought him posthumous fame that will not dim with the years. For in this book Kovrigin tells about Andrei Svetochev, and every word about the great Scientist is dear to Humanity.

Let us remind you once more: *Kovrigin's Chronicles* is a narrow-visioned narrative. The author is not interested in life-styles or science. He mentions the technology of his times only when he comes in contact with it personally or when the fate of his friends depends on it. In the course of the action he gives a rather detailed description of certain aggregates, or automatons, that existed in his day, but in these descriptions one senses not only a profound indifference to technology but a lack of understanding that occasionally borders on technological illiteracy. He doesn't even mention Space or Man's flights into it, as though he lived in the era of geocentricity. And he only understood the great scientific meaning of the discovery by his friend Andrei Svetochev at the end of his life, and then only in a purely utilitarian way.

The narrow-mindedness of the Author is also seen in the way he depicts Andrei Svetochev out of context, only from his personal point of view. He doesn't mention Svetochev's Collaborators nor his Teachers or Predecessors. If we are to believe Kovrigin, it would appear that Svetochev did everything alone, while in reality he was surrounded by like-minded men, many of whom (Ivannikov, Lemer, Karajarian, Kelau) were among the century's greatest Scientists.

The book's style is archaic, certainly not contemporary. As a specialist in 20th-century literature, the Author, unable to find his own creative style, imitates 20th-century writers, and not the first-class ones at that. There is one more defect that must be mentioned. Even when talking about his youth, Kovrigin talks of himself as though he were a Man who had lived, had many experiences, and was solid and settled. Do not forget that Kovrigin wrote the book at the sunset of his life.

Various Researchers have differing approaches to Matvei Kovrigin, author of *Kovrigin's Chronicles*. Some like him, others don't. Kovrigin is a paradoxical figure. Along with his sincerity, kindness, unquestionable personal bravery, and readiness to always come to someone's aid, coexist petty pedantry, grumbling, and a lack of self-criticism that borders on self-adoration.

"A Mediocrity's Tale of a Genius" and "Mozart and Salieri of the 22nd Century"—that is how some Critics describe this book, forgetting that we are indebted to Kovrigin for the most complete description of the life of Andrei Svetochev. We must remember that Kovrigin was the friend of the greatest Genius of technological thought and told us about him as best he could. Let us be grateful to him for that.

Since many concepts, names, aggregates, and mechanisms mentioned by the Author have long since become obsolete, forgotten, and replaced by others, the new generation does not know about them, and we have taken it upon ourselves to add footnotes giving the historical significance of these concepts and objects.

With sincere respect,
Planeta Publishing House
Russian Edition

2301 A.D.

Introduction 1

. . . The girl stood on the cliff on the shore of the river. This was in the fall, when dreary rains fall, and the shore's clays get soggy and show footprints clearly. The girl stood on the cliff and stared meditatively at the autumnal river, along which floated yellow leaves.

A young man walked by, and he saw the girl standing on the cliff and fell in love with her at first sight. And she loved him at first sight, for that was the way of love in fairy tales.

This young man lived by the river, and when the girl called a plane and flew off to the big city, promising to return in the spring, he was left alone in the hut on the river's shore to wait for her return. Why he lived alone on the riverbank and who he was is of no import, for this is a fairy tale.

Every day the young man came to the cliff where the girl had once stood. He trampled a narrow path in the clay near her footprints. He did not step in her footprints, and each time it seemed to him that the girl invisibly walked next to him to the cliff and stood next to him and looked at the autumnal river, along which floated yellow leaves.

Then the great rains came, and the prints left by the girl's shoes filled up with water, and they reflected the late autumn sky. Then the frosts came, and the footprints became ice.

And once the young man took out a footprint and brought it back to his hut. He set it on the table, and when he woke up in the morning he saw that the footprint had melted. And the young man was very surprised and saddened. Don't be surprised; in fairy tales people are amazed by the most ordinary things.

The young man grew sad and thought: *The footprints of my beloved are worthy of immortality. But ice is not immortal. Nor is metal, for it rusts; nor is glass, for it breaks; nor is stone, for it wears out and cracks in heat and cold. I must create a material that can be poured into any form and will not fear heat, nor cold, nor time.*

And the day came when he created such a material, which replaced stone and metal, glass and plastic, wood and concrete, water and flax. He created Sole Material, which is called aqualide. People began building cities on earth and under water with it, they made all their machines and everything else with it. And this is no longer a fairy tale, for we live in this world.

This is where the footprints of that girl led who stood at the cliff on an autumn day when yellow leaves floated on the river.

But once, the girl for whom the young man was waiting. . . .

And so on, and so forth.

You, dear reader, know this sentimental story yourself from your childhood; it's even taught in school. It was written by an idle Poet and dedicated to Andrei Svetochev and Nina Astakhova, and this semi-legend, semi–fairy tale is for some reason considered very poetic and touching, and perhaps some particularly naive people tend to think that this is precisely the way we arrived at our contemporary aqualide civilization.

It is so: the girl did stand on the riverbank. But the rest was not like that at all. The idle writer made it all up.

"Then how did it happen?" you will ask, my respected Reader.

Now I will begin my narrative, and you will learn how it started, what led Andrei Svetochev to his discovery, where and how he met Nina Astakhova. And you will learn many other things.

I have lived my MILS * and then some, my life is approaching its end, and the day is not far off when my ashes will fall like a light cloud from the White Tower onto the flowers growing at its base. But I still have time to tell you the true story of Nina Astakhova and Andrei Svetochev, whose friend I was, and of myself, for at one time my life was closely tied to the life of these two People.

* **MILS**   Minimum Individual Life Span. The standard lifetime guaranteed every inhabitant of the planet by medicine and Society. In the period described by the Author the MILS equaled one hundred ten years, but actually the average life span even then was considerably longer.

The Incident at the 2
Leningrad Post Office

I will begin with very distant times. My tale starts on the day they abolished money. You've all read about that day, but I remember it perfectly and I know that it's been made more colorful in the books. In actuality, nothing much happened that day. The point is, the process of the withering away of money had been going on a long time. Money didn't die suddenly—it passed away slowly, like a man who had passed his MILS and then some. Toward the end it had more of a statistical than a value significance. If you didn't have enough money markers to buy whatever you wanted, you simply tore out a piece of paper from your notebook and wrote "15 kopeks" or "3 rubles" or "20 rubles" and gave it to the Saleswoman or the ASPMID.* Or you could ask for the money from a passerby, who would give it to you and go on, without bothering to find out your name.

The day they abolished money we had a brief meeting at the University, and then we went on about our business. I remember that heading back from the meeting to the philology department, I walked along with Nina Astakhova, and we certainly weren't talking about money, we were talking about *The Anthology of Forgotten Poets of the Twentieth Century*, which I was working on then. Nina (she was in her second year) had been assigned to me, a Graduate Student, as a Technical Assistant and was helping me compile the anthology. She was conscientious, and spent a lot of time in libraries and archives, looking for poems and information on now-forgotten poets of the twentieth century, but I did not like her stubbornness and excessive independence. For instance, Nina insisted

* **ASPMID** Automatic Salesman, Polite, Mobile, Intellectual, Dependable. An ancient aggregate, long removed from production.

that the Anthology had to include the poems of one Vadim Shefner (1915–1984?), and I was against it. I did not like the note of sadness and excessive meditation in his poems. I preferred Poets with cheery, resounding poems, where everything was clear and simple. I felt that it was those Poets who should be in my Anthology so that the Reader would have an accurate picture of twentieth-century poetry. Nina continued insisting on the inclusion of that Shefner; she was stuck on him. And she would get heated, even angry as she insisted. She couldn't get it through her head that I was compiling a scholarly work, and scholarship demands the absence of passion.

But in general I liked Nina. We often went out sailing; she loved the sea. And sometimes we would take a plane taxi and fly out of town somewhere. We would walk in the allées. I liked being with her, but I was a little put off by her strange personality. Sometimes she was funny and even mocking, and then suddenly she would turn silent and thoughtful. Sometimes her face wore an expression as though she were anticipating something unusual, a miracle, to happen any second.

"Nina, what are you thinking about now?" I asked her once, while we were walking down a country lane.

"Well, . . . I don't know myself. You know, sometimes I think that something very very good is going to happen in my life. That there will be joy in it."

"You are probably referring to the fact that I will soon complete my Anthology and when it is published your name will be mentioned in the preface as my Assistant?" I said. "That truly is great joy. And well deserved."

"Oh, that's not it at all," she said reproachfully. "Even I myself don't know what kind of happiness I'm waiting for."

I was rather surprised and even saddened by her words. How can you wait for happiness without knowing precisely what happiness you're waiting for? Where's the logic in that?

"You have to develop scientific thought," I advised. "You haven't even lived a quarter MILS, you have a long life ahead of you—personal and scholarly. Someday you'll get married, perhaps your husband will be a Scholar, and your level of thinking should not be below his. Have you ever thought about that?"

But Nina pretended not to understand me. She said nothing in reply and instead jumped up and picked a leaf from an overhanging branch and peered through it at the sun.

"Today the sun is green!" she announced. "How amusing!"

I didn't try to convince her that the sun today, like every day, was completely ordinary, and not green. I was always lost whenever she said strange things like that.

Nevertheless, I liked Nina. But don't think that she was as beautiful as Artists and Sculptors now depict her. No, I wouldn't call her a beauty. She was slender and agile, with a very light step, with an expressive and even attractive face, but she certainly didn't have the beauty that they attribute to her now.

But back to the day they abolished money.

As I've said, after the meeting in the graduation exercises hall Nina and I headed for the philology department. Nina went to a lecture, I dug in at the library and worked a long time over my Anthology and then headed for the University cafeteria. When the SATYR* came over, I gave my usual order of cabbage soup, syntholiver, and fruit cocktail. After eating, by habit I called over the SATYR to pay. I was about to put the coins in the slots in its plastic chest when I saw that the slots were taped over.

"Dinner's free. Dinner's free," the SATYR said matter-of-factly.

"Not 'dinner's free,' but say "No charge for dinner," I corrected the SATYR. "Go get the FARO.**

* **SATYR** Serving Aggregate Taking Your Requests. A primitive aggregate of the 22nd century. Something like the ancient Waiter.

FARO Food Aggregate Running Others. 22nd-century aggregate. Did the work of the ancient Captain.

Soon the bulky FARO came to my table. I told him to fix the tape in the SATYRs under him, they were not completely grammatical. That was shameful, we were a University here, after all, a cultural center.

"I'm upset. Alarmed. I'll take measures," the FARO replied. "Are there any other complaints?"

"Unfortunately, yes. I was served an overcooked syntho-liver. Do you think that now that things are free you can feed people overcooked liver?"

"I'm upset. Alarmed. I'll take measures," the FARO replied. "Are there any other complaints?"

"No. You may go."

After dinner, I went on out the embankment and headed toward the First Line. Everything was almost as usual on the embankment, except for the flags dressing the ships and the crowds of boys and girls at the granite ramps. They stopped passersby and asked for money. When they got it, the children ran down the steps to the water and threw the coins into the river. They turned the paper bills into boats and sailed them out on the waves. Schools were let out to celebrate the abolition of money, which, in my opinion, was hardly a way of enforcing discipline.

When I turned into the First Line, I saw a Widrinkson.* Dancing and singing an inaudible song, he walked along the plastic cobblestones of the street, interfering with traffic, causing the elmobiles to drive around him carefully. People were staring at him with interest and amazement, and some with obvious fear. I too stopped to stare at a rare sight; the last time I had seen a Widrinkson was in childhood, when I was nine.

I stood around a bit, hoping that the Widrinkson would curse and I would be able to write down a new swear word. But the Widrinkson just hummed to himself. I went on, rather chagrined that I wouldn't be able to add to my DOWUBA.

* **Widrinkson** Wine-drinking person. A medical and partly popular term of the 21st–22nd centuries. Literally, drunkard, alcoholic. Widrinkson did not include people who drank moderate amounts of grape wine; as you know, such beverages are drunk to this day.

When I was twelve, I began a dictionary, which I called DO-WUBA (*Dictionary of Words Used By the Ancients*). My DO-WUBA consisted of four parts: (1) swear words; (2) underworld jargon; (3) hunting terms; (4) military terms. While I could add to the last three divisions through my reading of old books and archives, I had a lot of trouble with the first one, since swearing had long stopped being used on Earth and there were no written sources. I had to gather material for this section grain by grain, and it went very slowly.

It was crowded on Bolshoi Prospect. I could sense a holiday mood. Paper bills flew out of windows and balconies and landed at the feet of pedestrians. As I walked past a bank, I looked in. Children filled the bank. They were laughing, jumping, and throwing stacks of bills at one another. From time to time the kids ran up to the desk and the FEMIFA* gave them more money.

On the corner of Bolshoi Prospect and the Sixth Line I met my friend Andrei Svetochev. Yes, yes, the very Svetochev whose name is known to every Person on Earth. But then he wasn't famous for anything. However, among Scientists he was already well known.

I had known Andrei since childhood; we lived in the same building and went to the same school. Then our educational paths diverged. Andrei was always interested in technology, and after graduation was accepted by the Academy of Higher Scientific Knowledge, while I went to the philology department of the University. And even though we could have lived at home, because our parents lived in Leningrad, we moved to dormitories; it was more convenient. However, we remained friends and met often. Since our school days we were avid stamp collectors, and that brought us closer too. When we met we bragged about our collections and talked about life

---

* **FEMIFA** Financial Electronic Multioperational Ideally Functioning Aggregate. An aggregate abolished after the abolition of money. Now seen in museums.

in general, our plans and aspirations. And we had very different plans and aspirations.

The last few months Andrei had been glum and silent. However, when I looked in on him at his dorm, he confessed that he had come up with a very important discovery, but it wasn't going well. He rushed from one experiment to another, but to no avail.

I felt for him and gave him some friendly advice, to take on a less complex work and not strive for unattainable goals. After all, the unattainable was unattainable and the impossible was impossible. One must set reasonable goals and march from milepost to milepost.

But Andrei wasn't pleased by my friendly advice and pointed at a picture hanging over his desk. It showed Hercules chasing after the Arcadian stag. Hercules was running after the stag along snowy mountain peaks.

"Do you see how he runs?" Andrei said. "He's running on the highest peaks, and he doesn't set foot on the peaks and cliffs that are lower, he jumps over them. That's how he caught the stag."

"He could have not caught it," I countered reasonably. "He could have fallen to his death. And then, he's Hercules and you're a mere mortal."

"Well, that's another thing altogether," Andrei said drily and changed the subject to stamps.

That day I left him with the feeling that he had chosen a false path in science and didn't want to leave it, out of stubbornness. I even felt sorry for him. It seemed to me that he was running in place, while I took step after inexorable step forward. My Anthology and commentaries to it were close to completion, and I was already thinking about my next work: "Science-Fiction Writers of the Twentieth Century in the Light of Contemporary Ethical Views." Besides, I was constantly working on my DOWUBA. As I have already mentioned, this was very slow going. I had to chase after every swear word with foam at the mouth, as they used to say in the olden days. The work was further complicated by the fact that I couldn't ask my Assistant, Nina Astakhova, to participate in this work, because I was shielding her maidenly innocence. But in the long run I was moving slowly but surely forward, while Andrei was running in place, setting himself an unattainable goal, as I then thought.

But let me get back to the day in question. Thus, I ran into Andrei on the corner of Bolshoi Prospect and the Sixth Line. Andrei was gloomy again.

"Where are you hurrying to, Andrei?" I asked.

"To the Post Office," he replied glumly. "You know that they've abolished stamps. At least I used to have some luck with stamps, and now they've abolished them."

"Abolished?" I was stunned. "How can that be? What about our collections?"

"You didn't listen very closely to the announcement about abolition of money. They said: money is abolished and so are all signs of payment. And stamps are just that."

"That's right," I realized. "Since there is no more money, there is no need for stamps. . . . But what about philatelists?"

"Tough!" Andrei barked. "Let's go to the Post Office."

He waved his hand at a passing elmobile taxi and we got in.

"To the Post Office," I said to the AUTHOR.*

"Got it. Taking you to the Post Office. No fee," the AUTHOR said, leaning three of its eyes over the controls. The fourth eye—a large lens in the back of its head—was looking at us.

"Let's go with jumps," Andrei said. "We're in a hurry."

"I must warn you of danger," the AUTHOR said. "There's a lot of traffic to the Post Office today. Jumping is dangerous."

"I don't care," Andrei said. "Big deal, dangerous."

* **AUTHOR** Automatic Transport Hackie with Oral Responses. An ancient aggregate of the late 21st and early 22nd centuries. Long ago replaced by more perfected models.

"Do you want driving with conversation?" the AUTHOR asked. "The extra fee for conversation has been abolished."

"With conversation," I said.

"Before you I took a gray-haired old man to the Post Office; he was about MILS plus forty. The old man looked unhappy. He had a Humanitarian badge on his coat. The old man was very angry."

"Did he swear?" I asked hopefully.

"No, he did not do what you mention. But he looked unhappy."

"Aren't you tired of this chatter?" Andrei said angrily. "I can't understand what pleasure there can be in talking to machines!"

We shut up.

It was rather far to the Post Office; it was in the new center of town, which had moved in the direction of Pushkino. There were a lot of elmobiles at that hour. When there was a spot a few cars ahead, our elmobile expanded its wings and hopped over the cars to land in the available spot. Finally we reached the Post Office, a small twenty-story building in a small square.

There was a rather large crowd in the square. There were schoolchildren, and middle-aged people, and old people. Several had brought stamp albums and philately guides. They all looked unhappy. They were all looking at the gigantic screen on the Post Office wall.

Andrei and I also looked at the screen and saw Moscow. The square in front of the Moscow PO was also filled with stamp collectors. Then they showed the PO in Buenos Aires. It was night there, and the crowd of philatelists stood outside with torches. Some had pipes and were blowing into them. Then we saw the Rome PO. Thousands of philatelists were having a sit-in on the plastic roadway, stopping traffic. After Rome we saw a small town, somewhere in the Black Earth region of Russia. Here schoolchildren and adults stood in front of the Post Office with placards that read: POST OFFICE PEOPLE! WE NEED STAMPS!

Then the screen went black and the Announcer said:

"The Universal Post Office Council is meeting in Geneva. The stamp question will be resolved at any moment. We are tuning in to Geneva."

"Let's go inside," Andrei said and started making his way through the crowd.

I followed, listening to the conversations People were having, hoping to pick up a swear word or two to add to my DOWUBA. But unfortunately, no one was swearing, even though they were upset.

Inside the Post Office there were a lot of people, but not as many as I had expected. We went up to the windows where just yesterday stamps were sold. Now there was a sign: IN CONNECTION WITH THE ABOLITION OF MONEY, STAMPS ARE ABOLISHED. LETTERS CAN BE MAILED FOR FREE

The girl attendant was explaining to the little old man of two MILS or so that since money was abolished, stamps were unnecessary and letters would arrive at their destination without stamps. Earrings dangled from her ears. They were very simple—two metal balls on thin chains—but they struck my eye immediately: in our times these ear ornaments had long gone out of style. But the girl was good-looking and the earrings became her.

"Stamp collecting is a historical tradition," Andrei said as he got his turn at the window. "And it's not up to you people to abolish it."

"Stamps have been abolished by the times, not the Post Office," the girl with the earrings said modestly. "Stamp collecting is an unnecessary, obsolete superstition."

"As long as there are People interested in stamps, stamps must exist," Andrei said loudly and angrily.

"How silly you are with your stamps!" the girl answered angrily.

"And you're silly with opinions on stamps and your prehistoric earrings!" Andrei yelled back. "You're just a stupid harpy!"

The girl looked at Andrei, frightened and insulted.

"Andrei! What's the matter!" I said. "You're swearing! I'm ashamed of you!"

"Forgive me," Andrei said to the girl with the earrings. "This has never happened to me before. Forgive me for insulting you."

"I forgive you," the girl said. "You're just very upset. . . . What's a harpy?"

"I don't know," Andrei said. "But that's what my great-grandfather used to say to my great-grandmother when he was angry."

"In deep antiquity harpies were mythical forest spirits," I said. "Later the word lost its original meaning and was used in folklore as a swear word, applied to shrewish women without an attractive appearance. I can assure you that you do not resemble a harpy in the least, and from that point of view my friend was mistaken."

"That's very interesting!" the girl said. "And how do you know these things?"

"I know not only that, but much much more," I replied modestly. And I went on to explain that my *Dictionary of Words Used By the Ancients*, or DOWUBA, contains many words, concepts, and idiomatic expressions. I also told her my name and who I was. The girl listened with interest and then told me a few words about herself. Her name was Nadya. Later Nadya became my wife, but that's another story.

When Andrei and I left the Post Office, we saw the Announcer on the giant screen, who told us this:

1. The Universal Post Office Council considers stamp collecting a vestige from the past that does not bring any benefit to Mankind.
2. The Universal Post Office Council considers stamp collecting a vestige from the past that does not bring any harm to Mankind.
3. Since collectors want stamps to exist, let them exist, but not as signs of payment.
4. From now on every Person has the right to issue his own stamps, for which purpose printing presses and so on will be made available.

5. Every Person has the right in the course of his lifetime to issue three stamps with no more than 1,000,000 copies.

"There, you see," I told Andrei. "Everything ended well. And you didn't have to insult the girl and call her such inappropriate names. You insulted a Person. You'll have to redeem yourself."

"I know that," Andrei replied. "I behaved in an unworthy manner. And it wasn't over the stamps, it's just that I'm so unlucky. At one time I thought that I was close to a great discovery, and now I'm beginning to think that I was taking a false path."

"In our age there can be no great discoveries," I countered. "In our age there can only be improvements."

Andrei said nothing in reply, and I thought that he agreed with me silently, but didn't say so out of false pride.

But I was wrong. There was much in Andrei that I didn't understand. And yet I had known him since childhood.

Childhood 3

In my earliest childhood I lived with my parents in a house on the Eleventh Line of Vasilyevsky Island. Father taught literature in grammar school, mother worked as a craftsman at a factory of women's jewelry. They poured rings and other jewelry out of chemically pure iron (gold had been out of fashion a long time). They also made brooches and diadems with Mars stones. It was at this factory that mother befriended Anna Svetocheva, Andrei's mother. Then our fathers became friends, and we moved to a single apartment in the Wharf District, right by the sea. The process of the so-called secondary communal housing life had just begun. You see, once upon a time, many People were forced to live in large communal apartments. Since People of differing personalities, professions, and habits lived in these apartments, arguments and discord broke out among them. But in the meantime the tempo of construction grew, and finally the year came when anyone who wanted to live in his own apartment could. But after some more time People and families who were friends began moving into common apartments, but on a new basis, on the basis of friendship and mutual love. This was taken into account and they began constructing buildings with large apartments. The People in such apartments lived as one family, putting money into one kitty, no matter the size of salary. Now this natural process continues, accelerating constantly, particularly since money has been abolished and everything is much simpler.

The house we moved into with the Svetochevs, exchanging apartments with a large family, was an old brick building. Compared to the buildings of solid concrete that surrounded it, it looked ancient. Our house even had locks on the doors that opened on the landings, and I loved that touch of antiquity. The doors were shut without locking them, naturally—the keys had been lost or turned in—but the very existence of those strange mechanisms gave the apartment a mysterious air.

Our families got along very well. Andrei's father, Sergei Ekaterinovich Svetochev, was a jolly man. He worked in a paper factory and was very proud of his profession. "Everything flows, everything changes, but paper production goes on," he used to say. "Without us People can't live." How could he have known that his son would make a discovery so great that even paper would become unnecessary!

Andrei and I were settled into a large room, the nursery, and our beds stood next to each other. The apartment wasn't large, but cozy—but which of us, honored Readers, hasn't been there! The house is preserved untouched as a Memorial Museum to Andrei Svetochev, and everything is kept as it was in the past. They do change the floor-covering twice a year;

it's worn down by the feet of the innumerable Tourists from all the continents of our planet. The visitors to the Museum find the apartment quite modest, but as a child I thought it was very large. In those days we didn't have such large living area allowances and the norm was one room per person. It's only now when a gigantic house of aqualide can be raised overnight that you can, if such a crazy idea should come to you, order a personal palace for yourself, and while they'll be surprised at your whim at Housing and Construction, they'll fill your order and a day later you can move into your palace, only to leave it a week later out of sheer boredom.

But getting back to Andrei. So, we lived in one house and went to the same kindergarten, and then entered grammar school together. We got along and shared our secrets and future plans. We helped each other in school: I did well in our mother tongue, Andrei was good at math. However, he manifested no signs of genius at that stage. He was a boy like any other. In the beginning classes he was average, and his notebooks were never kept up well and I was often held up as an example to him.

I must add that even though we were friends, Andrei had some personality traits that I disliked intensely. I always felt that even though we were close, Andrei never told me everything, as though he were afraid that I wouldn't understand. I was also hurt by the need for privacy and silence that came over him from time to time. He could sit for an hour or more without moving, staring into space and thinking about something. He would answer my questions with non sequiturs, and that naturally angered me.

He also liked to wander alone on the shore of the bay, where the beach was. In the fall the beach was deserted and when we came back from school I always headed straight for home, while Andrei sometimes turned off to that empty beach, where there was nothing interesting.

Once when I came home from school without Andrei, which happened often, his mother sent me to get him. "It's

his birthday today," she said. "How could he have forgotten?"
I went to the beach. It was damp and cloudy. It was drizzling.
The water was still, and tiny needles of rain pierced its surface
and disappeared. Andrei stood at the very edge in his raincoat.
He wasn't staring into the distance, he was looking down at
his feet, at the water.

"Why do you hang around this beach?" I said. "It's not
summer now. Go home, your mother is calling. Or did you
forget that you turn ten today? And what are you thinking
about anyway?"

"I'm thinking about water," Andrei replied. "Water is very
strange, right? It's not like anything else in the world."

"What's so strange about water?" I said in surprise. "Water
is water."

"No, water is strange and inexplicable," Andrei repeated
stubbornly. "It's liquid, but if you hit it flat with a stick, it will
even hurt your hand, that's how firm it is. Now if you could
make water completely hard—"

"When winter comes water will turn to ice and be hard," I
interrupted.

"I'm not talking about ice," he said, in an insulted tone.

We silently went home.

At home Andrei's mother hugged him and gave him a
packet of stamps, and my mother gave him *The Philatelist's
Guidebook.*

"Hurrah! Nicaragua! Nicaragua!" my comrade shouted, ex-
amining his stamps. He jumped up and down with pleasure
and ran around the rooms calling: "Nicaragua! Nicaragua!"

As he ran past the couch, I tripped him and he fell down
on it. I flopped down next to him and we started scuffling, and
then we each grabbed a bolster and began hitting each other.
Naturally, this was in fun.

"Beat the animalists!" I shouted, swinging my nitrolon
bolster at Andrei.

"Beat the portraitists!" he shouted, lowering his bolster on
my head.

Our school stamp club called portraitists those who collected stamps with portraits. For instance, I collected stamps with pictures of famous People. Andrei belonged to the "animalists"—he collected the so-called pretty stamps; he particularly liked depictions of various exotic animals. He had strange tastes: he liked the brightest, even the gaudy, stamps, he liked colorful birds and animals. He treasured his collection, but if one of the gang asked him for the brightest, most colorful stamp in it, he'd give it away. He rarely asked anyone for anything himself, and some kids thought he was stuck up. But he wasn't, he was simply quiet, controlled, and this trait grew with the years.

His interest in abstract discussions grew with the years as well. These discussions, to tell the truth, bored me to death.

Once, when we were in fourth grade, we made a field trip to St. Isaac's Cathedral—rather, to its colonnade. That day a medium-size plane landed on the flat roof of our school, we quickly proceeded to its interior, and soon flew off to St. Isaac's. Stopping in mid-air by the upper colonnade, the heliplane lowered its ramp, and our class went down after our Teacher to the columns. We could see the entire city from the top of the cathedral, as well as the Neva River with its fourteen bridges, and the battleship *Aurora* in its eternal dock, and the bay, and the ships in it.

"How beautiful!" I said to Andrei. "Isn't it?"

"Very beautiful," he agreed. "Except that everything is made out of different things. There's stone, and iron, and brick, and concrete, and plastic, and glass. . . . It's all different."

"What do you want?" I asked in surprise. "That's how it should be. You make one thing out of one material, and another out of another. That's how it's always been and that's how it will always be."

"Everything should be made out of the same thing," Andrei said thoughtfully. "Houses, and ships, and cars, and rockets, and shoes, and furniture, and everything."

"Now that's nonsense," I said. "And then, lots of things are made out of plastic."

"Not everything, though," Andrei said. "A plastic has to be invented so that you can make everything out of it."

"Don't act smart!" I grew angry. "We're just schoolchildren and there's no point in thinking about what can't be."

After my criticism, Andrei was hurt and didn't talk to me about abstract things for a long time. But he did drag home all kinds of scientific books, which concentrated primarily on water. When we were passed to the next grade, Andrei spent almost all his evenings at the Free Laboratory—such labs exist at every school today as well. There were all kinds of machines and apparatus, and he puttered around, forgetting to eat. Strange as it may seem, neither my parents nor his did anything to stop this fascination. When I hinted to them that Andrei was just wasting his time and damaging his health and general well-being, they gently told me that I was missing a few things. But I was not at all stupid for my age, and I did rather well in school. As for Andrei, the further he went, the better he did in science and the more mediocre in all other subjects. He even cut some classes because of his experiments and, strange as this may seem, the Pedagogues allowed him to get away with this. For instance, he went to gym class very rarely, and to swimming class at the school pool even more rarely than that. Just think: he never did learn how to swim!

Despite the few peculiarities of his personality, Andrei was a good pal. Sometimes we argued, but we never fought. Once, though, he blew up over nothing and insulted me. In seventh grade we were studying Einstein's theory and I didn't understand it all at first, so at home I turned to the ERASMMUS.* I know that nowadays this aggregate is not used— it's considered a poor teaching aid and has been discontinued —but in my youth some students used its help. Andrei looked upon ERASMMUS severely and called it Crammer.

---

* **ERASMMUS** Electronic Reading and Study Machine Making Understanding Simpler.

I put the book in the opening, turned it on, and the mechanical fingers turned the pages. ERASMMUS began reading the book aloud, explaining it visually on the screen, and giving its own simplified and comprehensible explanations.

Suddenly Andrei, who had been sitting quietly at his desk, doing nothing and staring into space, said angrily:

"Will you turn off that darn Crammer! Can't you understand such simple things?"

"Andrei, you're crude," I said. "This machine is called ERASMMUS and not a crammer."

"And who thinks up these names for all this aggregates? ERASMMUS! Really!"

"The names are thought up by the Special Volunteer Naming Commissions, composed of Poets," I replied. "Therefore, in insulting the aggregate, you insult the Poets who voluntarily and without recompense give names to these mechanisms. And since I used ERASMMUS, you insult me as well."

"Forgive me, I didn't want to insult you at all," Andrei said. "Give me the book, and I'll explain the chapter to you."

He began telling me the meaning of the Theory, but his explanations were strange, paradoxical, and totally incomprehensible to me. I told Andrei this, and he was sincerely surprised.

"But it's so simple. I came across this book accidentally when we were in second grade, and I didn't see anything hard about it then."

"You don't, but I do!" I replied and turned on ERASMMUS again.

But this argument didn't destroy our friendship. And when we turned sixteen and we received the right to use the Amplifying Station of Thought Transmission, Andrei and I chose the same wavelength and became "twins" in thought transmission.* Soon this came in handy. Andrei needed my help.

* Thought transmission in those days could only be done by two subscribers on pattern A-B, B-A. The Amplification Stations used tremendous energy reserves and the use of thought transmission was considered an extreme emergency measure to be used only when all other communications systems were unavailable.

This is what happened. In early spring our parents took a vacation and flew to Madagascar, leaving us with rules and warnings. Andrei, taking advantage of their absence, stayed late at the Free Laboratory. He would go there alone and do experiments with water, on which he was fixated, as they used to say. As it later turned out, some of his experiments were far from safe, and the DRAGEN* often had to lecture Andrei and even turn off the circuits at the lab to stop the experiments. For this reason Andrei came to hate the innocent DRAGEN and even called it Beanpole.

Once Andrei was held up at the lab until very late, but I wasn't too worried about him since I was sure that he was in no danger since he was doing his experiments under the supervision of the DRAGEN. And I calmly went to bed.

I was falling asleep, when I heard Andrei's mind signal.

"What's wrong?" I asked.

"Danger," Andrei announced. "Come to the lab. That's all. Over and out."

I got dressed immediately and ran out on the street. The FACA** hailed me at the gates.

"Are you upset? Any orders?"

"Thank you, no," I replied and ran down the glowing plastic road in the direction of school. The street was empty; just a few couples sat on the benches of the boulevard here and there. I ran into a BONUS.*** It had a bouquet of pink flowers in its hand, and a pink light glowed in its forehead. The pink light meant that a girl was born, and the BONUS was on its way to inform the father. I almost knocked it over, I was in such a rush.

But here was the school. In the daytime a statue of Nike

---

* **DRAGEN** Directing and Regulating Aggregate Governing Experiments by Neophytes. Old-fashioned aggregate, now replaced by a new model.

** **FACA** Factotum Aggregate for Communal Apartments. A mechanism of the 21st–22nd centuries. Did approximately what Superintendents used to do in antiquity.

*** **BONUS** Bearer of Official News, Unlimited Smiles. An ancient aggregate, long off the market.

hung in the schoolyard, and the head had been restored through the most precise cybernetic calculations, and the entire statue (rather, its copy) looked just as the sculptor had made it. It was cast from nonrusting metal and was suspended by electromagnets high above a low pedestal, as though flying forward. At night the electromagnets were turned off, and the statue was gently lowered to its pedestal. In the morning, when the sun's rays caressed the on switch, Nike smoothly rose into the air, continuing its flight. In the days of my youth there were many such floating statues. Now, unfortunately, electromagnets have been rejected, considered in poor taste, and people have returned to regular pedestals. That's a shame! I fear today's youth rejects the creative achievements of the past too quickly.

A light burned in the windows of the large building of the Free Laboratory. I went into the technology section. Here, amid the apparatus and machinery, I saw Andrei. He was sitting on a plastic stool, and blood was dripping from his hands. Above him, bending down clumsily, the DRAGEN was giving him medical advice. Andrei was very pale. I rushed over to the first aid chest, got the necessary equipment, and proceeded to give first aid. Andrei had been injured in the shoulder and had lost a lot of blood. The wound was not large, but rather deep. I poured Universal Balm on it and bandaged it, and then called a Doctor by phone.

"What happened here?" I asked Andrei.

"A small miscalculation," he replied. "I expected a completely different effect. You see, I had to know the behavior of water under certain special circumstances. I overcooled it under pressure and sprayed it into a heated gold pipe. I thought that the change in temperature—"

"And what were you looking at?" I turned severely to the DRAGEN. "You're supposed to stop dangerous experiments!"

"The experiment is not dangerous," the DRAGEN answered indifferently. "The experiment is worthwhile, necessary, needed, obligatory, beneficial, and not dangerous."

"How can that be when the man is injured?" I was angry. "And look what's going on here!"

The floor was covered with broken dials, shards of plexiglas, pieces of metal, a burst gold pipe with rather thick walls.

"It's not Beanpole's fault," Andrei said. "If anyone's at fault, it's me. I convinced Beanpole that the experiment was safe."

"You tricked him! He may not be a Person, and only a mechanism, but you still fooled him. Tricking the mechanism, you trick Society!"

"I didn't trick him, I convinced him. I made corrections in his electronic circuitry. He even helped me with the experiment."

"Experiments are necessary, safe, approved, on solid ground, objective, full of promise," the DRAGEN muttered.

"Well, talking to you two is like grinding water in a mortar!" I said angrily.

"Water in a mortar? Grind? A new experiment?" The DRAGEN was interested.

"No experiments," I said. "Why don't you clean up in here."

The DRAGEN quickly bent down over the vent of the disposal, pulled out a plastic shovel from his foot, and, hopping about, threw out all the shards and pieces. Once the pieces of the gold pipe went down the disposal, he shut the vent.

"There. May I unplug?"

"Yes," I replied. "And tell the Humans to replace you. You're irreparable."

The Doctor came just then.

Andrei's wound healed quickly, leaving a scar. The strangest part is that Andrei was not punished for his prank. He was kept away from experiments for a short time, and then he went back to them. Say what you will, he had more than enough stubbornness.

From Our Youth 4

One day in early autumn Andrei and I were walking along a bay. As we approached a rowboat dock, Andrei said:

"Let's take a boat. We haven't been on one in a long time."

We took a boat and began rowing out into the bay. Yachts and recreational electric boats passed us, and farther out we could see the slow-moving passenger ships, freighters, and large sailboats. The sailboats were beautiful; they looked just like ancient engravings. Except these had no crews: the sails were raised and lowered by mechanisms controlled by CAP-TAINs.* The sailing ships carried nonurgent freight and proved to be invaluable. Of course sometimes, as a result of the extreme complexity of the controlling mechanism, strange things happened to some of these ships. They would suddenly start wandering around the seas, never coming in to any port. These wandering ships were a danger to other craft, and they tried to catch up with them, but that wasn't so easy. The CAP-TAINs began developing a resistance factor, and they tried to elude their pursuers.

Andrei and I rowed out further into the bay. But a two-deck atomic cruiser came alongside, creating a large swell. Andrei lost his stroke—he wasn't a good rower anyway—but I managed to turn the prow into the wave. We were shaken, and some water splashed into our boat, but we were all right.

"It could have been worse," I told Andrei. "We could have landed in the water, and you still don't know how to swim. That's weird: you're studying water, experimenting on it, and you don't know how to swim. Perhaps you want to tame storms and squalls?"

"No, storms and squalls will remain. But water, I'm con-

---

* **CAPTAIN** Cybernetic Antiaccident Pilot Tops in Actual Inwater Navigation. A highly perfected aggregate for its day. Modernized now.

vinced of it, will become servant to Man. And the time for that is not so far off."

I said nothing. I'd known for a long time that water was Andrei's hobbyhorse and I didn't want to argue with him. It was pointless.

"That conclusion can be reached by means other than research, science, and technology, you know. Logic of life maintains it," Andrei continued. "Man has friends: metal, stone, wood, glass, plastic—tried and true friends. But Mankind is growing, it needs a new strong friend and ally. There is no such friend for now. But he does have an enemy. Water. Water is a hostile element, water is antistability."

"Water is water, and there's nothing you can do about it." I put in my bon mot.

"But when Man subjugates a strong and dangerous enemy, that strong and dangerous enemy becomes the most faithful and dependable ally. And Mankind needs a new ally now. Only when he's conquered water will Man become the complete ruler of the planet."

"Go on, Zeke, it's your week," I said, after listening to Andrei.

"Who's Zeke?" Andrei asked.

"That's just an ancient saying. I won't explain it to you."

In those days I had already developed a serious interest in the history of literature and folklore of the twentieth century and had made definite successes in the field. I found ancient sayings, expressions, and jokes in old books and copied them out into a special notebook. Also, I was studying twentieth-century Poets, hoping with time to write a historical work on them. At the same time I worked on my favorite child, DOWUBA.

In our school, eleventh and twelfth grade were specialized, and after tenth I went to the liberal arts division. Andrei went to the technology division. We set off for school together as usual, but once we got there, we were separated until the end of the day. We were friendly as before, went to movies and the theater together, and during our vacation traveled in

America, Australia, Switzerland. But I best remember our walks together in our home town. We wandered along the old streets, which retained their character untouched since the twentieth century, and down to the New City, where the new buildings loomed, and which seemed so tall to me—there was no aqualide construction then.

Once, walking past a building I saw a sign:

ORPHIUS, meaning Official Readout of Potential Human Intelligence Unlimited Scores.

I had long wanted to verify my mental capacity, which, with all my modesty, I didn't doubt for an instant. And so I jokingly suggested to Andrei:

"Let's go in and find out what scores our brains get."

"All right, if you like," Andrei agreed. "But I don't have much faith in their accuracy."

"Maybe you're afraid one of us will turn out to be a potential idiot?" I teased.

"Anything's possible," Andrei said. "Sometimes I feel like such a fool."

We went inside, and soon we were taken to separate cubicles, each filled with equipment. The Assistant offered me a chair, and placed a plastic helmet with protruding wires on my head.

"Think about what interests you most and what you think about most often," the Assistant said.

I started thinking about my favorite child, DOWUBA, and needles moved on dials, lights went on and off. Then the Assistant checked a screen and turned off the equipment.

"Ready," he said. "You have a tendency toward systematics."

"And what's my score?"

"Four. Not bad at all."

"What, only four?!" I was incensed. "On a scale of ten? There must be a mistake. Obviously, your ORPHIUS needs repairs."

"Four is a pretty good score," the Assistant told me. "There are many People who get a much lower score and they work in science, arts, and literature and are considered smart People. Directors and Screenwriters often get a one from OR-PHIUS, and yet you watch their movies and like them."

"That just confirms my theory that your aggregate is inaccurate. If a Director makes a film, and Critics write about it, that alone proves that ORPHIUS is wrong in giving them ones."

"That doesn't prove anything," the Assistant countered. "You can be a stupid Scholar and you can be a wise Worker."

"Does your ORPHIUS ever give high scores?" I asked. "Does it give eights, nines, tens?"

"ORPHIUS has never given a ten from the day it was invented. Ten is the state of genius. Geniuses aren't born every day. Even nine is the threshold of genius. Do you know the story of Nils Indestrom?"

"I know the Theory of Inaccessibility. We studied it in eighth grade. Do you think that if your ORPHIUS gave me a four I'm so stupid as not to know Indestrom's TI?"

"No one doubts that you know the TI," the Assistant soothed me. "I just want to remind you about his life. Thirty years ago in the small Swedish town of Ultafjord, a young Worker was repairing the equipment in a fishnet factory. He had the minimal Earth education, twelve grades with a technical specialty. In his free time young Nils attended theoretical courses in general physics, and read books on the quantum theory and cosmography. Besides, he could do such complicated and fast calculations in his head that he could beat a computer of middle range. He was planning to go on to school, but since he was extremely modest, he was in no hurry to apply. One day his friends, knowing his modesty and his extraordinary abilities, dragged Nils to ORPHIUS, which gave him a nine. Soon after, Idestrom was accepted in the second year at the Academy of Higher Scientific Knowledge. Memorials in his honor stand in every major city in the world."

"I know all that," I said. "But it's always seemed strange to me that they erect statues to the creator of a negative law."

"Wisdom can be negative," the Assistant said. "Particularly since the TI, with all its negativism, plays a positive role. It prevents Mankind from making useless attempts to reach the Distant Stars. So he's earned his statues."

I went out into the reception hall and waited for Andrei. He was held up for some reason in his cubicle and I had to wait almost an hour. Finally he came out, accompanied by his Assistant and two other elderly Men who looked professorial.

"Let's go," he said. "The torture is over."

We bade farewell to the workers at the research center and I thought that they were treating Andrei too respectfully, incommensurate with his age. One of the Professors even walked him out.

"Why were they working on you for so long?" I asked.

"They gave me various additional problems and forms. They exhausted me. And then they called my school. And then the Universal Academy of Sciences."

"Obviously, their ORPHIUS is very imperfect, and so they needed additional information," I said, to console Andrei. "That ORPHIUS only gave me a four, that's an obvious error."

"Yes, it is imperfect," Andrei agreed. "It gave me a ten. I certainly don't deserve that. Sometimes I feel like a brainless puppy."

After school, I entered the University in the philology department, and Andrei went into the Academy of Higher Knowledge, into the third year. We now lived in different dorms, but we saw each other frequently.

A Deserved Punishment **5**

But I return to where I began my narrative.

A few days after the "stamp revolt" Andrei came to visit me. He looked sad.

"Tell me, what's happened?" I asked. "Another failed experiment? You should be used to failure by now. You're like a fish in water with them."

"No, this is a different sort of unpleasantness," Andrei replied, not noticing my barb and missing the hidden pun. "You see, at the general meeting I reported my behavior, how I yelled at that girl—"

"Well, to think that you might have kept quiet about it! He who hides evil, lies. And what did the general meeting decide?"

"They decided to punish me with hunting. I have to go to the Luzhsky Preserve and kill one hare. There are too many there now and they're damaging gardens in the area."

"That's unpleasant, all right," I grimaced. "But it's a deserved punishment. Just think: telling a girl that she's a harpy!"

"Would you consider flying over to the preserve with me?" Andrei asked. "It's dreary setting out on this alone. Naturally, I'll carry out the punishment myself."

I remembered that a Student had told me that the Ranger of the preserve was an ancient old man who knows ancient folklore, old curses, jokes, and swear words. *Maybe I'll be able to add to DOWUBA,* I thought and agreed to accompany Andrei. Andrei left, cheered up by my decision.

I immediately informed Nina that I was leaving in the morning for two or three days, and asked her not to interrupt her work on the Anthology. But when she learned that I was going to the preserve, she wanted to come along.

"What, you want to see an animal killed?" I was stunned. "I didn't expect that!"

"No, don't be silly! I just want to be in the great outdoors. And to see some live animals."

"Well, that's another matter," I said. "I'll come pick you up in the morning."

In the depths of my heart, I was very happy that Nina decided to come with me to the preserve. I decided that she wasn't interested in nature, she was interested in me. Perhaps she was waiting for a declaration of love from me. And she had agreed to go to the hunt just to hear it.

Hunting had long ceased being a pleasure for People and had turned into an unpleasant obligation that arose from time to time when there were too many animals in the preserves. When wars had stopped and poverty and social inequality had disappeared from Earth, People's mores had softened and crime had been reduced to nothing. No longer cruel to one another, People changed their attitude toward animals as well. Long before I was born, a worldwide law was passed forbidding experimentation on animals. They were completely replaced by electrobionic models. Keeping animals locked up, that is in so-called zoos, was recognized as cruelty, and zoos were closed down. This did not upset anyone, since the perfection and speed of transportation made it possible for everyone to see animals in their native habitats, in preserves. Man did not need to hunt—not for meat, nor hides, nor furs. Animal furs had been replaced by synthetics, and synthurs (synthetic furs) were much more attractive and warmer than natural furs. Thus, the economic need for hunting was gone, and morally it was repugnant to man, as was any violence or murder. I remember when we read the classics in school, we were always surprised by the beautifully written descriptions of the hunt. We thought this love of cruelty very strange.

The next morning I went to Nina's. She didn't live in the dormitory, but at home with her mother. Nina's father had perished during an underwater expedition, and even though it had happened long ago, Nina's mother always acted as though it had just happened yesterday. Nevertheless it was cozy at their house, and I enjoyed being there. That morning Nina and her mother greeted me warmly, as usual. I remember that morning very well, because it was on that day that great changes began in our lives.

"You must eat before you set out," Nina's mother said. "At the University cafeteria, you eat what the SATYR offers you, and they don't have vivid imaginations. I programmed our DIVER* myself, and it's had vast experience."

"I would truly enjoy some home cooking," I agreed. "Please ask the DIVER for two syntholamb chops."

"You'll have to earn those chops yourself," Nina's mother laughed. "Program it yourself. Come on, I'll teach you. You'll marry one day, and this will come in handy."

She led me to the kitchen. At our approach, the DIVER came out of its niche and extended a simulation of a metal hand that had a keyboard with numbers, letters, and signs.

"Here's lamb for you," said Nina's mother, pressing some buttons, "and here's veal chops for Nina. It's so simple."

The DIVER lowered its hand and froze in a position of readiness.

"Is it dangerous, flying off to hunt?" Nina's mother asked. "I'm so worried about Nina, she's so reckless, just like her father."

"Don't worry, I wouldn't have taken her with me if it were dangerous."

"Yes, yes, you're right. When she's with you, I don't worry. You're a sensible and controlled Man."

"My profession demands no less," I replied modestly.

"I would like for Nina to marry a man in a safe profession, like yours." Nina's mother confessed. "But let's get out of the kitchen, we're keeping the DIVER from its work."

We left the kitchen, and the DIVER started working. It couldn't work when there were People around, because it was programmed to feel shame. In the last centuries women had grown so tired of working in the kitchen, cooking and washing dishes, that now this work was considered unesthetic, and the DIVER could not work in the presence of People for fear of ruining their mood. If you came into the kitchen, it stopped working and awaited your orders. When it got them, it waited respectfully until you left to do the work.

We went back into the living room, and Nina started talk-

* **DIVER**   Domestic Individual Versatile Electronic Robot. Ancient kitchen aggregate. Long ago replaced by newer models.

ing about *The Anthology of Forgotten Poets* and about how we should include Vadim Shefner.

"What kind of man was he?" Nina's mother asked. "Was he a Widrinkson?"

"I couldn't say for sure," I replied. "But he was definitely a Tobsmokson*; he mentions cigarettes in one of his poems. But it's quite possible that he was a Widrinkson as well. Anything is possible with these twentieth-century Poets."

"You should judge People by their good points, not their flaws," Nina suddenly announced.

"That is not scholarly," I countered. "For me and my work it is important to know not only what the Writer wrote, but how he behaved in life."

"How right you are!" Nina's mother exclaimed. "Tell me, this Svetochev with whom you're going hunting, is he a balanced Individual? After all, a Man who is being punished so severely might be capable of anything."

"Andrei is a good friend," I soothed her. "He's never let anyone down. Except for himself."

"Don't worry, Mama," Nina interjected. "I've never seen this Andrei, but I can picture him well from Matvei's stories about him. I think he's a fine Man, but doomed to be a failure. He keeps seeking something and going wrong. I feel sorry for him."

"Yes, he's a good Man," I added. "He won't get the stars from the skies and he won't invent gunpowder, but that doesn't keep him from being a good Man and my friend."

On the Way to **6**
the Preserve

Soon Nina and I left her house and headed for the plane stop that was located on top of a tall building. Going up to the

* **Tobsmokson**   Tobacco-smoking person. Medical term of the times.

roof by elevator, we ran into Andrei. I introduced him to Nina, and we got into a four-seater. I took the seat next to the ERP,* and Nina and Andrei sat in the back.

"The flight is free," the ERP said. "Give me your flight plan and indicate the speed you wish: excursion, business, high, or ultra."

We gave the plan and ordered excursion speed. The weather was good, and it was a pleasure to fly. The city floated slowly below us, then we saw the huge white cubes of the synthetic products factories and the towers of the grain elevators. Soon we saw green fields below us; every few rows apart stood the command posts for long-distance electrotractors. Beyond the fields, in the distance, stretched the highways for distance driving, covered with yellowish and gray pieces of plastic; we could see the lacquered backs of the multiseat elmobiles. Parallel to these roads and sometimes running off from the highways into the woods, circling riverbanks and so on, meandered the narrow dirt roads for horseback riders. Small inns, where riders could rest and feed their horses and show them to the MOLE** on duty, were located on the roads. Even though Earth's population was growing, the shift to synthetic meat had freed so much land that Mankind could indulge in the pleasure of horseback riding. Actually, our Scientists proved that this wasn't a luxury but a benefit. Horse clubs and mass riding competitions were founded in my time. Many preferred covering short distances by horse. Young People dropped their elcycles and studied riding in their spare time. Some riders wore cloth helmets with red stars and long cavalry coats with horizontal stripes, resurrecting the uniform of Budyonny's Men. The old Men preferred mechanical means of locomotion and were unhappy with the paradox of the development of transportation. However, the number of horses and riders grew, and continues to do so.

* **ERP**   Electronic Responsible Pilot. 22nd-century aggregate. Replaced by more modern type.

** **MOLE**   Medical Organized Labor, Efficient. Veterinary aggregate.

Sitting next to the ERP, I couldn't hear what Nina and Andrei talked about. But they were having a lively conversation, of which I heard bits and snatches, as well as laughter. Not only Nina laughed, but Andrei as well.

Strange how can Andrei laugh, I thought. *He's being punished, he's headed for such an unpleasant task—and he's laughing!*

"What was so funny in what Nina told you?" I asked him, leaning over my seat.

"Nothing special," Nina replied for him. "I just remembered how once for a joke I inserted five stanzas from Omar Khayyam into the *Anthology* manuscript, and you read them and said quite seriously that these decaying poems did not reflect the twentieth century."

"I was thinking about something else at the time and made a mistake," I replied. "I know when Khayyam lived. But does Andrei know his poems?"

"Just imagine, he does," Nina said.

"He shouldn't be thinking about Khayyam now, but about the punishment he deserves. And you, Nina, shouldn't be changing his mood. Everyone who is punished should not only take the punishment but have a sense of his guilt."

After my totally just, by the way, remark, the laughter in the back seat stopped. They did go on talking, but in quieter tones.

Soon we landed at the boundary of the preserve. The ERP, commanded to return to the station in town, flew off on its return flight.

Here, in the neighborhood of the preserve, it was against the law to build contemporary buildings or constructions, and we crossed the river on a log bridge and went down the forest path. We had to find the house of the Forest Ranger, from whom Andrei had to get the weapon with which to fulfill his task.

Andrei stalked on ahead, and Nina and I followed at a slight distance. Hares bounded across the path; in one spot a fox gave us a sly look from the underbrush and ran off. Forest birds sang in the branches and our approach did not frighten them in the least.

"You know, I pictured your friend very differently," Nina suddenly said. "He's better than you made him out to be."

"I never said anything bad about him," I countered. "I don't know what you want from me!"

"You didn't say enough good about him," she replied. "I think that he's not an average Person. You don't know him well."

"How can you say that, Nina?" I said calmly. "I've known him all my life, and you only met an hour and a half ago."

"Nevertheless, he's not like the others."

"Every Man is not like others in some respects."

"I can sense in him a determination to reach an important goal."

"You can set yourself important goals and still be a failure," I explained reasonably.

"Well, maybe he is a failure," Nina said thoughtfully. "But an important failure is better than a minor one."

"I don't understand you, Nina. Success is always success and failure is always failure."

"I don't think so. One Man, say, decides to climb to the top of a mountain, and the other to stand on a swamp mound. The man who doesn't get to the peak will still go higher than the one standing on the mound."

I didn't argue with this aimless discussion, particularly since we had reached the Ranger's house. This was the home of the old man who supposedly knew ancient folklore. So I turned on my pocket microrecorder, hoping to use the transcription of our conversation with him in my DOWUBA.

The Old Widrinkson 7

The Forest Ranger's house stood in a green meadow by a stream. This was a real wood and plastic hut of the late twenty-second century, with an ancient television antenna on the roof, a porch, and a shed. An old motorcycle stood next to the house. To one side, under the trees, lay feeding stations for deer and gazelles and small boxes on the tree trunks, bird feeders. It was all so different from the city!

A stately old man came out of the house, smiling broadly, greeted us respectfully, and led us inside. The room we entered was very cozy. It radiated antiquity: the beat-up TV in its cracked casing, the porolon sofa of old-fashioned construction, the high wooden table, and the chairs with cane backs. Topping off the impression, completing the picture, were a gleaming electric samovar on a marble-topped table and two rifles hanging on the wall.

"This is so interesting!" Nina said. "I would love to live here."

"Who's to stop you?" the Ranger replied. "Come and live with us, the old woman and I will make room. We're always glad to have company."

"You see," Andrei interrupted, "we're here on business. We, that is, I have to kill one hare."

"Yes, I applied for the killing," the old man confirmed. "We have too many hares. There's a garden farm ten kilometers from here, and they've started chewing up the plants. And what did you do for such a punishment?"

Andrei explained what he was being punished for, and the old man said with a kindly smile:

"They're strict in the cities! The wife and I argue a lot out here in the woods. If I had to kill an animal for every 'fool' I've said, there wouldn't be any animals left in the preserve.

Well, take the rifle, then. Let's go to the shed, I'll teach you to shoot."

The old man and Andrei went outside and headed for an outbuilding. We heard a shot and then another. Then the old man returned and Andrei followed with the rifle.

"Quick fellow," the ranger praised Andrei. "The first time he's got a gun in his hand and he understood everything. Hit the bull's eye."

"Well, I'll go kill a hare," Andrei said to us. "I want to get this unpleasant business over with. What do I do with it then?" he asked the old man.

"Bring it here, there's no point in letting it go to waste. We'll eat it, that's what."

"May I go with you?" Nina asked Andrei.

"No, Nina, what are you thinking of? Why should you see all that? I'll go alone."

He went into the woods, and Nina went outside and sat on a bench. A fawn came over to her and nuzzled her knee, and she patted its back. I watched her out the window, and at that moment she seemed more attractive than ever.

"Fine gal," the Ranger said, seeming to read my thoughts. "Just what a gal should be."

"She's no gal. She's in her second year already," I corrected the old man.

"She could be in the twenty-second for all I know. She's a gal to me. I hit a hundred eighty-seven next week."

"Hitting, that means turning an age," I said with comprehension. "You look younger. Just think, MILS plus seventy-seven! You must have applied to the Commission on Life Extension?"

"I didn't apply anywhere. I extend my life on my own. We Rangers live a long time."

"How do you do that?" I asked. "Maybe you use ancient herbs and potions?"

"I know only one medicine and I don't think about death and that sort of nonsense, and my life extends itself. What's your handle?"

"Handle, that means name," I said. "My name is Matvei Ludmillovich."

"I'm Stepan Stepanovich. I have no truck with those maternal patronymics," he added with a kindly aged cackle. "All these new-fangled things: women's patronymics, ships with sails, galloping down the roads on horses . . . No, I'm an old man and I'll never get used to these things."

Finishing his speech, the Ranger opened a desk drawer and took out a leather sack and pack of papers.

"What's that?" I asked interestedly.

"It's a pouch, and in the pouch there's *makhorka*, home-grown stuff."

"What, could you possibly be a Tobsmokson?" I was amazed. "And at your age!"

"I'm no Tobsmokson, I'm a smoker. What stupid words they come up with!"

He folded over the edge of one paper, placed some tobacco in there, and then rolled the paper into a tube—and lit up. The heavy blue smoke crawled toward me, and I sneezed. A shot rang out in the woods just then.

"The hare was, now it isn't," the old man said, inhaling. "Your friend won't miss. And you—you're a fuddy-duddy."

"What's a fuddy-duddy?" I asked. "What does that folk idiom mean?"

"Nothing," the old man replied. "I just said it. A joke."

"Perhaps it's a swear word?" I was overjoyed. "Don't be embarrassed, please, call me another name."

"Why should I, you haven't done anything bad to me. And then I'm not under the influence either. I'll take some medicine and then I'll cuss. Come on, I'll show you my apothecary, where I cook up my medicine."

He took me to the kitchen and from there to a small annex. There was a strong smell in there. It was strange—unpleasant yet pleasant at the same time. There were vats on the old electric range with tubes and hoses going off in all directions. Something rumbled in the vats. An odiferous liquid dripped from a hose into a plastic bowl.

"What's this?" I asked. "A chemical laboratory?"

"The same," the old man answered heartily, pouring the liquid out of the bowl into a glass and offering it to me.

I hesitated, suspecting the very worst.

"Take it; drink. Like a teardrop! I'm distilling some for my birthday. You drink, and then I'll take a shot."

"You're a Widrinkson!" I exclaimed. "How inappropriate at your honorable age!"

"Drink," the old man insisted gently. "Or you'll hurt my feelings."

"Will you tell me some swear words?"

"I will, I will. But drink. I'll tell you everything."

I decided to sacrifice my health for science, and not wanting to insult the old man, I took a few sips. At first I was disgusted, but then the feeling began to pass.

"Drink and eat!" the Ranger said in an avuncular tone, handing me a piece of cheese.

I took a bite, and then, not to hurt his feelings, finished the glass. I felt very good and very happy. It was a new sensation for me, physically and spiritually. Then the old man had a drink, and we went back into the room.

"Our little hunter is slow coming back," the Ranger said. "And the girl is gone, too, probably ran off into the woods. That fellow has a head on his shoulders. He's going to steal her away from you. I saw the way she looked at him. She'll give you the heave-ho."

"What's a heave-ho?" I asked.

In reply the Old Widrinkson sang in a quavering voice:

> Ah, I planted the garden myself
> And I blossomed like the cherry myself,
> I loved my sweetheart my own way
> And I gave him the heave-ho myself.

And he finished:

"She's going to write you off, that's for sure. She'll forget you and it's over."

"You promised to cuss me with some folkloric expressions," I reminded him.

"With pleasure, I can do it in my sleep," the Widrinkson replied. "I remember lots of that. Sometimes, my father would start in and I would memorize it."

And the Ranger began saying swear words and I repeated them, and my pocket recorder got it all down. The DOWUBA was expanding. But then Andrei came in and Nina with him, and my conversation with the Widrinkson was interrupted. Andrei put the rifle in the corner and turned the dead hare over to the Ranger, who took it to the kitchen.

"It was unpleasant killing it," Andrei said. "They're quite tame. What's the matter with you?" he asked, looking at me closely.

"Nothing," I replied and to my own surprise began singing:

> Ah, I planted the garden myself,
> And I blossomed like the cherry myself . . .

"What's going on with you?" Nina laughed. "I've never seen you like this."

"Ah, he's had a drink! He's become a Widrinkson!" Andrei guessed. "Some future Professor!"

"Only in the name of science!" I said, tongue twisting. "Only to fill in my DOWUBA!"

At that moment the Old Widrinkson appeared, carrying a full glass of his "medicine." He handed it to Andrei.

"Drink half and then give it to the girl," he said. "If you don't drink to my coming birthday, I'll be hurt. Only we don't have a good meal, my old woman went to Australia to look at the kangaroo preserves. And our DIVER is broken—I tried to teach it to make moonshine, and it went and broke! Stupid robot!" With those words the Ranger set several cans on the floor and opened them with an ancient hunting knife.

Andrei drank his half of the glass and handed it to Nina.

"Nina, Nina, what are you doing! Think, Nina!" I cried

out, for even though I was intoxicated, my reason had not left me.

"Ah, don't be silly!" Nina laughed and, to my horror, drained the glass.

"Right!" the Old Widrinkson shouted. "Fine work, children! Do you know what ancient omen we used to believe in? If a boy and a girl drank out of the same glass, it meant a wedding."

I felt very sad then for some reason and began weeping. But the old man brought me another glass and after I drank it I felt fine. In the meantime, the Old Widrinkson pulled out an old-fashioned phonograph, plugged it in, and began dancing to some bizarre ancient music. Andrei and Nina joined him. And I just sat and smiled. Everything seemed very sweet and pleasant, but I couldn't get up from my seat. Then my head started spinning, and I don't remember anything else.

A Bridge Without **8**
Railings

In the morning I was awakened by a squirrel jumping through the open window onto the ancient sofa on which I slept. My head ached, but the Old Widrinkson gave me an elixir and I felt healthy again.

Everyone had gotten up long before me. The Ranger gave us breakfast and some food for the road, and the three of us set out for the forest lake. The Old Widrinkson gave us directions and told us that it was very beautiful there.

We moved at a leisurely pace—Andrei and I with backpacks, Nina unburdened—down the forest road, then turned down a path that we followed for three kilometers or so, first through the woods and then through a mossy swamp. Then low hills began, covered with heather and juniper bushes. The sun was rising higher and higher, and it was quite warm, even hot. Soon from one of the hills we could see the lake and a small river falling into it.

"Let's go to that shore," Nina said. "Look how lovely it is!"

The other shore truly was beautiful. There were gray round stones on the sloping shore and the forest started again beyond it. However, it was all rather far.

"Is it worth going there?" I said. "Is this shore bad?"

"The other's better!" Andrei countered. And Nina concurred.

I agreed with the majority, and we went down to the river. The bridge across it was nothing like what we call a bridge. Spikes had been driven in two places, and three links, each two logs wide, were thrown from bank to bank. There were no railings.

Andrei stepped onto the bridge first, then Nina, and I brought up the rear. We walked carefully. The water was dark and deep below, foaming at the spikes, and we could see the power of the current. To the left of the bridge the river widened, and there was a whirlpool. Small funnels of water quietly moved on its surface.

"How gorgeous!" Nina said, stopping and looking down into the depths. And suddenly, losing her balance, she cried out and fell down into that deep dark water.

Andrei jumped in after her. He forgot to take off his knapsack and I realized that he might drown—he hadn't learned to swim, after all. So I threw off my backpack, set it down on the logs, quickly removed my shoes and threw them on the bank. Then I dived in. When I surfaced, I saw that Nina had been carried some distance by the current and she was swimming to shore. I wasn't worried about her, because I knew she was a strong swimmer. Andrei was nowhere to be seen. I began diving, and finally found him under the water. I pulled off his pack and dragged my friend to the surface and swam with him to shore. Soon I could touch bottom. I pulled Andrei out on the shore—the very one for which we were headed—and Nina ran up to me.

"What's the matter with him? How is he?" she yelled. "It's all my fault."

"No, it's not," I consoled her. "He shouldn't have jumped in after you. If you don't know the depth, don't get in—that's an ancient saying. He doesn't know how to swim! As for you, instead of crying over nothing, help me."

We removed Andrei's jacket and shirt. He didn't move or breathe, his body was very pale, and the small scar on his shoulder was blue—the traces of the exploded pipe, when he was doing experiments in the Free Laboratory.

We began giving him artificial respiration, but he still didn't stir. Realizing that things were serious, I decided to call a Doctor. I never removed my Personal Apparatus from my wrist, and now it came in handy. I pushed the button for the autocoordinator, the button with the red cross and exclamation point—an emergency call for medical aid.

"Nina, I'll give him artificial respiration and you run over to that field over there and wave your arms. Or, even better, take off your blouse and wave that. The Doctor will find us easier from his extracopter."

I looked at my Personal Apparatus. Next to my call button the green light was on, the signal that my call had been taken. But I went on with the respiration even though it wasn't doing much.

Suddenly I heard the rustle of the underbrush, branches being moved aside, and a Man ran out on the shore. He looked as though he had just jumped down from an old movie reel. His shirt sleeves were rolled up to his elbows, and in his right hand he held an antique duelling pistol, barrel down. On one wrist gleamed the Personal Apparatus, a perfectly contemporary attribute, but on the other was something resembling a watch. *He's suffering from a loss of his temporal sense, poor fellow*, I thought.

The man threw the pistol on the sand and, rushing up to the motionless Andrei, put the hand with what I thought was a wristwatch on Andrei's forehead. I realized then that it wasn't a watch but a QUACK.* That meant the Man was a Doctor.

No sooner had the Doctor placed the QUACK on Andrei's brow than a green line lit up on the apparatus. Then the QUACK spoke softly, but clearly.

"Seventy-eight pain units, rising. Mortal outcome avoidable. No internal injuries. Condition on Muller-Borshchenko scale: alpha −7.8. Give artificial respiration type A-3. Give artificial respiration. Mortal outcome avoidable."

"Well, I know that," the Doctor said, addressing either the machine, or us, or himself, and began giving Andrei artificial respiration according to the best medical practice.

Soon Andrei was showing signs of life. The Doctor put the QUACK on his forehead again. The green line was no longer quivering and was wider. The machine spoke again.

"Mortal outcome avoided. Eleven illness units, falling. Data on Stepanov and Brosius: beta one plus Z seven. The patient needs complete rest for four days. Normal food. Mortal outcome avoided."

In the meantime, Andrei had completely revived. He was just very pale after his experience.

"Let him lie still a bit longer," the Doctor said. "Then take him to that hut and let him sleep. And then feed him well. You don't need my help any longer. I have a much more unpleasant duty ahead of me: I have to go kill a hare. You see, I had just taken aim when your call came."

"What were you being punished for?" I asked.

"I? Didn't you hear about that horrible incident in the Nevsky District? A Man died who was only ninety-six years old. He missed his MILS by an entire fourteen years! I'm the Doctor in charge of Prevention, I answer for the life span of

---

* **QUACK** Quick, Utilitarian Absolute Cures and Knowledge. An ancient medical aggregate. Now replaced by a more efficient long-distance one.

People in the district. I demanded this punishment myself at the Doctor's meeting."

"And why did you choose such an inconvenient weapon?" I asked. "It's easier to make a hit with a rifle."

"I have a friend, Curator of the Museum of Ancient Objects, and he gave me this pistol and taught me how to shoot. It's easier to carry a pistol."

The Doctor picked up his gun and headed for the woods. Nina and I stayed with Andrei. Soon he felt well enough to move. I put on my backpack, then Nina and I took him by the arms and began leading him to the lake along the riverbank, where an ancient wooden hut with just one window stood on the pebbles.

"Wait!" I quickly returned to the scene of the accident, undressed, and dove into the water, where I rather quickly found Andrei's backpack.

We soon reached the hut. It was very old. Inside there was a stove, a chair, a table, and a thick layer of hay on the floor, kept here for winter feedings. A ladder led upstairs. There was hay there, too.

"Oh, I'm spending the night in the attic!" Nina cried. "It's so cozy here!"

"It's too early to think about spending the night," I said reasonably. "First we have to dry off and eat. Nina, you go to that side of the hut and undress there, and we'll take this side."

Soon Andrei and I were lying naked on the sand, our clothes spread out beside us. I lay on my back and looked at the sky. It was light blue, whitish, the way it is on hot, cloudless days. I thought about how the light, weightless sky, seeming to consist of nothing, always remained itself, while on the solid, material ground everything changed.

"While you went to get my pack, Nina told me how it all happened," Andrei interrupted my meditations. "I absolutely have to learn to swim."

I knew that Andrei was grateful to me, but in our day it

was no longer customary to express gratitude. For if A thanked B for behaving as he should have, that implied that B might have behaved differently.

We heard Nina's laughter from the other side of the hut. Then she cried out:

"He's coming toward you! He stole my scarf!"

"Who?" I shouted. "There's no one here."

"The hedgehog! He came over and took my scarf. He's so clever."

And a hedgehog did come around the corner. A scarf was stuck on his quills. I grabbed the scarf, the hedgehog grunted angrily, shuffled his feet, and left.

Soon our clothes were dry, and we started to eat. Andrei's pack was soaked, but the canned goods were in there, and nothing had happened to them. The bread and tableware were in mine. Forest birds flew and hopped around us, picking up the crumbs we tossed them.

The Girl on 9
the Cliff

I got up rather late in the morning, it was so good sleeping on hay. When I opened my eyes, I saw that Andrei was sitting at the table by the window and writing something. He felt my gaze and turned to me.

"Do you mind? I took a notebook from your backpack and took it apart into pages," he asked. "I had some paper in my pack, but it was soaked."

"Go on, work," I replied. "But I have a few thoughts on my Anthology written in there, and don't you even think about writing over them."

"No, of course not!" Andrei said. "I'm writing on the other side."

I got up and walked over to him. The entire table was covered with filled-up pages.*

"Only numbers, formulas, signs, and not a single human word," I said. "Did you get up a long time ago?"

"At dawn," Andrei said. "I slept very soundly, but then something seemed to give me a shove. I woke up and took my seat at the table."

"Do you feel all right?"

"Physically, not very well. I still feel weak and tired. But my head is working well. You know, I think I'm reaching an important solution."

"You've come to various important solutions many times, and then they turned out to be wrong."

"No, not this time. I think I've caught the devil by the tail this time. It's totally unexpected. I still don't understand how I could have come on it."

"I think that you need some sleep and rest. And then you can take this up again with a rested mind," I suggested cautiously.

"You must think I've lost my mind," Andrei laughed. "Even if I have, it's with a plus. You know, if you take a hundred computers and shake up their circuits before using them, ninety-nine will fall into technological idiocy, but the hundredth might fall into a state of genius and give a paradoxical but correct solution."

"I won't argue with you," I answered gently. "Is Nina still sleeping?"

"No, she's at the lake. There she is."

I looked out the window to the right. Nina was standing on a low sandy cliff and looking out over the lake into the distance. The wind was stirring her dress. The sun lit her from the side, and she was very clearly visible.

"The girl on the cliff," Andrei suddenly said. "Like in the poem."

* These pages are now in the Svetochev Memorial Museum. And on the reverse side are the notes by Matvei Kovrigin.

"What poem?" I asked with interest.

"Just a girl standing on the cliff and looking out in the distance. Before her the lake and water lilies; behind her the forest and the morning sun. And she stands there and looks out. And someone looks at her and thinks: 'Now the girl is standing on the cliff and looking into the distance. Now I'll remember her always. She'll go back into the forest, but I'll still imagine that she's here. And when I grow old, I'll come to this shore and see: a girl standing at the cliff looking out into the distance.' "

"I don't see what you like in that poem. I hate sentimentality. They wrote better than that in the twentieth century."

Andrei muttered something in reply and lost himself in his notes, and I went over to the lake. Water lilies and grasses grew at the shore. I walked along the rickety boardwalk to the open water and took a long bath. Then I went over to Nina. She was still standing on the low cliff and staring out aimlessly.

"Nina, did you sleep well?" I asked.

"Very well. At first I was bothered by the bats. They kept flying in and out the window. But they're noiseless. Now they're sleeping up there upside down. They're cute. Just think that people used to be afraid of them."

"Nina, you haven't forgotten the Anthology?" I reminded her. "We have to get back to town."

"No, I'm staying here for four days," she replied calmly. "Andrei needs four days of rest. I'll cook for him."

"Well, he's not so weak that he needs someone to do his cooking," I argued. "A sick Man doesn't get up at dawn and sit down to scribble endless formulas. If a Man is sick, he stays in bed and doesn't doodle."

"What?" Nina asked. "Stays in bed and what?"

"Doodle," I explained. "It's an idiomatic expression of the twentieth century."

"But I'm staying anyway," Nina said.

"Well, do what you think is best," I replied. "After all, we live in the twenty-second century and know that trying to change someone's mind is an unworthy act. If a sighted person walks to the abyss, the one who stops him is like a blind man."

"Ah, spare me the schooltime maxims," Nina said sadly. "And I'm not headed for the abyss yet." She jumped off the small cliff onto the sand and, tossing off her shoes, went into the water to pick water lilies.

"Here!" she shouted, throwing a flower at me. "And don't make serious faces."

I went back to the hut. Andrei was still struggling with his formulas.

"Here, look," he said when I came in. "Here it is."

He showed me a page scribbled over and crossed out. At the bottom, outlined with a thick line, was one formula, very long.

"So what?"

"I found what I was looking for. Now all I have to do is check, check, and double-check myself."

"Fine, you do that, but I have to go back to town. Nina's staying here."

"Nina brings me luck," Andrei said thoughtfully. "I never believed in things like that, but she does bring me luck."

I set out for town soon after that. I walked to the Ranger's Station and then called a heliplane and soon found myself back in Leningrad.

SAPIENS Said Yes! 10

Back in Leningrad, I was so immersed in my work on *The Anthology of Forgotten Poets of the Twentieth Century* that for a time I forgot about everything and everyone else. Of course, I did miss Nina (her help was very substantial), but nevertheless my work progressed. For days at a time I sat at my desk and left only to get an infrequent breath of fresh air.

Once I went out to the Islands. I walked down an allée and came out on the square with the monument to Ivanov and Smith, the Conquerors of Cancer, to the crew of *Mars 1*, and to Anton Stepanov, one of the greatest poets of the twenty-second century. The monument to Nils Indestrom, the author of the Theory of Inaccessibility, is here too. You all know the statue: a giant made of black metal standing on a black socle; his outstretched hand seems to be frozen in an imperious gesture nailing everything terrestrial to the Earth, rather, to the Solar System. In those years a bronze plaque was affixed to the pedestal with Indestrom's words: "The path to the Distant Worlds is closed forever. The body is weaker than wings." Underneath was engraved the Formula of Inaccessiblity—the sum of Nils Indestrom's life. We learned the formula in school. It proved that even if man could create the energy to penetrate beyond the limits of the Solar System, he would never be able to create a material that would withstand the flight. I never liked that statue. It always seemed strange to me that people erected it in memory of a Scientist who proved something negative.

I sat on a bench and shared my thoughts with the Man sitting next to me. Judging by the badge on his lapel, he was a Student in technical school. He disagreed with me and said that with his negative law Nils Indestrom had saved many lives. And he added that the statue must stand eternally, even if the law is proved false.

"The law is the law because it cannot be proved false," I countered.

"For now, but people are trying to undermine it even as we speak," the Student said. "All the specialized press is peppered with articles about how we are on the verge of a technical revolution. Mankind needs a single, superstrong, universal material. Man's metal-stone-wood-plastic-ceramic shirt is too tight for him. It's splitting at the seams."

"I don't know, I'm perfectly comfortable in it," I countered. "And where in our age will a Man be found who can create the material of which you speak?"

"Many Scientists are working on it," the Student replied. "Particularly, Andrei Svetochev. Of course, he's chosen a very difficult path—"

"Does he really have any real achievements?" I interrupted.

"In the usual sense, no. But if—"

"If only, if mushrooms grew in your mouth," I replied with an ancient folk saying, which made my interlocutor shut up for, as they used to say in the past, "he couldn't beat that."

I didn't know then that Svetochev's formula would soon turn into technological reality.

The next day, while I was working on my *Anthology,* Nina came to see me. I noted immediately that she had a festive air about her and that she had become much prettier lately.

"The fresh air did you good," I said, and she looked embarrassed.

"I was there ten days instead of four because Andrei was so busy," she said in an apologetic tone. "I cooked his meals. If you don't feed him, he doesn't think to eat. But he's moved along in his work. He checked his formula, and its—"

"You had enough food?" I asked. "You can't call for transport from the preserve."

"I went to the Ranger's twice. He's such a sweet man. And his wife was back from Australia."

"Nina, I'm not interested in Australia but in the Anthology," I said gently. "And even though your help is purely technical, your participation is desirable. But finish up about Andrei. So, he checked his formula, and it, like all the others, was a mistake? Right?"

"For now nothing is clear. He turned the material over to the Academy, and they turned it over to SAPIENS.* But the calculations Andrei turned in are so complex and paradoxical that SAPIENS has been struggling with them for over

* **SAPIENS** Specialized Aggregate Investigating Experimental and New Stuff. An ancient 21st-century aggregate.

twenty-four hours now and still can't support or reject them. Usually it takes SAPIENS a few minutes to determine whether or not a Researcher is correct."

"I'm not an electronic SAPIENS, just a plain *Homo sapiens*, but I can predict the result," I joked. "It'll be another failure."

Nina said nothing, pretending to be engrossed in reading material for the Anthology.

"I'm not too thrilled with your choice of authors," she suddenly said. "You're oversimplifying the twentieth century. It was more complex than you think. That's what I think."

"Your remark amazes me!" I said. "Don't forget that I'm compiling the Anthology, and you're only my Technical Assistant."

Nina's attack on my work depressed me so much that I couldn't fall asleep for a long time that night. I fell asleep at two in the morning, and at three I was awakened by a thought signal from Andrei.

"What's wrong?" I asked. "Do you need help? I'm on my way."

"I don't need help," Andrei's thoughtgram said. "Congratulate me. Three minutes ago SAPIENS confirmed the correctness of my formula."

"Congratulations, I'm happy for you," I replied. "Is that all?"

"That's all. This thought transmission is over and out."

I was very happy that Andrei finally had some luck. Of course, I was rather surprised that he didn't let me know about it in some other way, for in our day thought transmission was used only in extreme emergencies. It was only later that I realized what enormous changes Andrei's discovery brought to our world.

ANTHROPOCE *Predicts* **11**

The next morning, while I was working on my Anthology, Nina came over once again. She told me the news on the doorstep.

"You can't imagine what's going on at the Academy with Andrei! The Head of the Universal Academy of Sciences flew in immediately, as well as an entire delegation from the Space Institute! They're giving Andrei a special institute and lab, they're giving him the right to choose any number of coworkers he wants!"

"You had time to go over there, too?" I asked.

"Yes," she replied. "Why?"

"Just asking, no reason."

"You'd think that you're not happy for your friend!"

"I'm very happy for him," I replied. "But I'm rather perturbed by this sensational atmosphere that's growing around Andrei. You could think we were back in the twentieth century."

"Great discoveries are possible in the twenty-second," too," Nina countered.

I didn't argue, knowing it was pointless. Instead I reminded her that vacation was coming up and suggested that we go to Hawaii together.

"No, I want to spend this summer in Leningrad," Nina said.

"Well, to each his own, and heaven to the saved," I parried with an old saying. "I'm going over to the Bureau of Vacation Planning."

"I'll walk you," Nina said. She obviously wanted to make up in some way for the sharpness of her refusal.

We went out to the street. As we passed the metro station,

I called Nina's attention to the stately and modest sign that said ANTHROPOCE.*

"Let's go learn the future," I said. "Have you ever visited ANTHROPOCE?"

"No, I haven't," Nina replied. "Let's, if you want."

We went down into the metro, but instead of taking a train we continued our descent, away from the platform, down a ramp. ANTHROPOCE was situated significantly below the subway level. This aggregate was so sensitive and accurate that it could work only underground, where the soil does not shift and the temperature is steady.

We walked a long time down that ramp. Then, before us, silently sliding into the wall, a door opened and then shut behind us. "Take off hard shoes, put on soft slippers," a sign flashed above us on the wall, and a robot came over with slippers of synthetic plush. When we had changed, another door opened before us silently, and we went into the reception area. An Assistant came over and led us to a desk. We sat down and the Assistant gave us a tablet with the rules to read. The rules were:

1. The main purpose of the ANTHROPOCE is to warn People about misfortunes, failures, and catastrophes, with the aim of allowing People to avoid them.

2. The Subject must not see the depiction of his life on the screen of ANTHROPOCE.

3. Only the Intermediary has the right to do so, that is, a Person chosen by the Subject and whom the Subject trusts completely.

4. The Intermediary, seeing the Subject's future on the screen, must then retell what he has seen to the Subject about his future, but only that which he feels he can recount without causing the Subject sorrow.

5. The Intermediary does not have the right to tell the Subject about his life span or circumstances of death, so as not to cause a depres-

---

* **ANTHROPOCE** Aggregate of the Newest Type and the Highest, Retrospectively Offering Predictions Of Coming Events. A highly complex aggregate for its period. Now replaced by ANTHROPOCE-2.

sion in the Subject. Tactful hints and friendly acts on the part of
the Intermediary will help avert the causes of unhappiness if it
threatens the Subject.

6. The Subject can not be the Intermediary for the Person who was
   Intermediary for him.
7. Close relatives may not be Intermediaries for one another.
8. ANTHROPOCE is not completely perfected. It gives incorrect
   prognoses twenty times out of a hundred.
9. The ANTHROPOCE works in the international language code,
   based on Latin and Ancient Greek. Therefore it sometimes gives
   only approximate visual explanations. The Intermediary must
   mentally supply synonyms in his native tongue.
10. ANTHROPOCE does not give a consistent picture of the Sub-
    ject's life, but only key moments.

"Therefore, according to these rules, only one of us can
learn his future today," I said.

"Not future, but a picture of the future," the Assistant corrected me. "Man creates his own future. ANTHROPOCE just
gives a series of stills from the movie of that future."

"Well, Nina, since I 'hooked you' on this, as they used to
say, I'm willing to be your Intermediary."

"What do I have to do?" Nina asked the Assistant.

"Come with me," he said.

He opened a door and led Nina to a room filled with equipment. One wall had a large, matte white screen. The door shut
behind Nina and the Assistant returned and sat down with
me.

"Will she be in there long?" I asked.

"Approximately a half hour. ANTHROPOCE will research
her health, heredity, learn her handwriting, hear her voice,
ask about the past—in a word, it will learn a thousand things
from her. On the basis of all that, using very complicated calculations and juxtapositions, ANTHROPOCE will make a prediction on the future of your friend. But only an approximate
one, keep that in mind."

"Tell me, if this work were entrusted to four, rather than just one, ANTHROPOCE, would the accuracy be greater?" I asked the Assistant.

"You obviously are not a Man of Technological bent," the Assistant smiled, "or you would not have asked that question. ANTHROPOCE is the aggregate of aggregates. It consists of one thousand two hundred separately functioning computers. They are dissimilar: they all accept the same input, but they handle it differently. Each of the twelve hundred computers creates its own picture of the future. Then they automatically plug into the argue machine, that is, the machine for arguments. They begin arguing wordlessly among themselves, and each computer, using logical proof, defends its variant of the future and at the same time, during the argument, makes certain changes in its version. Gradually, several computers, crushed by the logic of the others, drop out of the game. When there are only ten left, the computer judge steps in. While the computers argued among themselves, the judge listens without interfering, but catching everything. It develops its own opinion. It takes a grain of truth from every defeated computer. On the basis of what it knows, the judge enters into negotiations with the remaining ten computers and declares the one with the version closest to his own as the winner. Now, as you see, there are two computers left: the winner and the judge. Then predictions go on to the arbitration function, where the basic prediction is developed. This prediction goes to the transformer, which transforms it into visual images and records it on videotape. ANTHROPOCE does not give a sound tape. The videotape goes to the correcting computer, which deletes episodes of an intimate nature. After that the Intermediary can go to the screen. You see, it's rather simple."

"Some simplicity!" I exclaimed. "It's pure abracadabra."

"What?" The Assistant was confused. "Pure what?"

"Abracadabra," I repeated. "In ancient times this word was used to describe incomprehensible speech and phenom-

ena. You know, I still don't know on what the computers base
their predictions."

"On the basis of knowledge," the Assistant answered.
"They are stuffed with millions of bits of information. They
know the most unusual things: how many millimeters of pre-
cipitation in the city of Armavir in June; how many millimi-
crons the sole of the shoes of a Man weighing so much is worn
down over the course of a kilometer; how the coming close-
ness of Mars will affect exact navigational instruments; how
many meteorites fell on any day in the Pacific Ocean; how the
coming Olympics will affect fashion—"

"Thanks," I said. "That's enough for me. I'm up to here
with wisdom."

Soon Nina came out of the room in which ANTHROPOCE
reigned.

"Now you will see some events from the future of this girl
on ANTHROPOCE's screen," the Assistant said to me.
"Come."

He led me to the room that Nina had just vacated. Then he
left and the door closed silently behind him. I sat in a chair in
absolute silence. "Be quiet! If it's funny, don't laugh. If it's
sad, don't cry. The keyboard is on your left." The sign on the
wall went out.

The bluish rectangle of the screen was barely visible in
the darkness. Then the keyboard, which was to my right,
shone with a greenish phosphorescent light. There were a lot
of keys. The first said "this year"; the next "next year"; and
then "two years later"; and so on for one hundred twenty
years.

I pushed the first key. Nina appeared on the screen. She
was standing on the street with me and we were talking about
something. Then she looked sad and said something with a
determined and embarrassed look. Then she took my head in
her hands, kissed me on the forehead, and I went one way and
she another. Then the screen grew foggy and I saw Nina
again, but this time with Andrei. They were walking on the

beach and they both looked happy. I pushed the "hold" key, and Nina and Andrei froze, as in an instant photo.

"Yes, it's all clear," I said to myself. "But what will happen in forty years? Will she be happy with him?"

I pushed "Forty years from now." Nina and Andrei disappeared from the screen. Dark horizontal stripes moved across the screen.

"Something must be out of order with ANTHROPOCE," I decided and began pushing the keys in reverse order: "Thirty nine years from now," "thirty-eight," "thirty-seven" . . . There was nothing but the lines on the screen. There was something very depressing about them, and I went back to pushing the keys in reverse order, but skipping two or three or four years at a time, finally by fives. When I reached "Three years from now" and still saw the dark lines, I came to the conclusion that the ANTHROPOCE was broken.

So much for our marvelous technology, I thought. *Humanity hasn't moved far beyond our great-grandfather's televisions, which were always breaking down and served as a constant theme for twentieth-century humorists. I'll go to the Assistant and tell him to rename ANTHROPOCE Pithecanthropus, and then it'll have some meaning.*

I was just about to go, when, just for my own conscience, I pushed "A year from now"—and Nina appeared on the screen. She stood in a large room with Andrei. The room was filled with strange machinery and equipment. Then the fog came in and then I saw Nina again. She was alone this time. In bright sunlight, smiling happily, she walked to a small dock, where a row of small electromotorboats stood in the smooth, still water. She passed the *Aquilon,* and hopped into the *Eos,* a small red boat, and took it out into the bay. The screen blinked and faded, and then I saw Nina again in the same boat. But it was dancing in the waves, and the gray rollers were chasing it toward a craggy shore. Suddenly the image on the screen quivered and faded and then exploded in light. Now I saw Nina on land, on a craggy island. She stood

by a low cliff and looked into the distance. Then something
dark moved in on her, and I could not see her. Red and yellow
threads moved across the screen. And then came the dark
horizontal stripes, rolling one on another.

I pushed the "Oblivion Relay." The screen went dark, and
the lights went on. But I didn't leave the room; I pushed the
"Assistant Call" button, and he appeared immediately. I told
him all I had seen.

"This is very serious," he said. "ANTHROPOCE has predicted a tragic accident."

"Is there a possibility of avoiding it?" I asked.

"That's what ANTHROPOCE was created for, to look into
the future and give Man a warning signal. The year before
last, an Astronaut was taken off all flights after ANTHRO-
POCE had predicted a catastrophe. The Astronaut is alive to
this day. But the situation here is more complex. You can take
an Astronaut from flight duty, but you can't keep a Person from
boat rides if the Person loves the sea. And you certainly can't
forbid him to walk on the ground, and the danger here was
predicted to take place on land."

"So the accident is unavoidable?"

"No, it can be avoided. But for that, apparently, the Subject's entire lifestyle must be changed. The entire paradigm of
events, causes and effects must be remodeled. And then the
life of this girl will be long and happy."

"But how can that be done?" I asked.

"Forgive my asking," the Assistant said softly, "but do you
love this girl?"

"Yes," I said.

"Then it all depends on you."

"Well, tell me, did you see anything interesting?" Nina
asked in a rather frivolous tone when we left the building
where ANTHROPOCE was housed.

"Nina, you are in danger," I said. "You must change the
paradigm of your life."

"And how do I do that?" Nina asked.

"You must forget about Andrei. There is another Man who has loved you for a long time and with whom you can live a long and happy life."

"But I love Andrei," Nina said. "There's nothing that can be done about that. And please don't say anything to Andrei about the prognosis."

"I give you my word that I'll keep silent about it," I said. "But the danger threatens you. And here's what I have to say to you: never get in a boat or ship or any other form of water transport if it is called Eos."

"Eos, eos . . . What a strange and beautiful word," Nina said thoughtfully. "I've heard it or read it somewhere before. In a poem, I think."

"Some poets like to make up these meaningless but mellifluous words. . . . Well, I'm off to make a reservation for my vacation trip. Should I make two?"

"No, I'm staying. Go get yourself one ticket. And don't be mad at me." She put her hands on my shoulders and kissed me on the forehead. "Go on. I wish you happiness."

The Plot Thickens **12**

I walked along the busy prospect in deep thought. I was sad. The Old Widrinkson had been right: he knew right off that Nina didn't love me and never would. Somewhere I had made a mistake, but I didn't know where. And so I walked down the bright street amid happy and merry people, but I wasn't merry, nor very happy.

I was surprised and upset by ANTHROPOCE's prediction. The first part of its prognosis looked very much like the truth. But would the second part of the vision come true? Thinking about it, I remembered how Andrei and I had gone to OR-

PHIUS and that aggregate had obviously made a mistake in analyzing my mental capacity as just a four. And in general these aggregates and mechanisms were not perfected and even ANTHROPOCE itself was wrong one time out of every five. Therefore the second part, more removed in time, had to be wrong. "The dream is terrible, but God is merciful"; I remembered the old saying, and I felt better. However, I no longer wanted to fly far away, and I decided to spend my vacation working and merely change my location temporarily. Knowing that Novosibirsk had a large library with many ancient books, I decided to spend my summer there. And on the way I would stop in Moscow, where I had to do some research at the Lenin Library. Having made the decision, I went home, picked up my briefcase, and headed for the underground station to take the pneumatotube. In those days, that was a new form of speedy transportation and I used it often.

"Are there any free seats?" I asked the conductor.

"One," he replied. "Departure in four minutes. Get in the collective pressure ball."

He opened the hermetic door and I went into a long cylindrical vat made of very thick, glowing rubber. There were seats made of the same material. Passengers were already seated; I was the last one, the fiftieth.

"The pressure amortizer of the underground ballistic car is completely filled with passengers!" the conductor said into a microphone. "The doors are hermetically sealed, we're waiting for departure. Start up!"

Our car began rocking lightly. This meant that it was being placed in a hollow metal container. Then the rocking increased; that meant the amortizing fluid was being poured into the space between the outer wall of our rubber car and the inner wall of the metal container. Our car floated inside the container.

"Everything's go!" I heard the loudspeaker announce.

"Shoot!" the Conductor called into the microphone.

I felt a light jolt, as usual, and then I gasped as we increased speed. It felt as though I were in a superfast elevator that was moving horizontally instead of vertically. Then a pleasant lightness entered my body, and soon I was floating in the air, holding on to the safety straps, like the other passengers. The underground ballistic car flew down the ideally smooth tunnel pipe. Soon our speed decreased, and we lost weightlessness. Then it stopped, the doors opened, and I took the elevator up to the Moscow streets and headed for the library. I was in there until evening, taking the notes I needed. I sat in the quiet room and worked, but the prediction of AN-THROPOCE kept floating up in my mind. "No, it won't happen, this is just another technological error," I said, chasing away the upsetting thoughts and stubbornly returning to my work, knowing that Mankind needed it.

When I left the library it was dark, and the self-glowing sidewalks gave off a steady, soothing light. It was time to think about a place to sleep.

Luckily, by my day, it was no longer a problem for people arriving in familiar or unfamiliar cities. Hotels still existed then, but they were used primarily in resort cities, while in other large and small settlements they were no longer popular. Any Person could walk into any house, and everywhere he would be greeted warmly and welcomed as a friend. It was considered impolite to ask your guest where he was from, who he was, or why he came to this city. The guest, if he cared to, talked about himself, and if he didn't, then he didn't.

A small house on the bank of the Moscow River caught my eye, and I went into the lobby and up the elevator to the twentieth floor—I like higher stories, there's more light. Four apartment doors opened on the landing, and I thought for a moment about which one to enter. I loved these moments, when you don't know the people who will greet you, what their specialties are, but you do know that whoever it is, you will be a wanted guest. In the olden days this was called a no-lose situation. However, one of the four doors was out of the running: a sign of solitude hung on the door. I opened the door opposite and went down the hall to a room from which came voices.

Walking in, I saw a group of People around a large television set.

"Hello!" I said. "I want to be your guest."

"Happy to have you!" several voices replied.

A young woman moved away from the group and came toward me.

"I'm Hostess today," she said. "Come with me, I'll show you the spare room and the apartment. And then, you must be hungry?"

"And tomorrow we'll show you around Moscow," one of the seated men said.

"No, I don't need a tour of Moscow, I know it well, I'm from Leningrad, you know." Then I told them about myself.

The others told me their names and professions.

In my day People no longer hung around in front of the TV for hours on end, watching anything that came on, the way they did in the twentieth century, judging by old books and magazines. Therefore I was surprised that everyone in the apartment was watching a rather mediocre film—alas, there are many of those nowadays too. I asked them why they were all so interested in that movie.

"What, don't you know?" They were all amazed. "You of all people should know, you just came in from Leningrad. We're waiting for a special announcement."

"What special announcement?" It was my turn to be amazed. "What special announcements can there be in our day and age?"

"It's about the discovery by Andrei Svetochev," they explained.

But nothing special was happening on the screen yet. It was an ordinary movie, which you can watch, not watch. Some young man and girl were fighting, then making up, planning to go to Mars together, then changing their minds.

"What happened at your neighbor's?" I asked. "Why is there a solitude sign on their door?"

"A tragedy. A young construction engineer lived in their apartment. A month ago he went on a business trip to Venus and died there. Some construction fell on him. You know that our Earth materials don't do well in the conditions on other planets."

"He wasn't even sixty," one of the men said. "And AN-THROPOCE had predicted a full MILS for him."

"All these complex aggregates make mistakes often," I said.

"Aggregates make mistakes, buildings collapse on Mars, spaceships are lost, and all because materials are imperfect," the Hostess said.

Suddenly the movie was interrupted, and the Chief Announcer appeared on screen, surrounded by translating machines. The Announcer was excited.

"Attention! Attention!" he said. "Listen to the Special Bulletin. All terrestrial and nonterrestrial transmitting systems are operating.

"The Universal Scientific Council has studied the theoretical work done by Andrei Svetochev and checked the accuracy of his formula. Svetochev's Theorem on the possibility of creating a fundamentally new sole universal material has been pronounced correct and technically feasible. Andrei Svetochev is granted unlimited technological power.

"I give the floor to Svetochev."

Andrei appeared on screen. He was pale and in general seemed more agitated than happy. He spoke in a hollow, inexpressive voice about the essences of his discovery. He stuttered, couldn't find the right words, repeated some words without any need—basically, his oratorical ability was not too great. I remembered that in school his grades in oral Russian were always lower than mine. But now he was really doing badly, a C, or maybe even a D. It was only when he went over to the lightboard behind him and began scribbling formulas and tables that his voice sounded more confident and sure. Now every schoolboy knows that speech of Andrei's by heart, but in a cleaned-up version, without those pauses, stutters, and repetitions. When I first heard it, strangely enough, it didn't make a great impression on me. Andrei used too many scientific and technological expressions that I couldn't understand. The essence of his discovery, as you all know, came down to the fact that he had proven theoretically that it was possible to create a sole universal material from a single raw material: water.

But Andrei stopped, the screen went black, and silence reigned for an instant in the room. Then all my new friends, without discussing it, stood up in respect. I had to stand up too, even though deep in my heart I thought this expression of feeling rather much.

"A new technological era is beginning," someone said softly.

We went out on the balcony. From the twentieth floor we could see the lights of Moscow stretching to the horizon. To our right were the Kremlin towers, spotlit with special sunlight projectors. It always seemed like noon over the Kremlin.

When I awoke the next day in my room, I immediately sensed that it was nine-eleven. The apartment was empty, all its inhabitants had gone to work. I washed up, ate the breakfast they had prepared for me, and looked at the morning paper, which was devoted almost entirely to Andrei and his discovery. Then I went out on the balcony.

Below on the embankment of the Moscow River, a human river flowed, and all in one direction—to Red Square. This river didn't fit on the sidewalks, it washed over the street, and it stopped the elmobiles and elbuses.

Strange, I thought. *It's not May 1, nor November 7 nor Space Day. Could this be because of Andrei?*

I turned on the TV. They were showing Leningrad. "A turbulent meeting on Palace Square," the Announcer said, and I saw many people on the square. They all had happy faces, as though some miracle had happened. Groups of Students carried rather crude, hand-lettered posters: LONG OVER-DUE! CHEMISTS ARE HAPPY, AND PHYSICISTS, TOO! HURRAH ANDREI! and so on. The crowd behaved in the most undisciplined manner. It sang loudly and shouted. I tuned out Leningrad and turned on Irkutsk, but it was the same there. People crowding the square, bearing homemade signs. One said: METAL, STONE, WOOD, GLASS, and all the words were crossed out, and one over it said: SOLE UNIVERSAL. Then I switched to London, Paris, Berlin; it was the same there, too, only the placards were in foreign languages.

This hubbub all over the world must not interfere with my work, I thought. *Everyone must do his own work.*

Soon I left the apartment and twelve minutes later was at the air terminal.

Self-made ATILLA 13

In those days the trip to Novosibirsk could be made by extraplane, speed rocketplane, regular dirigible, or dirigible sanatorium. Since I had no reason to hurry, I chose the dirigible sanatorium and soon found myself on board. The Doctor on Duty took me to my double cabin and showed me my bed. Then he placed a QUACK on my forehead, which showed only three illness units rising.

"Well, well, comrade, you'll live two MILS," the doctor smiled. "But you are slightly overtired, and I'll have to prescribe certain procedures. Do you have any special wishes?"

"If possible, I would like my cabinmate to be a Man of the humanities," I asked. "My head aches from all this technical talk."

The doctor left, and soon after a Man of middle years

walked into the cabin. He had a rather large suitcase and that surprised me; as a rule, People traveled without hand baggage. My fellow traveler told me that his name was Valentin Ekaterinovich Krasotukhin and that he had two specialties: he was an Ichthyologist and a Writer. To tell the truth, his name meant nothing to me, even though I knew more than just twentieth-century literature, I knew contemporary literature as well. Introducing myself and my profession, I asked my cabinmate what works he had written.

"You see," Valentine Ekaterinovich replied, "I'm an Ichthyologist by education and work. But I'm a Writer by calling. Of course, I look truth in the eye and realize that I have no talent, but I've built a cybernetic machine and with its help I hope to create a poetic-prose-dramatic epic, which will bring me fame—"

"But listen," I interrupted my new friend, "everyone knows that back in the late twentieth century it was proven that no machine, no matter how advanced, can replace the creative process. That's as obvious as the fact that there can be no perpetual-motion machine."

"But I built my own creative aggregate," Krasotukhin countered. "I believe that my ATILLA will not let me down! Here, take a look!"

With those words the Writer-Ichthyologist opened his suitcase and pulled out a rather large machine with many buttons and keys, and set it on the table.

"Here it is, my ATILLA!"

I was a bit depressed: I couldn't avoid technology, even here. But I didn't want to upset my cabinmate.

"Why is it called ATILLA?" I asked.

"ATILLA means Aggregate Transmitting Impulses of Literary Logic Automatically," Krasotukhin explained. "Of course, it hasn't hit its creative stride yet, it's still studying. Every day I read it the classics and contemporary authors, teach it grammar, read dictionaries to it. Besides that, I take it to lectures on ichthyology, to which it listens with great attention. I also read it chapters from the poetics textbook and from art history. A year from now it will know everything and be able to create on the level of the average beginning Writer."

"Could you demonstrate ATILLA in action?" I asked.

"With pleasure!" Krasotukhin cried out. "Give me a creative assignment."

"Well, let it write something for children, something about a kitty-cat," I suggested, picking something easy.

Krasotukhin pushed the "Attention" button on ATILLA. A green eye went on, and the aggregate hummed softly. Then Krasotukhin pushed the "Poetry for Children" key. The machine hummed louder. A black microphone came out.

"ATILLA, dearie, take a creative assignment. Write something about a cat," the Writer-Ichthyologist said in a wheedling tone.

"Creative commission taken!" a voice from the speaker said and the tableau with "Creative Output" in green letters lit up. Then a sheet of paper came out of a slot. On it was printed:

THE CAT AND THE KIDDIES

"Hello, hello, kitty cat,
How are things with you?"
The Kiddies asked the billy goat
While the flat fish weep and float.
And the kitty told the kids,
Giving his old beard a shake,
"Go to school and learn some things!"
The mackerel cries without his wings.

Created by ATILLA

"That's not so bad," I said comfortingly. "I've read similar things in children's magazines of the twentieth century. But it needs some corrections. Your ATILLA seems to confuse a cat with a goat. And what the fish have to do with it, I don't know."

"ATILLA still confuses some concepts," the Writer-Ichthyologist explained abashedly. "The weeping flounder is poetic license. But the line about the mackerel without wings has something of high tragedy in it, I can feel a naturophilosophical conception in it. But in general, it's harder for ATILLA to write poetry than prose. You'll see that for yourself in a minute."

And Krasotukhin ordered ATILLA to create a story with a lyrical ending. The story had to mention a man, a forest, and animals. Soon the aggregate let us see its creation.

THE FOREST FILLED WITH MIRACLES

The forest rustled gloomily (sadly? bitterly?). The forest animals were all over that forest. At the same time a man and a mannette (mankin? mannye?) were walking along the riverlet (riverette?) to the river. In the forest they met a fox and a foxette, a wolf and wolfette, a fish and a fishette, a bear and a bearette.

"I'll eat you up, Peoples!" the bear said.

"Don't feed on us, Theodore (Victor? Grigori?), we want to live a long time!"

"All right," the bear replied, "I won't dine on you."

And joyously, synchronously and unitedly the snowbirds, pheasants, blowfish, trout, and skates sitting on the branches sang a hymn to the rising sun (moon? light?). The forest rustled merrily (satisfied? fully?).

Created by ATILLA

"The story is rather primitive," I said. "And then there's the fish again."

"Yes, my ATILLA likes mentioning fish," Krasotukhin confessed sadly. "I'm afraid I went a bit overboard on his ichthyological studies. Wouldn't you like to try ATILLA on dramaturgy?"

"Look at the marvelous view," I said to Krasotukhin to get his mind off ATILLA. "And the visibility is fine, too."

Our dirigible sanatorium had undocked a long time ago

and was floating at 800 meters. We could look out the large porthole at the city garden moving below. Its straight streets with houses roofed with blue plastic looked like canals dug in the greenery. Only the black spheres on the poles—the thought-transmission amplifiers—bespoke a city of several thousand people. Then fields stretched out below us again, with long-distance control towers for the electrotractors.

Soon we were called to bathe. The swimming pool was covered with a huge plastic dome; a bit higher, almost touching it, a few summer clouds floated past. The pool's bottom was also transparent, light blue plastic. Swimming, we saw beneath us meadows, forest, rivers, road with elbuses on them. It seemed that we were swimming not in a pool, not in water, but in the sky itself, in the endless, smoky blue infinity. We soared in it, like birds, free and easy, and this ease was intensified by the silence, for the dirigible moved noiselessly, as in a dream. A diving board was attached to one side of the pool, and every time I dove headfirst into the pool, I had the eerie sensation that I was falling into space, into an abyss, at the bottom of which were trees, and meadows bisected by roads. And suddenly the water would catch me and keep me from falling further.

In the evening, after dinner, I got into a conversation with the Writer-Ichthyologist. He was no fool; as long as we didn't talk about ATILLA, he was logical and normal. For instance, he told me about this project of using ancient warships—the ones that hadn't been recycled—for fish nurseries. All these ancient battleships, aircraft carriers, useless in dry dock, would be perfect for this. A few changes were required, quite minor. And then, in my turn, when I spoke of *The Anthology of Forgotten Poets of the Twentieth Century,* the Writer-Ichthyologist agreed that this was very important and necessary work, and made a few suggestions that evinced his reading and his lively mind. And when he heard that I was working on filling up my DOWUBA, my new friend heartily approved and told me that I was doing something important and needed for posterity, since there are almost no people left on Earth who use swear words and this form of folklore should be written down for posterity.

But then my interlocutor got back on his hobbyhorse and brought up ATILLA, and asked me to teach ATILLA to curse.

"It would present little difficulty," I replied. "But would it be wise?"

"The future prose-poetry-and-dramatic-lyric epic that I will create with my coauthor, ATILLA, will require swear words as well. The epic will cover all centuries and, as you know, in the past centuries swear words were used quite often. And then, as you yourself have seen, I've overloaded ATILLA with ichthyological knowledge, and a few choice expressions will balance him out, so to speak."

"All right, I'll give your ATILLA a lesson in impolite conversation, but I must ask you to leave the cabin. I can't pronounce crude words in front of a Human."

That night we had crossed the Urals and were now flying over Siberia. By evening we passed industrial timber forests, with clearings and logging camps. But then the true taiga showed up more and more frequently below us. These were preserves, kept in their original condition. We flew at low altitudes, and we could smell the firs and pines. I was in an excellent mood, and I so informed my cabinmate.

"I think that I will not spoil your mood if I ask you to give ATILLA another assignment," the Writer-Ichthyologist said. "Tomorrow we will part, and I would like to leave you with a pleasant impression of my child. Yesterday ATILLA was not at his creative peak for some reason. I want to rehabilitate him in your eyes."

I thought that dealing with ATILLA was the one way to definitely ruin my mood. But then I remembered what they taught us in morals lessons in fourth grade: "Never sadden a Person if special circumstances don't call for it. The weaknesses of good People don't make them bad People." So I gritted my teeth and agreed to one more creative assignment with ATILLA.

"I often give him specialized tasks," the Writer-Ichthyologist said, pleased by my acquiescence. "For instance, to find rhymes for "flounder" or write a story in which all the words begin with one letter. That way it's easier to check on the progress of his vocabulary. Wouldn't you like to give him a specialized assignment?"

"Let him write a story with a lyrical melancholy bent and let all the words begin with S," I said.

My cabinmate gave ATILLA the assignment immediately, and the machine blinked and hummed.

"Well, little ATILLA, don't let me down this time," the Writer-Ichthyologist said. "Make it soulful and lyrical."

Soon ATILLA was finished. The page, just like the two others, is in my archives even as I write.

SUNNY SARDINE

The sunny sun set sickly, shining soulfully. Slack skates slithered and skeptically sized up the situation. Singing silkworms sang on silver maples and the silver hake shook sensitively as the shark swam by.

"Son of a bitch! Sucker! Skunk!" the salmon said, shyly, stammering and staring at the stars.

"Son of a bitch! Stinkpot! Stumblebum!" scattering sugar the silver hake said.

"Saboteur! Speculator! Suffragette! Scandalmonger! Superfool!" shouted the salmon from the sycamore.

The sun set slowly, subtracting sunshine. Sneezeweeds and sneezeworts swayed, and snaggletoothed snails sniggled at snakes. The sardine sank.

Created by ATILLA

"Fish again!" the Writer-Icythyologist said sadly. "And then words I've never even heard of."

"But those are obsolete words! They're words from my DOWUBA," I explained. "Your ATILLA mastered them and is introducing them into the text in disproportionate amounts."

"In the olden days did people really use so many unnecessary words?" my new acquaintance asked.

"Not all swear words were empty," I replied. "Many of them implied a completely definite negative event."

"What's a scandalmonger, speculator, and stinkpot?"

"It would take too long to explain," I replied. "When my DOWUBA comes out, you'll be able to learn the derivation of all these words."

"Wouldn't you like to try my ATILLA once more?" he asked with feeble hope in his voice.

Luckily, the Doctor on duty knocked at the door and invited us to the salon to watch Andrei Svetochev's latest appearance on TV. Choosing the lesser of two evils, I quickly followed him.

All the passenger-patients were gathered in the salon in front of the large TV set. Soon Andrei appeared on the screen. His statement seemed rather colorless to me. He announced that he was appearing only because he had received many questions. There was nothing new that he could say at the moment. He made only one concrete statement: the Main Laboratory for creating the Sole Material would be built on a desert island in the Baltic Sea, fifty kilometers from Leningrad. The island would be enlarged with dredged sand. The work would begin tomorrow.

That insignificant announcement, particularly made in a tired and expressionless voice, did not seem to bode success for my friend. But the audience, as I had noted, was satisfied with his scant information.

The Press Conference. 14
Meeting Nadya.

It was the third week of my stay in Novosibirsk. I spend the whole day in the library, finding material for my Anthology, and the work was coming to an end. One morning the Chief Librarian came into the reading room and invited all who wanted to to come into the TV room, saying that Andrei Svetochev would be speaking. I went with the rest to the TV.

Andrei appeared on the screen. He was sitting in a small room at a table with a number of translating machines. All the chairs and aisles in the room were filled with People, primarily Reporters. This was something like a Press Conference. The questions were asked without any system, and I relay them in that way and order, just as I recorded them on my pocket tape recorder.

ANDREI: I am ready to answer your questions.

REPORTER 1: When will the idea of a sole material be realized by you?

ANDREI: It may take a year, perhaps.

REPORTER 2: Can your sole material be described briefly as a type of plastic with universal characteristics?

ANDREI: It can, if you like. But actually, this is essentially a new material.

REPORTER 3: Some newspapers have expressed the thought that the use of the sole material might create non-hungry unemployment. Many professions will become completely unnecessary.

ANDREI [*digging through some papers*]: I'm not competent in this field. But Economists Sergeev, Tropinius, and Maorti maintain that there will be no unemployment as a result. There will be work for everyone, but some will have to learn a new job.

REPORTER 4: How will this affect the length of the work day?

ANDREI [*digging through the papers again*]: Here are the calculations. Not mine, the economists'. Three years after the total changeover to aqualide, the average work day on the Planet will be reduced to two hours eighteen minutes.

REPORTER 5: What is aqualide?

ANDREI: That's what I've decided to call the sole material.

REPORTER 6: How do you feel about Nils Indestrom?

ANDREI: I have the greatest respect for him.

REPORTER 6: However, your discovery, if it can be realized practically, will disprove Indestrom's Theory of Inaccessibility?

ANDREI: Yes.

REPORTER 7: Therefore, a material will be created that will permit the construction of spaceships that will be able to go beyond the Solar System?

ANDREI: Yes. But that is the concern of Builders and Cosmonauts. I'm more interested in Earth and underwater matters.

REPORTER 8: What do you mean, "underwater"?

ANDREI: Aqualide will make it possible to build underwater with water.

REPORTER 9: Therefore man will receive a large new living space under the ocean and can go on growing quietly? Is that what you're saying?

ANDREI: Yes. We will build tunnels, industries, and residential buildings on the ocean floor.

A long pause. Then they all rise. Applause and cries of bravo.

After the pause:

REPORTER 10: Why is your experimental Laboratory being built on an island? Why not on the mainland, in Leningrad?

ANDREI: I asked for that myself. It's safer that way.

REPORTER 10: For whom?

ANDREI: For the city. You see, at one point in the production of aqualide as I foresee it there is danger of explosion. The theoretical calculations are correct, but in the technology I'm taking a certain risk.

REPORTER 10: If there is an explosion, does that mean you were following a false path and the creation of a sole material will remain an unobtainable dream of Mankind? Is that correct?

ANDREI: No. I repeat, the theoretical calculations are correct. If there is an explosion, then someone in my footsteps will find a better technological method.

REPORTER 11: What's the name of your island?

ANDREI: For now it's nameless. But I suggested they call it Matvei Island, in honor of my friend.

REPORTER 12: Your friend—is he a Physicist, Chemist, Mathematician?

ANDREI: No, he's a Literary Historian.

REPORTER 13: What made you think of a sole material?

ANDREI: It always seemed strange to me that cars, ships, houses, and household objects were made of various materials. Even as a child I thought this was silly, irrational.

REPORTER 14: What will we be able to manufacture from aqualide?

ANDREI: You will not be able to make food products, fuel, or fertilizer. Everything else can be made from it.

REPORTER 15: Therefore, everything Mankind needs in terms of machinery, buildings, and objects can be made from it?

ANDREI: Yes. Everything except coffins and matches.

REPORTER 16 [wearing a badge from a humor magazine]: But we haven't manufactured matches in a long time.

ANDREI: I was joking.

REPORTER 17: How are things going on the island, on Matvei Island?"

ANDREI: You'll see right now.

Andrei disappeared from the screen. The sea appeared. We seemed to be flying over it. There was an island. Now it was closer. We saw temporary wood piers and many small boats tied to them. We flew over the island. It was small and deserted. In the distance, out at sea, we saw pumps dredging sand. There were no major buildings on the island, only long plastic barracks. The island was teeming with People. Some were digging trenches with simple shovels, others were smoothing out the shoreline, and still others were busy with earthworks and so on. It was noisy, and they were singing songs in various languages. The Workers, primarily young People, were of all nationalities and skin colors. But there were older People among them.

Then the island disappeared and Andrei reappeared on the screen. The reporters began asking questions again.

REPORTER 18: I was amazed to see that they were using such primitive tools on the island. You would think we had returned to the early twentieth century. Which museum did they get those picks and shovels from?

ANDREI: I didn't get them out of any museum. They had them made at the Leningrad factory to their specifications, from ancient blueprints, and they brought them to the island themselves.

REPORTER 18: Who are "they"?

ANDREI: The volunteers. They've come from all parts of the world.

REPORTER 19: But you do have contemporary technology on the island for earthworks. You do, don't you?

ANDREI: We do. But they won't use it. They've pushed it aside. They want to work themselves, with their hands.

REPORTER 20: But there are Doctors for Health Preservation on the island? The Doctor's word is law.

ANDREI: They won't listen to Doctors. And then, there are so many volunteers that they don't work more than an hour each. So it doesn't harm their health.

REPORTER 21: Have there been any traumas as a result of using imperfect tools?

ANDREI: No major traumas. But there are bruises and cal-
louses. Yesterday a Chilean student injured his toe with a
shovel.

REPORTER 21: I hope he was immediately evacuated to a hospital on the mainland?

ANDREI: Not immediately. His friends decided to allow him
an extra hour of work for an honorable injury.

REPORTER 21: In allowing People to work with primitive
tools, you are shortening their MILS. How do you feel
about that?

ANDREI: The earthworks are almost over, and then specialists
will take over.

REPORTER 22: Could you please try to explain the essence of
your discovery in brief and popular form?

Here Andrei began explaining his discovery, but he spoke
so obscurely and abstractly that I couldn't understand a thing
and walked away from the screen without hearing my friend
out. But I won't hide the fact that I was touched by Andrei's
thoughtfulness. I was pleased that he named the island after
me.

That day I decided to go down to the local post office. I was
interested in their stamps. I took an eltaxi on the street and soon
entered the Post Office. The first thing I saw was an endless
array of stands displaying stamps. The Decision by the Universal Postal Council permitting every Person to issue his own
stamps was in force and many philatelists had their personal
stamps out and offered them to others. The stamps varied
wildly in themes and colors. Even though the mails were free,
tradition called for a price on the stamp. The price depended on
the Person's whims, from a penny to a hundred million rubles. I
chose a few stamps for myself and a few for Andrei and sent
them off to him right away, adding a friendly note. Then I went
to the Bureau of Fulfilling Wishes, organized by the Post Office, with the aim of ordering my own stamp. I had decided
what it would look like. I wanted to depict myself holding a

manuscript of DOWUBA in my hands. Walking across the hall to the Bureau, I heard my name pronounced by a pleasant female voice. I turned and saw—now who would think, dear reader? I saw Nadya, the girl we met at the Leningrad Post Office under very strange circumstances.

"What are you doing here?" I asked. "Did you transfer to the Novosibirsk Post Office? Were you so traumatized by the incident that took place in the Leningrad PO?"

"I'm not doing anything here. I just dropped in to see how things are here," she smiled. And then she explained that she was in Novosibirsk on vacation, visiting her brother.

I, in my turn, told Nadya that I was in Novosibirsk to work in the library.

"And how is your DOWUBA going?" Nadya asked.

I confess that I was flattered that she remembered my work and was interested in it, and I told her that it wasn't filling up well, because there were no more People in Siberia who still knew how to swear, and that recently I've been busy with my Anthology.

"And you dropped in here as a philatelist?" Nadya asked.

"And as a mailer of letters. I just wrote to Andrei Svetochev, the man thanks to whom we met."

"Was that really Svetochev?" Nadya exclaimed. "I never would have thought he was like that! I didn't even get a good look at my insulter. The next time you write to him, wish him luck and tell him that I'm not mad in the least."

"He's already been punished for his action," I said. "He had to kill a hare."

"What? He was punished with hunting?" Nadya was sad. "That's so unpleasant."

"Don't worry about him," I said softly. "He insulted you, he was sent to hunt as punishment, but thanks to coincidental circumstances he met a girl and fell in love with her and she with him."

"But why aren't you happy about it?" Nadya asked. "You sounded sad."

"I'm happy for him and happy for her," I replied. "But not for myself."

Nadya said nothing, she didn't try to console me, and I liked that. We left the Post Office silently and walked down the street quietly.

"Do you have far to go?" I asked. "I'll walk you."

"Please do," Nadya replied. "I love to walk. I'd love to be a girl mail carrier, like the one I read about in a historical romance. This girl mail carrier didn't like to ride her motorcycle and she walked from village to village on foot. I'd like to be like her, walking in sandals from village to village on the old asphalt, knocking with my staff on fences and handing people their letters and radiograms."

"Only you knock on gates, not fences," I corrected her.

"You must know history very well," Nadya said respectfully. "It's so pleasant to chat with a highly educated Humanities Major."

I won't conceal the fact that I liked hearing that from that pleasant girl, who even though she barely knew me, understood just what a man I was. *Has Nina even once treated me so fairly?* I thought. Nevertheless, I modestly told Nadya that even though I was tops in the history of the twentieth century, I still didn't know all there was to know. For instance, my linguistic baggage needed adding to. Of course, besides my native Russian I knew English, German, and the Romance languages, as well as a group of Slavic languages and Latin, but I still didn't know Ancient Greek.

"But you know so much about everything," Nadya countered softly. "You see, besides English and French, I don't know any languages. Of course, I do know the international code."

"Well, that's no language," I countered. "Many years will go by before the international code becomes a language. For now it's just a parcel of technical terms."

"Where are you staying?" Nadya suddenly asked.

"Since I've come for a fairly long stay, I took a hotel room."

"Move to our place," Nadya offered. "No one will disturb you, including me. Our apartment is almost empty, everyone's gone for the summer. My brother won't disturb you either, he's quiet."

"What does your brother do?"

"He's a Memorial," Nadya replied.

"What do you mean, a memorial?" I was stunned. "Obviously, you mean that figuratively: your brother was once a famous scientist and then he died and they raised a memorial to him? Yes? But why is there no sadness in your voice for the deceased? With your attractive looks, such heartlessness does you no credit."

"My brother's alive and well," Nadya laughed. "His profession is Memorial; he's working on problems of increasing memory."

"Live and learn," I said. "And is your Memorial brother getting along in his work?"

"Yes. Several years ago he constructed a machine that increases memory. But this machine needs lengthy experimentation and only after that can it be mass-produced."

"I would love to take a look at the apparatus."

"You see it on me," Nadya replied and touched her earrings.

"What, those little earrings are the machine you mentioned?"

"Yes. Two microaggregates are mounted in them, and they create a force field around my head."

"And what is it called?" I asked.

"The complete name is Increasing Memory Practically. IMP, for short."

"IMP!" I exclaimed. "What a silly name! Silly acronyms like that were often used in the twentieth century but nowadays, with the Naming Commission, which is composed of Volunteer Poets . . ."

"I understand," Nadya interrupted. "But my brother hasn't registered his apparatus with the Naming Commission. And he couldn't come up with a better name himself. But after all, the name isn't important. The machine works well."

I doubt that an apparatus with a terrible name like that can be successful, I thought, but I didn't say anything to Nadya so as not to upset her.*

Nadya and I parted at her gate, and the next day I moved into her apartment and settled in a quiet corner room. Her brother was a very taciturn man. If out of politeness I asked him about his work over dinner, he would answer readily, but his speech was so full of scientific terminology that I couldn't understand a thing. It all seemed simpler and more understandable in Nadya's version.

I was working at the house now. I brought books home from the library and selected the poems that I felt were appropriate for my Anthology. Then I read them aloud and the TRAP** wrote them down. Once I worked until late at night but still didn't do all I intended. In the morning I had to return the books to the library, as I had promised the Librarian, but I still had eleven poems by one author that I hadn't had time to dictate into the TRAP. At breakfast I asked Nadya for a favor: could she dictate those poems into the TRAP while I returned the other books to the library? And then I would take the last book back after lunch.

Nadya agreed willingly, but added that I could return the book in question as well. She would read the eleven poems now, memorize them, and then read them into the TRAP.

"What are you saying, Nadya!" I exclaimed. "A Person can't just sit down and memorize eleven long poems!"

"You'll see," she said calmly. Then she took the poems I had marked, read them quickly, and I thought, not very care-

* It's typical of Kovrigin to rave about Nadya's memory further on, attributing it to Nadya personally and refusing to recognize that it was her brother's invention that was responsible. In this Kovrigin exhibits his prejudice against technology and his distrust for new things.

** **TRAP** Typing, Recording As Promised. A very imperfect aggregate of the 22nd century. Something like a dictating typewriter.

fully, and handed me the book. "Go to the library and don't worry."

I took the books to the library, but I didn't return the last one, I extended it for one more day. You can imagine my surprise when I found the eleven poems on my desk, neatly typed in triplicate by the TRAP! I took the book out of my briefcase and checked the text. And what do you think? I didn't find a single mistake! Nadya had memorized a difficult ancient text in a few moments and dictated it without error.

"Nadya! Nadya!" I called and ran out of the room looking for her.

I found her in the kitchen where she was programming the DIVER for dinner.

"Nadya! I'm astounded by your phenomenal memory," I cried.

"Yes, thanks to my brother's machine I have a good memory," the girl replied with a smile. "I'm a ninety-nine out of a hundred. But my brother says that's nothing to brag about; you can be stupid and still have a wonderful memory. When I went to ORPHIUS, it only gave me a four."

"Nadya, your memory is not simply excellent, it's super-phenomenal," I said. "I envy you your memory."

"And it's my only merit, I think," she replied modestly. "If I can ever be of any help to you with your Anthology, don't hesitate to ask."

And from that day on, Nadya began helping me with my work, and her help (of a purely technical nature, of course) was quite substantial.

The Gingerbread House 15

One day, Nadya suggested that we go off to a taiga forest preserve.

"With an excursion group?" I asked.

"No, just the two of us. They don't allow groups in there, it's a Class A preserve. I was planning to go for ten days with a girlfriend, but she changed her mind. The reservations are going to waste."

"And what will we do there for ten whole days?" I inquired.

"Nothing," Nadya replied. "It will do you some good, you look tired."

"All right," I said. "And what will we live in?"

"A container house. They'll drop us off in it into the taiga. There are no roads there."

The next morning we went to a special airport. The man on duty explained that Preserve No. 7 was one of the world's largest. Since it was a Class A, you not only couldn't build there, you couldn't even use a radio. Then he gave us some bug spray and two pistols.

"But why the pistols?" I asked. "We haven't committed any crime, and you want to send us hunting!"

"Don't worry," he replied. "You can't kill with them. But if a bear attacks you, you shoot at him, and he'll sleep for forty-seven minutes. That'll give you plenty of time to get away."

Soon we were taken over to the container house, and Nadya and I went in. The house had two rooms separated by a folding door, and a kitchenette. Each section had a folding couch, chair, and clothes closet. The kitchenette had a chest with plates, pots, and so on.

A metal ring was affixed to the roof. A heliplane flew over, an aluminum claw came down from its belly, grabbed the ring —and we were off. The quiet heliplane flew low. The container house swayed slightly, but it was more pleasant than not. I looked out the window and everything seemed pink to me, the sky and the earth. I figured out that that was caused by the glass and I asked Nadya why they used pink glass.

"It's made out of peppermint," Nadya explained. She went

on to tell me that these container houses were intended for transport to Venus. They would be parachuted down into the Venusian jungle. Our scouts often got lost in the jungles, and they could seek temporary shelter in these houses, to get some rest and food.

"But why peppermint windows?" I asked.

"The house is edible," Nadya said. "If the person seeking shelter runs out of food, he can eat the house. The container house is made of highly compressed food concentrates. And it's covered with a very thin waterproof shield."

I took out the technical description given to us by the Man on duty and I read that the walls were made of bread concentrate, the ceiling of pressed chocolate, the chairs of egg powder, and that even the blankets were edible: just cut off a square and toss it in boiling water, you got a glass of cranberry gelatin.

"Of course, hunger is no auntie, as they used to say in the past, and hunger can teach you to enjoy cake, but I hope we won't have to eat our domicile?" I joked to Nadya, who smiled in reply.

Finally the heliplane descended, carefully set us down in a clearing near a brook, and flew off. I opened the door, we came out and found ourselves waist-deep in grass.

We wandered through the taiga all day, and near evening we lit a fire on the bank of the brook and ate canned food. Then we went into our sections, and fell asleep immediately. I was awakened by Nadya knocking on the window.

"Get up, Lazy Bones, breakfast is ready!"

After breakfast we went walking through the taiga some more. When we got back to our gingerbread house, which we had left with the doors open, we saw that someone had been inside: the leg of one chair was chewed off, and the corner of the chest had also been nibbled. The caramel windows had been pecked through in places. This little incident did not spoil our good mood; it actually made us laugh.

In the evening over dinner I told Nadya it was a shame that we hadn't brought any books.

"What would you like to read?" Nadya asked.

"I had started a novel in Leningrad, Meridini's latest, in translation from the Italian," I said. And I went on to explain that I was interested in it because the translator had turned to me for consultation. The novel, rather, one of its chapters, used words that had been popular in the criminal world in the past, and the translator couldn't find the Russian equivalents. When he learned that I was working on DOWUBA, he turned to me for help, and I graciously let him familiarize himself with the section of criminal folklore. But I hadn't had time to read that chapter.

"You're referring to the novel called 'The Second Alien'?" Nadya asked. "How far did you get? I read it recently."

"I got to the part where Santiano crosses the Pacific and gets to Lamst. . . . But don't tell me how it ends, Nadya, that will spoil it for me."

"But I can read the novel to you word for word, from memory," Nadya said. "You stopped at the fourth chapter."

"I know that your memory is phenomenal, Nadya, but is it that good?" I was amazed.

In reply, Nady seated herself more comfortably by the fire and began:

" 'Let's start with the multiplicity of worlds,' Santiano said to himself, sitting on the veranda. 'The multiplicity of worlds assumes the existence of worlds similar to our Earth. Because it is infinite, the Universe does not limit their number. Therefore, there are worlds similar to our Earth. Because it is infinite, the Universe does not limit their number. Therefore, there are worlds similar to Earth. Because of their multiplicity, some of them are its copy. Thus, on Earth 2 at this minute the same Santiano sits, like me, but on his head there are say 998,760 hairs instead of my 998,761 hairs. On Earth 347 my double is absolutely perfect, but some little girl from Melitopole has a drop of jam on her cheek while our girl from Melitopole doesn't. And Earth 6,798,654,267 is exactly like our Earth except that is has one more frog.

" 'I think we're getting at the truth here,' Santiano said to himself. 'But let's continue the monologue. Besides the worlds that are very similar, there are those that resemble us, but not so much. Some have outstripped us in their development, others lag behind. The former have probably overcome the Formula of Inaccessibility and those aliens can come to our planet. But these are kind visitors. Visitors can't come from the other group of worlds because they are technologically backward. Therefore, these two are not from a planet like ours. They come from another system of worlds, and their human appearance is merely a mask. A kind visitor doesn't need a mask.'

"Santiano leaned over his desk and began reading the ancient *Detective's Guidebook*. This profession had long since disappeared from Earth, and our hero had to learn everything from scratch. He read for a long time, repeating the unfamiliar ancient words. Sometimes he would drop his reading and rush over to the bookshelf with the dictionaries. Finally he said to the ULSS* by the desk:

" 'Bring in the prisoner.'
" 'Who?' the aggregate asked, without moving.
" 'Bring in the arrested.'
" 'Who?' asked ULSS.
" 'Bring in the perpetrator.'
" 'Who?'
" 'Bring in the creature locked in the cellar. Understand?'
" 'Now I understand,' ULSS replied.
"It brought in the Alien. He looked in fear at the ULSS.
" 'Why did you set such an animal on me?' he asked Santiano.
" 'Sit down!' Santiano told the Alien.
" 'I know that routine! "Sit down, sit down," and then you slap me with a five-year stretch. I'll stand, thanks.'
" 'How old are you?' Santiano asked. 'What year in Earth terms were you born?'

* **ULSS** Universal Logical Special Servant. A highly primitive aggregate of the 20th century.

"The Alien looked confused.

" 'It's all in my passport,' he said, taking a book out of his pocket. 'It's all in there, without lies. Read for yourself.'

"Santiano took the book, opened it, looked at it, and put it on the edge of the desk.

" 'Listen,' he said to the Alien, 'you're giving me a document, and documents have been banned on Earth. They were banned long before you were born, according to that book.'

" 'Cut the bull, buddy,' the Alien said. 'It's valid. And I've never been tried, or even arrested, and I've done no time. What are you picking on me for?'

" 'You couldn't have been in jail even if you wanted to,' Santiano countered. 'When you were born, there were no prisons left on Earth. If you were born on Earth—'

" 'And where else would I be born?' the Alien cried. 'You think I'm from the Moon? Look, pal, let's wrap this up. I give you a pig in a poke, you set me free.' The Alien took out a pack of money from his pocket and put it on the desk.

" 'Where is your accompanist?" Santiano asked. Then he looked in the dictionary and corrected himself: 'Where is your accomplice, your confederate?'

" 'This is it!' the Alien shouted and pulled out a gun.

"But the ULSS grabbed him and took away the weapon.

" 'Now it's all clear to me,' Santiano said. 'You're not Human. You weren't born on Earth, or on an analogical planet. You arrived here from a world in a different system. You possess great powers of disguise, but your problem is that your information on Earth is very old. You came to the wrong place. Am I correct?'

"The Alien said nothing. There was a puff of smoke, not unlike a quick bolt of lightning, and he disappeared. Two footprints were burned into the ceramic floor. The gun in the ULSS's cobalt hand also exploded and disappeared. And the passport and money left rectangular burn marks on the desk.

"Meanwhile the second Alien wasn't napping. A man was observed in Ankabus with something akin to an ancient flashlight in his hand. He shone the light on houses. Four days

later the houses fell apart without an explosion. They turned
to dust. The Alien was also noted in the port. Not one of the
light ships that went out to sea that day returned. They disappeared in the ocean, without even sending out an SOS. . . .

"You're not tired of listening?" Nadya asked. "Am I reading too fast?"

"No, no, go on, Nadya!" I exclaimed. "I'm listening to you
with great pleasure."

It was a pleasure to listen to Nadya. The quiet burbling of
the brook blended with her voice, and I was thinking how just
recently I had been sitting around a campfire, but in a different preserve. And now the circle was complete. Another fire,
another preserve, but back there I was an extra person, in the
way. But not here. Something told me that I wasn't in the way
at all.

A Storm in **16**

the Taiga

I was awakened by thunder in the night. Lightning flashed
beyond the pink windows. Rain lashed the wall. The wind
was growing. In the flashes of lightning, I could see the trees
bending. I dressed hurriedly and knocked on the partition.

"Get up, Nadya, and come out in the kitchenette. There's
danger."

"I'm dressed. I couldn't sleep."

We went into the kitchenette and took turns drinking hot
tea from the thermos. It was cold in the house, which shook
from the gusts of wind. Suddenly, in the light of the storm, I
saw through the small window that a pine tree at the edge of
the clearing was leaning strangely. I grabbed Nadya, kicked
open the door, and carried my burden to the middle of the

clearing. Behind me I heard growing noise, a dull thump, and the crackle of breaking branches.

I set Nadya on the ground, and we both looked at the house. The pine had fallen on it, but the house was intact.

"For give me, Nadya, for dragging you out so roughly, right into the rain," I said. "I thought the house would collapse."

"Why apologize," Nadya said reproachfully. "You wanted to help me."

Soaked, we returned to our abode, but the entrance was blocked by the crown of the fallen tree. I made my way through the branches, but I couldn't open the door; the pine, falling, had blocked it and lodged it shut. I couldn't get to the window of my part because of the branches, but Nadya's window was reachable. Luckily it could be opened from the outside, and I got in the house and then helped Nadya up.

"Lie down and go to sleep," I said. "You're completely chilled, and it's all my fault. I'll go take care of the tree."

"All right," Nadya said. "I am very cold."

I went out into the foyer and saw that the tree had broken the window there. And right at the spot where Nadya stood when we were drinking tea.

So, I was right to have dragged her out. She would be dead otherwise, I thought and, getting an ax, I opened the door and went outside. The first thing I did was to chop off the branch that had broken the window, so that Nadya wouldn't see how close she had come to death. Some people relive past experiences, and it's better for them not to know what could have been. Then I gradually chopped off all the other branches, hacked up the trunk, and thus cleared the entrance to our house. I worked without paying attention to the rain and wind. The ax handle was made of compressed cafe-au-lait concentrate, but the ax blade was normal, luckily, and inedible, otherwise it couldn't have handled the workout I gave it.

When I was through I went into my section, undressed, and got into bed. Soon I felt chills. I was hot, then cold, but fell into a light sleep. When I woke up, I was shivering again.

"Why aren't you up?" Nadya called, knocking on the wall. "It's broad daylight."

"Nadya, I think I'm sick," I said.

Nadya came in and put her hand on my forehead. Her hand felt very cold to me.

"You have a high fever," Nadya said. "You're sick. But don't worry, everything will be fine." She brought me some hot tea and gave me some pills and I fell asleep.

I woke up because my forehead was cold. A stream of water was pouring down on me from the ceiling. I looked up; the ceiling was waterlogged and sagging. The wall looked abnormal, too: it was cracked and damp. I figured out that when the pine tree fell, its branches and needles had torn the moisture-proof shield and our edible abode was absorbing water, especially since it was still raining. As you know, the container houses were intended for use in the jungles of Venus, and even though the trees are tall there, they are not solid, they're grass. Trees like that could fall every day and still not harm the house. But our Earth trees have a solid mass, and that's another thing altogether.

"Nadya!" I said softly, and the girl, who had been napping in the chair, awoke immediately.

"I just slipped off for a minute," she said. "I've been sitting by you all the time. You were delirious. I never thought this vacation would come out like this. It's my fault."

"No, it's not, Nadya. But what did I say in my delirium?"

"You kept talking about Nina, and ANTHROPOCE, and DOWUBA . . . But I can quote it back to you."

"No, Nadya, it's just delirium. Try to forget it."

"I promise never to bring it up. And now we must call a Doctor. You're seriously ill."

"The only way to call a Doctor here is by the Personal Apparatus," I replied. "But that's a radio. And you can't use radios in Class A preserves."

"But this is a special case," Nadya countered. "We can make an exception."

"Nadya, don't you remember the morals lessons in fifth grade? 'One permitted exception may lead to thousands, and thousands of exceptions may lead to chaos.' "

"What should we do?" Nadya asked, in tears.

"We can use thought transmission," I said. "Thought transmission has no relation to radio. One of us will send a thought-gram to our twin, and the twin will radio the excursion center that I'm sick. But I'd rather not bother my twin, Andrei. He's up to here with work right now. Perhaps you could contact yours?"

"I don't have one," Nadya said in embarrassment. "Once I was in love with a young man, we were twins, and then we parted forever."

"Forgive the tactless question," I said. "I'll signal Andrei."

"I'm receiving you," Andrei said. "What's the matter?"

"Danger," I said. "Are you very busy?"

"Very," Andrei said. "I haven't slept in two days. Problems with the construction of the main building. But that's no matter. Tell me what I have to do."

I told him I was sick. He had to call the Novosibirsk excursion center and have them send a heliplane ambulance.

"It'll be taken care of," Andrei replied. "Buck up. I'll do it. Is that all?"

"That's all. Thought transmission over and out."

Nadya watched me anxiously, trying to guess the results of my transmission by my face.

"Everything will be fine, Nadya," I said. "Help is on the way. And you know, there is no bad without some good, as the old saying goes."

"What good is there in this bad situation?" Nadya asked.

"I'll tell you some other time," I replied and pulled the blankets over my head, because the ceiling was dripping more now. I felt chills again and I fell into a deep and troubled sleep.

"Get up!" Nadya woke me up. "They're here!"

She went out, I got dressed and left the house. It had

stopped raining and was getting lighter. It was 5:32. We were amazed by the number of birds on the house. They were pecking the walls and the soggy roof. The ambulance, a heliplane with a red cross on its belly, was hovering over the clearing. A sling came down from the belly. We got on, they lifted us, and we found ourselves in the heliplane, which immediately headed back.

The first thing the Doctor did was take me to the shower, and I stood under the hot water for a long time, washing off the sticky, chocolaty mess that had been pouring on me from the ceiling of our gingerbread house. Then I dressed in clean linens, and they put me in a cot. The Doctor put the QUACK on my forehead and it printed out the following:

"Fifty-one illness units descending. Condition: A-2 on the Greenwald and Vorotkevich scale. Treatment on the lambda-prime schematics: 7.5. Additional recommendation: Karakulin's Mixture. The illness will not affect his MILS."

"There, you see, everything will be fine," the Doctor smiled. "Especially since you have such a pretty Nurse," he added, looking over at Nadya.

Then he left, after giving me a bitter elixir, which made me feel better immediately. I looked at Nadya, sitting next to my cot on a plastic stool, and said:

"Nadya, you go rest. You're tired!"

Soon we landed in Novosibirsk, and Nadya and Doctor accompanied me to the hospital. Nadya stayed at the hospital and took care of me, literally never shutting her eyes. The NANNA* tried to replace her several times, but Nadya ordered it to keep out, and it left. In the mornings, when my temperature was lower, Nadya read from memory from books by contemporary writers and historical novels, skipping the hunting descriptions. Once, interrupting the reading, she asked, "Back in the taiga, you said there was no bad without good. What did you mean?"

---

* **NANNA**   Nice Automatic Nurse, Never Angry. An ancient medical aggregate.

"I meant that if everything that happened hadn't happened, I wouldn't have met you."

"I'm glad that things worked out that way, too," Nadya replied simply. "And for that we must thank your friend Andrei Svetochev."

And I recalled the incident at the Leningrad Post Office, my first conversation with Nadya, then the trip with Andrei and Nina to the preserve, then my last conversation with Nina after visiting ANTHROPOCE, and my new meeting with Nadya. Yes, it had come full circle and, I think, happily—for me and for Nadya.

Soon I was well, and returned to Leningrad with Nadya. In the fall, Nadya became my wife. Our marriage was and is happy. And if my indulgent Readers like these Notes and find food for the mind here, they should know that they are obliged not only to me for these Notes, but to Nadya as well, who was of great help in work on the manuscript.

At the Publishing House   17

Besides my marriage, there was one more important event in my life that fall. I completed my *Anthology of Forgotten Poets of the Twentieth Century* and took the manuscript to the Publishing House, to the Historical Division. The Editor greeted me sympathetically and asked me to come back in a week. My Readers, even if they are not Authors, can imagine what I went through during those seven days while my fate was being decided. I was consoled only by the fact that in the past Authors had to wait much longer for an evaluation of their work and sometimes spent months in a state of uncertainty while their manuscripts were being read by Editors.

And exactly a week later, at the Publishing House, I learned that my manuscript had been read by the staff of the Historical Division and the Editor himself, and was given a positive evaluation. Of course, some of the comments were obviously prejudiced and unobjective, and the printing run was set at only five thousand copies, but all this faded before the fact: my Anthology would be published, and the Planet's literature would be enriched by one more valuable and needed book. When the agreement was signed (a purely symbolic act, since money had been abolished and there was no payment to me) and my first wave of joy had receded, I asked the Editor to give my manuscript to some aggregate to read. Perhaps it would be fairer and more objective than the Staff of the division and would set a larger printing run.

The Editor responded to my modest request in an injured tone that in his division, as in the others of the Publishing House (except for the Poetry Division), all the manuscripts were read by People, and they were no aggregates.

"Why are Poets exempt from the rule?" I asked. "Why do they get preferential treatment? My *Anthology* consists of poetry too. Of course, the authors are dead, having lived a long time ago in the twentieth century."

"There are too many Poets, and the workers in the Poetry Division can't keep up with the load," the Editor replied, "and that's why they use machines."

Then he expressed the thought that the continual growth in the cultural level, and the availability of higher education for everyone, in his opinion had 999 virtues and one drawback. The drawback was that many people were writing poems now and taking them to the Publishing House, considering themselves poets when they really weren't at all. Of course, the quantity of true Poets was increasing as well, but proportionately and absolutely, there were many fewer of them than People who considered themselves Poets. And since the Publishing House couldn't deal with the flood of manuscripts, they had to rely on DRIPs, URPPs, ELCs, and

TANCs.* It was a hard lot for these machines. No machine has the right to insult a Person, yet it must tell the Author the truth, and the truth is often bitter. And so the Special Volunteer Naming Commission, which consists of Volunteer Poets, had given the machines such horrible names.

I asked the Editor to take me over to the Poetry Division, and he readily took me through the quiet editorial corridors into a large and rather noisy room, where a sign over the door read: "Canes, umbrellas, and other dangerous objects must be left in the vestibule!"

"What a vicious warning!" I said to the Editor. "Is it possible that in our age there is still danger of violence by hand, cane, or umbrella?"

"Alas, Poets are capable of anything," the Editor replied. "Of course, they don't attack People, but the machines are always getting it. Last year a Young Poet hit a DRIP with his cane when it told him that the rhymes 'June-moon-croon-spoon' have been around for hundreds of years and were not a discovery of that Poet. And the year before last, a beginning Poetess hit an URPP with her umbrella when it rejected her poems."

"I never thought that such vicious mores could exist in our times," I said. "How lucky that I deal with long-deceased poets instead of live ones for my Anthology!"

The glass door in front of us opened and we went into the room. We were immediately met by a FAME,** which asked in a gentle voice what we were submitting to the division, verses or a narrative poem. Upon learning that we hadn't written any poetry, it modestly moved aside. I started looking around. In the middle of the room were couches and armchairs, all holding Poets. They were chatting amicably among

---

* **DRIP**   Disinterested Reviewer of Intended Poetry.
   ELC   Educated Literary Consultant.
   TANC Tactful Aggregate for Negative Criticism.
   URPP Unilateral Rejector of Poor Poetry.

** **FAME** Finds Authors, Meets, Elicits. A mechanism of the 22nd century; like the ancient Secretary.

themselves, and I did not see any cruel expressions on their faces. Around the periphery of the room were desks with DRIPs, URPPs, and ELCs; they certainly didn't seem like monsters. They were ordinary specialized mechanisms, rather frail and harmless looking. The TANCs didn't look like ancient killing machines, either. It made it all the sadder to see signs over their desks that reminded me that these defenseless mechanisms were sometimes subjected to rough treatment and even attacks. For instance, over an URPP's desk hung a poem, which must have been composed by it:

> I am only a machine,
> And everyone should know it.
> It's not the little URPP's fault
> If you're a lousy poet.

The ELC had a quatrain over its desk:

> O Poet! Lad or maiden,
> Or old practitioner of verse!
> Do not hit me in a spurt of anger,
> And heap me with your curse and worse.

"What does that sign mean:'Please turn in manuscripts without metal clips'?" I asked my guide.

"The sign was put up after an unfortunate incident," the Editor explained. "Once a Poet gave an ELC a lyric poem held together by a paper clip of magnetized metal. The ELC read the work and found that it was a work of genius and immediately ran with it to a Human Editor. He found nothing good about the poem. It turned out that the magnetized metal wreaked havoc with the ELC's circuitry. Afterward that ELC-27 thought all Poets were Geniuses, and it had to be taken apart."

"I hope that the Poet didn't do that dastardly deed on purpose!"

"The Poet wasn't at fault," my guide assured me. "He works in a laboratory that deals with magnets."

Unwilling to abuse the kindness of my guide, I told him
that I could continue on my own, and he left. I blended into
the crowd of Poets, and when one of them went over with a
manuscript to an URPP, I followed. The URPP read the work
with great speed and began commenting on it. Obviously,
constant dealing with Poets and bad poetry had made the
URPP forget how to speak prose. It read its review liltingly in
a soft baritone, trying not to hurt the Author's feelings.

> Your verse's like cotton.
> The rhyming's rotten.
> It's sad but true,
> I feel for you.

> I have to whisper a hint
> This stuff we certainly can't print.
> But don't give up, you'll get better.
> Read the classics to the letter.

I didn't listen anymore and went over to a DRIP that was
consulting with another Poet. The DRIP also spoke in rhyme:

> Your poem "The Waterfall" is dry,
> The rhyme scheme isn't even wry.
> Great respect I have for you,
> But your poem just won't do.
> With the sadness of a MARM *
> What I tell you might cause harm.
> We won't publish this, your works,
> But you great fame awaits and lurks.

I stepped away from the DRIP and headed for the aggregate called PUMA.** At the same time a Person of middle
years approached the mechanism and handed it a fat manuscript.

"Would you look over my book *Sighs and Sniffs?* It's a
hundred forty poems. . . ."

* **MARM**   Melancholy Aggregate Returning Manuscripts.

** **PUMA**   Pity Untalented Miserable Authors.

The PUMA took the manuscript and read it instantly.

"Have you seen the URPP?"

"I've seen them all. Humans and machines. They don't understand it," the Poet said glumly.

"*Sighs and Sniffs* can be published in an edition of one copy," the PUMA said kindly. "Will that satisfy you?"

"Couldn't you make it two copies?" the untalented Poet begged. "And have it say on the title page that there were two million copies printed. Or more."

What a disgrace! I thought. In the old days this would have been called showing off and bull. Of course the PUMA will refuse this wild request and give him a talking-to.

But you can imagine my surprise when the PUMA replied affirmatively!

"All right," it said, "We'll print *Sighs and Sniffs* in a fictitious printing of two million and an actual two copies. Please indicate preference of jacket, format, type, and grade of paper." It handed the Poet a sample kit. "Choose."

Incensed by the behavior of the Poet and the aggregate, I hurried to the Human Editor of the Poetry Division. Not wanting to embarrass the Poet in question, I asked a general question: "Are there instances when the PUMA makes mistakes and acquiesces to the amoral request of an Author? For instance, can it plan a printing run of two copies and indicate in the book that there were two million copies printed?"

To my surprise, the Editor replied that that was the way PUMA was programmed.

"An aggregate programmed to lie!" I exclaimed. "I've never heard of such a thing!"

" 'A lie that exalts us is dearer than all the base truths,' the classic said," replied the Editor. And added, "This lie hurts no one. The Poet fools only himself, finding comfort in the lie. There's no reason to hurt him."

"I just don't understand. Why publish a book that no one will ever read?" I said.

"You must be indulgent," the Editor said. "Society is

wealthy enough to publish a Poet's book, even though Society doesn't need it. Why not make the Man happy?"

I must admit that the logic seemed strange to me, and I left the Editor without being convinced. *I'm glad that I'm not a Poet,* I thought. *And my book will come out not with a phony two-million run but a real five thousand copies.*

The Island with **18** My Name

The winter of that memorable year was a harsh one. The Neva froze over early, and the bay was covered with permanent ice by November, and from my window I could watch skiers and aero-ice boats skimming its surface. Nadya and I were now living in the same house as my parents and Andrei's parents, but in a different apartment. My *Anthology* was being set, and I waited for galleys to proofread, and in the meanwhile I began a new project: *Science-Fiction Writers of the Twentieth Century in Light of the Ethical Views of the Twenty-second Century.* Nadya helped me in this work—naturally, in a purely technical way. Her ideal memory finally found a worthy application. I hadn't seen Andrei in a long time. I knew that he was very busy and I didn't want to bother him. Everybody was constantly talking about him. Poets were scribbling hasty paeans to Andrei Svetochev, in which they compared him to Prometheus and God knows who else; the papers devoted entire sections to him with huge headlines like THE AQUALIDE CIVILIAZATION, TECHNOLOGICAL REVOLUTION, and so on. Magazines printed long articles like "Aqualide and the Distant Stars," "The Era of Monomaterials," "A Fresh Look at Earth's Economy." I was amazed by this publicity, it seemed flippant and premature; after all, they still didn't have any aqualide. But knowing Andrei's character, I didn't worry. All these advance tributes wouldn't upset him and he needed them like a dog needs a fifth leg. (I hope the Reader will forgive my vulgar ancient proverb.)

Nadya had told me several times to go visit Andrei on Matvei Island—the one named after me. However, I was so involved in my new work that I kept postponing the trip. But, as the saying goes, if the mountain won't come to Mohammed, then Mohammed goes to the mountain. One evening Andrei came to see me.

"I have a favor to ask," he said bluntly. "Would you help me fix up an article? I wrote it for a children's popular science magazine; they kept asking. But I'm having trouble putting my thoughts into readily comprehensible form. Read it and make changes. Is it all right that it's in longhand? My handwriting is illegible."

"Your handwriting is legible," I replied. "It's all this technical stuff that I can't understand."

"No, this doesn't have any formulas in it; it's for children, after all. You only have to clean up the article stylistically. You write so well."

"Thanks, I'll do what I can," I said. "By the way, why didn't Nina take this on?"

"Nina is a help in many ways, but she was afraid she couldn't be objective. For some reason, she likes whatever I do. She's the one who suggested I ask you."

After Andrei left, I read the article, and I must admit that I didn't understand a thing. It really didn't have any formulas, but it was crammed with technical terms, tables, and references to works by all kinds of Researchers. When Nadya came home from work, I gave her Andrei's article to read, and she said that everything was understandable, but a few things had to be simplified. With the help of Nadya and some dictionaries, I substituted simpler terms for the most confusing expressions, and smoothed out the article's style, but its meaning remained a mystery to me.

"Don't worry," Nadya said with a smile. "The children will understand. You're simply an inveterate Humanitarian. Everything here is so simple as to be genius."

The handwritten original of the article is still in my keeping and upon my death will become part of the Svetochev Memorial Museum.

When the article was polished and I had dictated it into the TRAP, Nadya said to me:

"Why don't you bring it out to the island with your name yourself? Your friend named it in your honor, and you've never even been there."

"No, I'll mail it tomorrow," I replied. "Even though I've never been there, I know the island well from all the TV coverage and pictures in the papers."

Nadya seemed to agree with my conclusion.

The next day—it was Nadya's day off—we went out first thing in the morning to cross-country ski on the bay. We had almost had a fight choosing skis.

"Take the self-propelled ones," Nadya said. "I'm tired of the regular ones."

"Why take the self-propelled ones, there aren't any hills on the bay," I said sensibly.

"I want to take the self-propelled ones, that's why!"

"All right, all right, as they used to say," I agreed.

The self-propelled skis were just coming into fashion then. They looked like regular plastic skis, but they had micromotors installed. When you dug in your heels, the motors went on. They made it easy to go uphill.

We went out on the bay and soon found ourselves by the ice mountain that led to the island with my name. Elmobiles and elcycles were all traveling on it—and all going in the direction of Leningrad. We stopped an elmobile and asked why everyone was headed away from the island and no one was going to the island.

"Didn't you hear the bulletin?" one of the passengers asked in surprise. "It was issued a half hour ago."

"Banishment from aqualide heaven," joked another. "The heaven is getting dangerous."

"So that's it!" Nadya laughed. "We were just on our way there."

She turned on her skis and moved up the ski path next to the ice road. I had to turn mine on and chase after her.

"Nadya, it's too far!" I called out, catching up. "And they're evacuating the island."

"But the island is named after you. They'll have to let you in," Nadya said.

"That's strange logic," I said in amazement. "And then, if we do go to the island, we should take the article, and I didn't bring it."

Nadya took off her mitten and pointed to her head.

"The article is in here, don't worry."

"We might get frostbite on our faces," I said. "Look at the strong wind we have to ski against."

"I thought of that too," Nadya replied and took two face masks from her pocket.

"Nadya, this means that you planned this!" I was stunned. "You planned this!"

"Darling, how else could I have lured you out," Nadya laughed. "You're either working on your science fiction writers or your DOWUBA, and you never set foot in your friend's house. So I arranged this."

"It's not nice to trick people. Remember what we learned in second grade: 'A small lie is still a lie. A drop and the ocean are identical in essence.'"

"Well, my lie is just a tiny drop," Nadya said with a smile.

Soon we saw Matvei Island, and we saw that ULSSes* were posted at intervals along the shore. They held barriers and signs in their metallic hands: NO ADMITTANCE TO THE ISLAND. DANGER. They were shouting out the same words.

* A reminder: the ULSS (Universal Logical Special Servant) was an ancient mechanism of the pre-aqualide era.

"You see, we came here for nothing," I said. "The ULSSes won't let us pass."

"We'll just walk past them," Nadya countered. "No mechanism can use force against Humans."

"You can't take advantage of that characteristic of the aggregates," I said severely. "Mechanisms are servants of Society."

"The evacuation is over. You can't go on the island," an ULSS said as I approached.

But I asked it to go find Andrei Svetochev and tell him that we were there. The ULSS went off into the island and returned quickly. Andrei was with it. He was happy to see us, but asked in surprise, hadn't we heard the emergency bulletin? We replied that we had been en route. Then Andrei told us that tomorrow the Main Experimental Laboratory would go into service producing aqualide. As we knew, one of the stages in production was still technologically unclear. Only practical experience would make it clear whether that step in the process was correct. In short, there could be an explosion.

"If there is an explosion, that means that aqualide is a mirage, a fiction?" I asked.

"No. It will simply mean that the technological process is imperfect. Others will find the right path, taking my mistake into account."

"It will be an expensive mistake," I said.

"And what has Humanity ever gotten for free?" Andrei said.

The island was deserted. Occasionally an ULSS would cross our path, off on some task or other. Buildings, towers, and strange constructions rising up in stepped levels surrounded us. Thick pipes painted in glowing colors went from building to building, sometimes lying on the ground, sometimes traveling high on girders.

"The island is so big now!" I said. "And there has been so much construction!"

"The entire world has worked here," Andrei said slowly. "And tomorrow, perhaps, there will be nothing left of this."

"When will the experiment begin?" Nadya asked.

"Don't worry, I won't chase you off the island at nightfall," Andrei said with a smile. "The experiment will begin at ten in the morning. We were planning to start at two A.M., but we had to postpone it. Nina's not well."

"What does Nina have to do with it?" I asked. "And hasn't she been evacuated to the mainland?"

"No. She wanted to be with me during the experiment. Since she is firm in her decision, she can sit at the double control console with me. I need an assistant anyway. This way, in case of an accident, we'll have saved someone's life."

"Were there many volunteers to do the experiment with you?"

"No end of them. They drove me crazy."

"But working at the double control board can't be easy. You probably need special knowledge, no?"

"Not at all. Only health, attention, and elementary literacy. Not technical literacy, simply literacy. Even you, with your tender love for technology and your deep understanding of it, could handle it," Andrei joked heavy-handedly.

"What's wrong with Nina?" I asked.

"Yesterday she was riding in an ice boat, miscalculated, and hit a hummock. She hurt her shoulder. She's at home now, gobbling aspirins, and won't call a Doctor. She's afraid he'll have her evacuated from the island."

"Tell me, what color was the boat?" I asked Andrei.

Andrei looked at me strangely and said, "Red. But what a strange question!"

"There's nothing strange about it," I said casually. "You Technologists think everything is strange."

Of course, from the point of view of a normal Person, my question was strange. But I had seen Nina getting into a *red* boat on the screen of ANTHROPOCE. I pictured the red motorboat with *EOS* on its hull. The boat was red, so was the ice boat. . . . And suddenly I felt better. All those months I had secretly worried about Nina's future, remembering ANTHRO-POCE's prediction, and now it was clear that ANTHROPOCE had made a mistake. That is, it was correct to some extent, but the saddest part of its prediction was wrong.

My reasoning was as follows: ANTHROPOCE thinks in broad, universal categories. A bay, an ocean, it's all a body of water to it. Ice is a small, local phenomenon. So ANTHRO-POCE sees it as water. An ice boat is a small vessel that travels on the surface of water: on ice. ANTHROPOCE sees it as a boat. The ice hummock that Nina crashed into was the cliffy shore on which Nina allegedly died. But ANTHROPOCE didn't foresee the outcome of the accident; that's why it's wrong twenty times out of a hundred. Nina was alive, she had merely injured her shoulder.

A heavy weight fell from my shoulders. I felt much better. And the island named after me, covered with strange construc-tions, seemed sweet and cozy.

"Here we are," Andrei said.

We were standing in front of a one-story plastic house, in which Andrei lived. I won't bother describing it; you all know it well. Now it's a branch of the Svetochev Memorial Museum.

We went in. Nina greeted us. She was much prettier than she had been when we parted. Of course she was pale, but it became her. Her shoulder was in great pain, that was obvious, but she was being brave. I introduced her to Nadya. I was dismayed to see that they didn't take to one another. Not that there was any hostility between them; no, they simply didn't have a common language. And even when Nadya dictated Andrei's article with my corrections into the TRAP, Nina didn't rave about her wonderful memory. But both Nina and Andrei liked the article.

After dinner Nadya went straight to our bedroom, Nina stayed in the living room–dining room, and Andrei and I went into his study. He sat down at the table with some blueprints, and I looked at his stamp album. Time passed.

"Why don't you go to bed," I said to Andrei. "Morning is wiser than evening. And then, there's another old saying: 'You can't get enough air before death.' Just don't take it literally."

"Take the album with you tomorrow," Andrei said. "If something happens to me, you keep it. And if everything's all right, bring it back. I don't want it to go to waste!"

"All right, I'll take it, anything you say. And I'll return it. I don't need your gaudy animals!"

"I hear a portraitist speaking! Beat the portraitists!" He jumped up from his chair, grabbed a cushion from the couch, and hit me on the head. I grabbed another cushion, and we began a fight.

"Boys will be boys!" Nina said with mock severity, as she came in the room. "The whole house is shaking."

"Don't get in the way, Nina, this is a battle between good and evil!" Andrei shouted, accepting my blows and trying to respond in kind.

There was a knock at the outside door. I immediately surmised that it was a mechanism of some sort. People could enter without knocking.

"Come in," Andrei said, going out into the vestibule.

The door opened and an ULSS appeared in clouds of steam.

"Important message," it said. "In superreactor number three I discovered a failure type alpha-321."

"You have to bring that up to EDPO,"* Andrei said strictly. "How many times have I told you that problems under Level B do not interest me."

"Understood. I'm off to EDPO," the ULSS said quietly and left, neatly shutting the door.

"These ULSSes are amazingly useless," Andrei said. "I've had so much grief from them. When will we finally be spared this antediluvian technology?"

Less than a minute later the front door opened once more

---

* **EDPO** Electronic Deputy Organizer of Production. A rather complex aggregate for its day. Later replaced with EDPO-2.

and another aggregate came in without knocking. It was rather small—the height of a ten-year-old. Folded wings shimmered on its back.

"Why did you come in without knocking?" I asked him sternly. "You aggregates are really taking liberties."

"I'm allowed not to knock," it said in an injured tone and then, turning to Andrei, the mechanism announced: "The accumulation of the substratum is proceeding normally. But in the Main Building, in terminal delta-117 I've discovered a breakdown type A-21."

"I'm on my way," Andrei replied. Then, addressing me, he said: "This is an EROS,* the latest in our technology. It's permitted to enter without knocking. Wouldn't you like to see the Main Building?"

"Why not, I'd love to," I said, so as not to disappoint Andrei.

"I guess I'll come with you," Nina said. "Maybe the walking will help my shoulder."

"Some treatment," I said helping Nina with her synthur coat. "Medicine on the shaman level. You should call a Doctor."

But she didn't hear me. That was just like her.

We went out into the freezing cold. A red spotlight revolved on a pole, and the entire island was flooded by the reddish, alarming light. In front of us the strange aggregate with folded wings marched on. I sensed an unpleasant independence, even self-assurance, about it.

"We know the way very well," Andrei said to it. "But the light has to be turned on in the Main Building."

The EROS lightly pushed off from the ground, spread its wings, and flew. Soon the lights went on in the Main Building.

When we entered the building, I was struck by its size; the laboratory hadn't seemed so large from the outside. The huge,

---

* **EROS** Electronic, Ready, On Target. One of the most perfected aggregates of the pre-aqualide era. No longer used on Earth, but in a remodelled and improved aqualide version works in the radioactive plateaus on Mars.

brightly lit room stretched into the distance. Monstrous machines and apparatus stood on both sides of the aisle. ULSSes on duty stood at the machines, monitoring them. Up above, under the transparent roof, where thousands of cables and pipes intertwined, two EROes flew silently.

Andrei went to the far end of the room, and soon I could no longer see him; he was lost in the mechanized space. Nina took me over to a control board with numerous colored buttons, and sat in the chair.

"This is where I'll be working tomorrow," she said matter-of-factly. "I'll be pushing buttons at specific times."

"You won't make mistakes?" I asked.

"No, there's a diagram." She took a large table pasted onto cardboard out of a sliding drawer. "It's all here. A child could follow it."

The table showed each of the buttons just as they were on the board and indicated at what time to push which one.

"What's this big red button?"

"That's the critical drop. The one and only."

"And you'll push it?"

"I'll push it," Nina said with a smile.

"You look really sick," I said. "Does your shoulder hurt a lot?"

"It aches a bit," she admitted reluctantly. "But it will be fine by tomorrow."

"And if it isn't?"

"Then we'll have to call in a Volunteer. But I'll stay on the island anyway."

The Red Button 19

Nadya woke me in the morning.

"Get up, go have breakfast. I've eaten already. We have to leave for home soon."

I got up and looked out the window. It had warmed up overnight and it was snowing. The snow was very visible against the bright yellow tower of the settler tank. It was getting light, but the red alarm light of the revolving projector still fell on the island named after me. It was very still.

At breakfast I took a close look at Nina. She looked very sick. I said so straight out, but she said nothing.

"Yes, we'll have to call on Volunteers and choose the best one from the lot," Andrei said. "It shouldn't be hard to choose; it simply requires a Man with good nerves."

"What about me?" I asked Andrei.

"What about you?"

"I'm that kind of Man. Of course I'm not too literate technologically, but my nerves are good."

"Do you have any idea how risky it is?" Andrei asked softly.

"Yes, I do. But why should someone else take the risk and not me? I'm the natural choice. We're friends, after all."

Andrei thought. Then he said:

"I'd rather have you than anyone else. The consoles are far from each other, but you and I can use thought transmission. It's more convenient than radio or TV and better than phone connections."

"So it's settled," I told Nina. "You can go off to Leningrad with Nadya without worry."

Just then the door opened without a knock. An EROS came in. Snow glistened on its folded wings. The snow melted and fell on the floor.

"I'm here on orders from EDPO," the aggregate said. "The substratum is filled to capacity. System A must be brought into action in twenty-three minutes."

"I read you and understand," Andrei said.

The EROS left, leaving wet footprints on the floor.

He didn't even bother to brush off the snow before coming to see Humans, I thought. *It's so specialized and so spoiled.*

I went into the room assigned to Nadya and me and explained my decision to her. Upon hearing it, she began to cry. Then she asked:

"But you believe that things will go well?"

"To tell the truth, not really," I replied. "Andrei is a loser. Up to now, he's had small, medium, and large failures. Now, probably a complete and total failure awaits him. But when a friend is in trouble, one's place is at his side."

"Yes, you're right," Nadya said through her tears. "But I believe that everything will end well."

"Let's hope so," I replied. "If something should happen to me, try to find a worthy successor to continue my work on the DOWUBA. As for correcting the galleys on the Anthology, all my hopes rest in you and your memory."

A small plane came. Nadya left on it alone. Nina refused to leave, despite the fact that her presence on the island named after me was no longer required and was purely pointless.

When Nadya got in the cabin with the ERP, I whispered:

"Wish us luck."

"Break a leg," Nadya said out loud.

"Go to the devil!" I replied.

Nina and Andrei gave us a funny look.

"That's the way you're supposed to do it," I explained. "It's not a curse, it's a spell in this case."

Soon Andrei and I went over to the Main Laboratory and Nina went to the house. She wanted to lie down. She looked terrible.

At ten minutes to ten, I sat at the double console. Andrei went to the other end of the huge room to take his place at the main console.

At 10:00 I pushed the first button. It was green. The room filled with a hollow, vibrating hum. The ULSSes at their monitoring positions raised their metallic hands, a sign that systems were working normally. An EROS glided lightly down from the glass ceiling, with its endless jumble of cables and pipes, and, standing for a second by the console, spread its wings, which shimmered with a greenish hue.

"No trouble in the terminals," it reported, and flew up again.

Then a mechanism, the likes of which I had never seen, crawled out from a round hatch in the floor. It had a plastic scaly skin and crawled like a snake. There was a hook on its tail. Swaying smoothly, it moved over to the bottom of the console and raised its head. The metal grill of the head covered a glowing green eye.

"The underground world is in order," the aggregate snake reported. "The power cable lead-ins are in order, the beta group contacts are in order. Any command?"

"If everything is in order, what commands could I have?" I reasoned. "You may crawl back."

Eight minutes after the first button was pushed, I pushed the next one according to the diagram in front of me, a white button. The hum moved up to another pitch. Blue lightning jagged behind the crystal shield of a huge aggregate mounted on the floor not far from the console.

At that moment I heard a thought signal from Andrei.

"How are things?" Andrei asked.

"Everything's in order," I said. "There really isn't anything complicated in this at all. I have nothing against doing it, but I wonder why you didn't have some EROS or ULSS do it."

"It's too responsible a position," Andrei said. "A Human is a Human and an aggregate is an aggregate."

"Actually, I don't understand the principle of doubling here," I said. "You have the same console and the same buttons I do. Don't think that I want to take French leave, as they used to say. It just seems strange to me. Is this a form of overinsurance? There was that concept in antiquity."

"Not overinsurance, just insurance," Andrei replied. "The process of transformation, as I've told you, takes forty-five hours thirty-seven minutes. During that time one of us might get tired and make a mistake due to inattention. But since there are two of us, an error is almost completely ruled out."

"Well, one mind is fine, two are better," I agreed. "Tell me, what's that aggregate snake called that crawled over to me?"

"PITHON,"* Andrei replied. "Is that all?"

"That's all. Thought transmission over and out."

At 10:27 I pushed the third, a blue button. At 10:49, a yellow one. At 11:04, a striped one. Everything was going smoothly. Most intervals between button pushes were six or seven minutes, but some were as long as forty minutes and an hour and ten minutes. During one of the long breaks I took a shower; during another, Andrei and I had dinner. Once in a while a SATYR** came over with hot tea and food. Occasionally Andrei and I used thought transmission, cheering each other on. The day went like that, and then the night.

"We've covered the whole day. Congratulations!" Andrei said at ten in the morning.

"Another day, another dollar," I answered with an ancient foreign saying. "How do you feel?"

"All right," Andrei replied. "And you?"

"Also fine. How's Nina?"

"I just talked to her and saw her on the videophone. She's in bed. Apparently she not only injured her shoulder, she's also got a cold."

"Send her to the mainland before it's too late," I suggested as a friend.

"She won't listen! You know her. Is that all?"

"All. Thought transmission over and out."

The day passed as well, and the second night of our vigil began. I had already pushed many buttons of varying hues and shades. At 2:05 I pushed a black one. The next one was

---

* **PITHON** Pleasant, Industrious, Trouble-Hounding, Orderly, and Nice. An ancient aggregate, long out of production.

** We remind the reader, a **SATYR** (Serving Aggregate Taking Your Requests) is a primitive aggregate of the early 22nd century, serving food.

red: the one that so much depended on. It had to be pushed twenty-five minutes after the black one.

"Well?" Andrei asked through thought transmission. "How do you feel? Are you scared?"

"A little," I said. "But what can you do?"

"I'm a little scared, too," Andrei said. "Good luck. Is that all?"

"That's all. Thought transmission over and out."

I didn't hear Nina come up to the console. She was pale, but even pallor became her. It was amazing, everything became her.

"I wanted to see how you were doing," she said, lightly tossing her synthur coat on the console's barrier.

"You picked the best time," I noted with some irony. "What a lovely dress! You're ready for a ball."

"I barely got it on, my shoulder hurts so," Nina said with a smile. "But it's an important occasion. Everything all right here?"

"Everything's normal."

"Did Snake-Eyes come to see you?"

"You mean PITHON? It was here."

"It's so funny. Once I put a piece of paper on its tail and it crawled off into its underground with it."

"It's not nice to mock mechanisms," I corrected Nina. "Mechanisms serve Society."

"You're still the same."

"That's the way I am."

"Well, good-bye," Nina said, leaning over the barrier and giving me a quick kiss. "There. Good luck!"

She went down the bluish tiles of the floor to the other end of the room, to Andrei. In her bright orange dress she walked with light footsteps, past the ULSSes attentively standing before apparatus that made no sense to me, past all the devilish technology, past everything that might kill us in the next few moments.

But the time came to push the red button. I placed my

finger on it and thought, *What will I feel now?* Probably nothing. It will all happen instantly. In these cases, for posterity, people always remember something very important; I had read that in books. What should I think of: Nadya, my Anthology?

I pushed the red button and thought at that second of Nina. There she was on a low sandy cliff, reflected in the quiet water of the lake. . . .

Aqualide Is! **20**

I had pushed the button down as far as it would go. But nothing happened. The hum in the room was louder, that's all. It came in waves, ebbing and rising. It seemed that the innumerable aggregates were trying, panting, climbing a mountain. The ULSSes, next to their monitors, raised their metallic hands for a minute to signal that everything was all right. An EROS flew down from its glassy heavens and, spreading its wings, reported:

"The terminals of system omicron-2 are functioning. No failures."

Then the EROS flew off, and Snake-Eyes crawled out of its hole to announce that the underworld was fine.

I connected up with Andrei and congratulated him on escaping danger.

"Yes, it's clear now," he replied. "Aqualide will exist. Are you very tired?"

"I can hold out," I said. "It's just four more hours."

Some time later I pushed a dark blue button, and then a light blue one. And at 7:39 A.M. I pushed the final one, a white one with a green exclamation point. After that I leaned back in the chair and fell asleep to the low hum of the aggregates. It was steady and sleep-inducing now. Then through my sleep, I heard new noises. Somewhere in the distance, in the middle of the room, something fell in steady cadence, fell with a metallic sound of glasslike resonance. And suddenly I felt someone touch my shoulder. I opened my eyes. Nina was before me.

"Get up, sleepyhead," she said. "The aqualide is running!"

"What do you mean running? Where's it running to?" I didn't understand, I was too sleepy.

"Ah, come on! You're so silly!"

I awoke thoroughly, looked at Nina, and saw tears in her eyes.

"Is something else wrong?" I asked. "You're crying."

"No, everything's marvelous. I'm so happy for Andrei! You won't even let a girl cry a bit."

"Well, you should have cried earlier," I noted sensibly. "Four hours ago." And getting up from my chair, I followed Nina.

We walked for a long time down the room, then turned into an alcove. The replacement ULSSes were there, against a wall; they seemed to be sleeping standing up. The EROSes, wing folded and leaning against the mighty ULSSes, slept like little children. PITHONs lay motionless at their feet, with their lenses turned off.

"A sleepy family," Nina said and snapped her fingers at an EROS—right on its forehead.

I wanted to correct her and remind her that Mechanisms were the servants of Society and had to be respected, but I bit my tongue. I knew that she would simply laugh in reply. That's the way she was.

We were headed in the direction of the rhythmic sounds, the resounding falling sounds, that I had heard in my sleep at the console. The sounds grew nearer. Then we turned into a corridor between some machines, and I saw Andrei. He looked haggard, his eyes were sunken. He looked like a madman. He was standing before a large machine, and from the

square jaws of that aggregate fell little bricks that looked like
ice, right into a metal box on the floor. Andrei had one of these
ingots and he was tossing it from one hand to the other, as
though afraid of frostbite. The thought came to me that perhaps this was all a mistake and instead of his marvelous aqualide Andrei had obtained plain old ordinary ice. Afraid to
voice my doubts, I bent over and picked up a brick. But I
immediately dropped it. The brick burned my fingers.
It fell on the floor heavily, with a big thud—and didn't
break.

"Here take mine, it's cooled off a bit," Andrei said and
handed me his ingot. I hefted it in my hand. It was very heavy.
Then I looked at it from all angles. It resembled ice, and
semitranslucent metal, and glass—in a word, it didn't resemble anything at all.

"So, this is aqualide?" I asked.

"Yes. This is Grade A aqualide. There are all other kinds
of gradations and forms, with various characteristics. But for
now we'll be testing this. We're going over to see CAIN.* It'll
have the final say."

We went through a covered passageway to the neighboring
building. The walls of the passageway were transparent.
Mounds and drifts of snow lay beyond them. The green light
from the revolving projector illuminated them. The red alert
condition was over.

We entered a room. In the middle of it stood an enormous
aggregate. It went deep into the room, but we could only see
its facade, with two round, large dials. Over them was a white
TV screen, and below them a black opening. It resembled the
face of an angry giant.

"CAIN won't hold back on this," Andrei said and tossed an
ingot of aqualide into the square jaws of the giant. It rumbled
quietly and then roared. I felt the floor tremble beneath me.

* **CAIN** Catastrophic Aggregate Investigating New-materials. Was very necessary in its day, but lost all meaning after the discovery of aqualide. Now
it is displayed in the Svetochev Memorial Museum.

The two dials lit up with red light. The screen showed what was happening to the ingot.

Steel hammers came down on the ingot, diamond drills tried to penetrate it, it was grabbed by pincers of superhard alloys. CAIN heated up the ingot, threw it into liquid gasses, cooled to almost absolute zero. It lowered it into acids and biles, pushed it into an explosion chamber, showered it with death rays. The arrow on the right dial, showing the intensity of the test, always hovered on the red mark. But the arrow on the dial showing the degree of destruction of the material was still on white, not moving even a micron.

The testing went on for a long time. Finally CAIN roared, as though in anger at its impotence, and grew silent. The ingot fell out of its mouth. Andrei picked it up. The aqualide was exactly as it had been before the tests. It didn't have a single scratch.

"Now I can let them know on the mainland that aqualide exists," Andrei said.

After that we went to the restaurant located in the center of the island with my name. We sat at a table in the huge empty room. It was very quiet here, and my exhaustion and the unusual circumstances made me think that I was asleep and dreaming. I wanted to pinch myself, to wake up and find myself in my study, with my manuscripts and notes for my DOWUBA on the desk, the familiar rows of books on the shelves.

But a SATYR came over to our table and stopped, awaiting orders, and I became convinced that this was real.

"Why don't we have a bottle of champagne?" Andrei said. "We certainly deserve a bottle of champagne."

"I'll tell the FARO," the SATYR said.

It left and I hinted to Andrei that this way it wouldn't take long before he turned into a Widrinkson: champagne once, champagne twice. . . .

"There won't be another time like this," Andrei said.

"Aqualide exists; there's nothing left for me to discover." I heard a secret sadness in his voice. He seemed sorry that everything was done.

The SATYR returned to the table, carrying glasses and fruit. The FARO itself trod heavily behind it, triumphantly bearing the bottle. It opened it with finesse and poured the wine into our glasses. We moved the glasses toward one another and touched them lightly (it used to be called toasting) and then drank.

When we left the restaurant, I said farewell to Andrei and Nina and called a plane. I knew that there was nothing more for me there. The Journalists, Reporters, and Scientists would be swarming over the island. It would be Andrei's business to talk to them.

It was light, and when I flew in the direction of Leningrad, I saw that the road to the island was filled with elmobiles. A mass of People, carrying rousing posters, was walking toward Matvei Island, sinking into the deep snow, but stubbornly moving forward. I had never seen so many People in my life.

Back home, I fell into bed and slept for fourteen hours.

The Ship Lowers **21**
Its Flag

The subsequent months, all the way to July, I worked on my new literary research work, *Science-Fiction Writers of the Twentieth Century*. My Readers, who later read this significant (and, I dare say, not in terms of size alone) work would hardly believe that I had done this monumental bit of research in such a brief period.

Completely immersed in my work, I couldn't manage a visit to Andrei on the island with my name. Of course, I knew that my friend was alive and well. All I had to do was turn on the TV or open a paper to come across his name. The era of aqualide had begun. Plants to produce this Sole Material were being constructed all over the world, and Andrei was working on simplifying and perfecting the technological process.

Once, while on a walk, Nadya and I stopped by the memorial to the creator of the Theory of Inaccessibility, Nils Indestrom. The statue still towered with its old gloom, but the brass plate with the formula had been removed from the pedestal, since the Theory had been disproved by Svetochev. The memorial remains in that condition to this day.

Courses in aqualide studies were introduced in schools and colleges. The metalurgical industry was winding down. Mass classes for retraining Metalworkers, Ceramicists, Chemists, Builders, Woodworkers, and many other specialists were started. Luckily I didn't have to change professions.

At the end of June my Anthology was published. I must say with sorrow that it was not welcomed with a worthy response. Many magazines pretended not to have noticed it, and others printed short reviews that certainly could not be termed objective or well wishing. Their reviewers accused me with an energy that could have been put to better use, of narrow vision, of a one-sided selection of materials, of impoverishing twentieth-century poetry. But one way or another, the Anthology was in print, and I was very pleased by this major event, leaving it up to the Critics' consciences to deal with their unworthy attacks on my first-rate work.

On the eve of the memorable and sad day to which this chapter is devoted, Andrei called me on thought transmission and invited me to visit the island with my name the following day. He told me that they would be testing an underwater tunnel-laying apparatus. Not wishing to upset my friend by my absence, I agreed, even though every hour was dear to me.

Rising the next morning, I was not sorry that I had accepted Andrei's invitation. The weather was wonderful, not a cloud in the sky. Bidding farewell to Nadya (she couldn't accompany me that day) and taking my briefcase with a copy of the *Anthology* inscribed to Nina and Andrei, I left the house and headed for the bank, which was a hop, skip, and a jump away from my house. Here, going down to the boat dock, I chose a light blue motorboat and began untying it from its moorings.

At that moment the SAMSON* on duty came up to me. Honking a warning, it raised its right hand and a red light went on in its metal palm. That was a "forbidden" sign. With its other hand, the SAMSON pointed to the shore—actually to the cabin where the electronic meteorological map was found. I looked at the sky, at the horizon. There wasn't a cloud in sight. Thinking that the SAMSON had made a mistake, I untied the boat and got in.

My respected Reader! No one could ever accuse me of not observing regulations, and I always treated all mechanisms with respect, remembering that they were the servants of Society. But I had a personal quarrel with this SAMSON #871. Back in the days of my pleasant childhood this SAMSON #871 spoiled my mood more than once, forbidding me to take a boat when there was even the slightest disturbance in the water. Even then this aggregate was old and silly and didn't even have a speech module. Now its vision was going and it often mistook Adults for Children. That's why I decided to overlook its signals and, switching on the motor, rode out into the bay.

Seeing that I had disobeyed, the SAMSON ran along the dock, honking in alarm and raising its hands with the red light and pointing with the other at the cabin with the map. But I certainly didn't want my first day off in ages to be spoiled by senile stubbornness and perhaps even personal hostility on the part of SAMSON #871. I went farther and farther out into the bay, programming the boat to head for the island with my name.

* **SAMSON** Self-propelled Aggregate of the Meteorological Service on Navigation. An old aggregate considered unreliable even in the days of the Author's youth.

The sea ahead of me was smooth, lacquered looking, without a wrinkle, and very empty. I didn't see a single ship near me or on the horizon. I didn't attribute anything to this fact, completely engrossed as I was in my own thoughts. I should have paid attention!

When I approached the island, a light breeze came up from the south-southwest. It seemed rather pleasant; the weather had been too hot. I landed on the island with my name, and moored the boat. I was amazed to see that there were no People. I stopped a passing ULSS and asked where all the People were.

"They're all at the test. At the test," the ULSS replied.

I wanted to ask where the tests were held, but this slow-thinking thing kept showering me with terms and no hard facts. I released it and beckoned to an EROS that was flying past; I knew they had more sense. And the EROS came down, folded its wings, stood at attention before me, and gave me rather logical explanations that all the People were now at the Experimental Field, where the tests on NEPTUNA* were about to begin.

Afraid that I might get lost among all the buildings, towers, and strange constructions, I asked the EROS to show me the way, which it did. It flew ahead of me, and after a short time I found myself at a large, unpaved field that was located on ground reclaimed from the sea behind the Main Laboratory. There were many People on the field, and in the center towered a greenish monster some fifteen meters long and four meters high.

"So this is the famous NEPTUNA?" I asked someone.

"Yes, it's NEPTUNA."

I thanked the EROS for its kindness and let it go off on its own business, and making my way through the crowd, I got closer to NEPTUNA.

* **NEPTUNA** Newest Engineering Perfected TUNneler with Aqualide. The first underwater aggregate. Now on display in the Svetochev Memorial Museum.

The aggregate reminded me of a huge lizard, but without feet. It was made of aqualide. The monster's body was filled with tiny round openings, and below, near the belly, there was something resembling gills. The body ended in a flexible, flat tail on rollers. There was a small console on the tail with buttons, dials, and other technical things, and then there were several rows of seats, like benches, each seating three people. The NEPTUNA made a great impression on me. Of course, today's underwater aggregates are much larger, but this was the first one of its kind.

Soon I saw Andrei. Accompanied by Scientists and Journalists, he came out from behind the NEPTUNA and walked over to the console, explaining something to the Men with him. The faces of many of them were familiar to me from books, newspapers, magazines, and TV. The scientific luminaries of our planet, as well as several famous Cosmonauts, were here. The reason for their interest in that underwater monster was not totally clear to me then, I must admit.

Andrei's appearance brought on cheers, and the crowd stirred, and somehow I found myself in the first row. At that moment Andrei, looking away from the console, straightened and looked at the crowd. Our eyes met. Leaving the circle of luminaries, Andrei ran over to me, took me by the hand, and brought me over to NEPTUNA. He introduced me to his colleagues and then brought me over to the console.

"Just in time," he said. "You'll be underwater now—and you won't get wet. We'll try out the aggregate. What's in your briefcase?"

I told him that I had a gift copy, inscribed, of my Anthology. But I wanted to give the book to both of them, Nina and him, at the same time. Where was Nina?

"She went over to Isle Seven a half hour ago to check on the equipment inventory."

"Will she be back soon?"

"About an hour and a half. I sent her over there intentionally. She wanted to go for a boat ride around the island, but I said, 'If you want to go for a ride, then go over to Isle Seven and do some business.' "

"Is there important apparatus there?"

"Not at all. She's just very tired of all the company. This will give her a rest, keep her at sea a bit longer. We're overrun with guests."

"Isn't she interested in the tests of NEPTUNA? Or is there some danger involved?"

"None at all. She's tried it out before. We had an unannounced trial three days ago. And now there'll be a demonstration—for everybody."

In the meantime the light breeze, which I had barely felt when I arrived on the island with my name, became stronger. A storm cloud was moving in from the south-southwest. A vague anxiety stirred in my breast.

"Andrei, what boat did Nina take?" I asked.

Andrei looked at me in bewilderment, puzzled by my question. Then he said:

"She always takes the electric motorboat that's moored by our house. It's a red one. Why?"

"Does it have a number or a name?"

"It's called *Dawn*. But why are you asking?" Anxiety sounded in Andrei's voice.

In my memory a line from the ancient but always young Poet rang through my mind: "When rosy-fingered Eos . . ." "When rosy-fingered Eos . . ." But why was I afraid of the word *Eos*? After all, the boat was called *Dawn*. But in ancient Greek, Eos meant Dawn! ANTHROPOCE's prediction showed a red boat with *Eos* written on its hull.

"Andrei, hurry. Get the rescue cutter! Postpone the tests!"

Andrei went pale. My anxiety was transmitted to him, and he sensed that something was wrong with Nina.

"Announce that the tests on NEPTUNA are being postponed," he said quietly to the Lab Assistant.

We ran to the dock. The SAMSON on duty, #223, raised its hand with the red light and didn't want us to take the rescue cutter.

But we had no time for the SAMSON. We set off, switching the motor to top power and programming the boat for Isle Seven.

"This is where *Dawn* usually sits, right here," Andrei said pointing to a small dock near the house. There was no SAMSON there to keep Nina from going out in the bay.

The wind was getting stronger. Waves moved across the bay. Whitecaps, too. Clouds covered the entire sky. It grew dark.

"I sent Nina out into this bad weather," Andrei said. "When I suggested she go out to Isle Seven, I was sitting at my desk, and the electric meteorology map was behind me. I didn't even turn around. I didn't look to see what the weather would be in the next few hours. The sky was so clear this morning . . ."

The sky was clear no more, alas. The wind kept mounting. Rollers, not waves, moved across the sea. Our cutter was tossed around, its bow diving underwater, the water washed up on the deck. Rain drops and spray, flying almost horizontally, stung our faces.

"I'll call the BIRDs," * Andrei said. "Let them fly out to Isle Seven."

He used his Personal Apparatus to call the disptacher at ARP** and gave the coordinates. The dispatcher replied immediately that the BIRDs were on their way. Then he added that he would get in touch with the shore patrol of the Swedish and Finnish ARP.

"But why didn't Nina call the BIRDs herself on her Personal Apparatus?" I asked. "Maybe she's sitting on the isle right now in complete safety, waiting for the storm to blow over."

* **BIRD** Bringing Initiative to Rescuing Drowners. A very powerful and maneuverable vehicle for those days.

** **ARP** Air Rescue Patrol.

"She's always leaving it on her bureau," Andrei said. "And this time, apparently, she didn't take it."

It gets worse and worse, I thought and suddenly realized that I was still holding my briefcase with the Anthology. I opened the hatch to the cockpit and tossed the wet briefcase in there. *Will I ever get to hand the book to Nina?* I thought anxiously.

"Where's Nina's twin in thought transmission?" I asked. "I seem to recall that her friend lived in Leningrad."

"She married a sailor a long time ago and lives in Vladivostok now," Andrei replied.

"It all fits," I said softly.

Soon we heard noise coming from the sky. We could hear it even through the storm. Then we saw five BIRDs. They were flying from Leningrad; they were part of the famous Second Baltic Squadron of the ARP. They flew up into the clouds, then swooped down and almost touched the rollers with their wings. They reminded me of the "destroyers" from historical films. The resemblance, naturally, was purely superficial: these were very contemporary and maneuverable machines. They were driven by two pilots: a Human Pilot sat next to the ERP. If the Pilot got into trouble, the EOL took over. The BIRDs often crashed; the risk of danger was much higher for Pilots in the ARP than for Cosmonauts. But for each lost Pilot's place there were thousands of young Men begging to take it. They gladly took young Cosmonauts who had been mustered out for a lack of caution in dangerous situations to be Pilots for the ARP. On a BIRD excessive bravery could harm no one but the Pilot himself, but at least in taking risks he could save someone's life. ARP had its own insignia, and the personnel wore clothing reminiscent of the uniforms of military Pilots of the twentieth century.

When the BIRDs flew over us and disappeared in the distance, I felt a bit better. But now, however, we were having our own trouble. The storm was mounting, we were tossed and heaved, we were making slow progress forward—we were still in the channel. Suddenly a huge roller picked up our cutter and slammed it into the channel buoy. Our speed fell. Soon we realized that we had sprung a leak on our starboard side. I opened the hatch and looked below. It was full of water.

"We'll be on bottom in a half hour," I told Andrei. "Maybe we should call for a BIRD here?"

"They're needed there more," Andrei replied. "The engine is working well. We'll manage somehow."

I went to the cockpit. It was knee-deep in water and my briefcase was floating. *My* Anthology *is lost,* I thought, but strange as it may seem, I didn't feel particularly sad about it. I opened a cupboard and took out two life jackets and brought them up. I gave one to Andrei and put one next to me.

"What's this for?" Andrei said.

"Just in case you sink like an iron, as they used to say in antiquity," I joked, trying to cheer up my friend.

But my rather crude joke had no effect. Andrei didn't seem to have heard it.

"I see something ahead," he suddenly said. "I think it's a ship."

I tried to see through the rain and spray. Finally I saw the outline of a sailing ship.

"Looks like a ship," I said. "But what's it doing at sea in a storm? All ships are in a safe harbor now, and certainly sailboats are."

We were out of the channel and in the open sea. The ship was coming across our path. Its black hull gleamed wetly, and the sharp bow sliced through the waves. It was a large, three-masted clipper. It showed a Dutch flag. Not all its sails were up—and what madman would raise any sails in a storm like that!

Soon the ship took in almost all the sails and, slowing down stood to our windward side. The deck was clear of People. Then a MARS* showed up. Leaning over the rail, it lowered a Jacob's ladder and shouted to us:

---

* **MARS** Marine Aggregate of the Regular Service. An uncomplicated, but well-constructed, 22nd-century aggregate.

"Heave this way, Accident Victims!"

Sheltered from the wind by the ship's bulk, we brought the cutter over to the side and clambered up the ladder to the deck. I took my briefcase. As I scrambled up, I held it in my teeth so that my hands would be free.

"Where's the CAPTAIN?" Andrei asked the MARS. "I must see the CAPTAIN!"

"The CAPTAIN is stationary," the MARS replied. "I can take you to it. Come with me."

Barely keeping our balance, we followed the mechanism. It walked smoothly, as though there were no storm; its heavy legs with the rubber suction cups for feet strode quietly over the wet deck.

"The CAPTAIN is in here," the MARS said, Bringing us to the pilot house and pushing on the doorbell. "The CAP-TAIN is waiting for you. Go in."

We entered a room with flickering equipment, black and blue arrows moving across yellow squares on the wall.

"Turn your faces to me!" the CAPTAIN* said.

We turned to the large black shield with the lens eye. The voice was coming from there.

"I see you. You are People. I'm reporting on the situation. I'm carrying freight from Amsterdam to Vyborg. I'm in a storm. I want to wait it out at sea. I'm afraid of getting close to shore and crashing. I saw you on radar. I went off course to aid you. Do you have any wishes?"

"Help us!" Andrei said and began explaining to the CAP-TAIN what he wanted.

"I heard you. I understand everything. A difficult situa-tion," the CAPTAIN said. "Wait for a decision in one minute seventeen seconds."

There was a silence. I suddenly heard my heart beating, and until that time I had thought that only invented heroes in bad novels heard their own hearts. A mysterious life went on

---

* A reminder for the Reader: **CAPTAIN** (Cybernetic Antiaccident Pilot Tops in Actual Inwater Navigation). An ancient aggregate, quite complex for its time.

around me. Lights went on and off on the consoles, equipment hummed. A thin metal hand came out of the wall, turned a black cylinder, and a white cardboard card fell out. The card was immediately sucked up by an opening in the same wall, and numbers and signs lit up above the opening. Everything was moving, but moving almost noiselessly, as in a dream.

"I've decided," the CAPTAIN's voice said. "I'm changing course to the one you told me. The probability of danger is fifty-seven point three percent. Spare me fear. Turn off the caution relay."

Suddenly all the lights in the pilot house went out, and a glass on the wall to our right lit up with the sign. "Caution relay. Break glass and turn knob to red line."

Andrei ran to the glass, broke it, and turned off the CAPTAIN's fear effect. All the other equipment lit up again.

"Go up to the forecastle for visual observation," the CAPTAIN said. "Hold tight to the handrails."

"Will you find it, will you notice the isle?" Andrei asked.

"I see farther than you do," the CAPTAIN replied. "I see everything, hear everything, understand everything."

Accompanied by the MARS, Andrei and I went to the forecastle. In the meantime, tubular telescopic constructions came out of openings in the deck and snakelike, twisted outgrowths moved out of them and stretched to the yards. The clipper opened sail, changed course, and sailed before the wind. Its bow burrowed deep into the waves, and we were covered with spray. The hull and rigging vibrated from tension. Andrei looked forward, never taking his eyes from the sea. Drops of blood fell from his right hand onto the wet deck; he had injured his hands breaking open the glass.

We should put some disinfectant on the wound, I thought and turned to the MARS next to us.

"Where's your medicine chest? Do you have drugs?"

"The freight you mention is not on board," the MARS replied. And I realized how incongruous my question had been. On a ship with no Humans there would be no medicine. I took a handkerchief out of the pocket of my soaked jacket and bandaged Andrei's hand as best I could. But I don't think he even noticed my minor medical aid.

Some time passed, and in the distance we saw the outlines of Isle Seven. It was coming closer. Actually, it was nothing more than a piece of cliff sticking out of the sea. The BIRDs were circling it. There were planes from the Second Baltic Squadron ARP, and Finnish BIRDs with blue wings, and Swedish ones with heraldic lions on the sides. But when we got closer to the isle, the planes were gone, returned to their bases. Only two BIRDs of the Second Baltic bobbed in the waves near the shore.

A building of some sort, apparently knocked down by the wind, lay across the island. It must have been a tower or derrick. Someone was lying near the fallen derrick, and someone else was kneeling next to the body. Farther away, at the water's edge, stood a Man in the Pilot's uniform.

The clipper pulled in its sails and dropped anchor. The MARS lowered a dinghy, and Andrei and I got in it and, fighting the waves, reached the island. The Pilot helped us land.

"What happened to her?" Andrei asked.

The Pilot said nothing in reply, just looked over at the man in the Airborne Doctor's uniform kneeling over someone. We ran over.

"Is she alive?" Andrei asked in a choked voice. "Why aren't you giving her artifical respiration?"

"She didn't drown. She was struck by this ledge on the derrick. Look." The Doctor pulled back the hair from Nina's temple. The wound was very small. There was almost no blood.

"It was instantaneous. An easy death," the Doctor said consolingly, and in order to make things perfectly clear, he placed the QUACK on her forehead.

"Zero illness units," the apparatus said. "Zero pain units. Cause of death on Haritonov and Barmey scale: 5-beta prime 2.3 with total incontrovertibility. Death occurred twenty-eight

minutes two seconds ago. Death occured twenty-eight minutes three seconds ago. Death occurred twenty-eight minutes
four seconds ago. Death—"

"That's enough," I said, touching the Doctor's shoulder,
"It's clear enough. . . ."

The Doctor and I walked away and stood near the Pilot, by
the water's edge. The storm was abating, the wind was dying
down. The ship awaited us patiently. And suddenly its siren
went off, anxious and pathetic. I saw that the flag on its main
mast was being lowered; it remained at half-mast in sign of
mourning.

I recalled the CAPTAIN's words: "I see everything, I hear
everything, I understand everything."

Two days later I came to the House of Farewells, to a large
room with marble walls. The funeral rites were simple; long
orations had been dropped many years ago. After a brief farewell, the coffin was taken through the glass passageway to the
White Tower's elevator, and it went up.

The immediate family and friends, including me, went up
to the open observation platform on the Tower, placed the sad
package on the flat bier made of dark metal, and set down the
flowers. Then we went down to the courtyard paved with
white stones. We heard sad music, and a light cloud of ashes
floated up over the White Tower and quietly settled at its
base, where red and white irises bloom.

It was over.

Several AUGURs * offered to join the relatives and friends,
but we sent them away. These aggregates were irritating in
moments of great sorrow. I hold many things against the
young generation—its obnoxiousness and lack of respect for
elders—but I can't help but approve of its rejection of several
unneeded aggregates, created in an era of excessive zeal for
technological novelties.

* **AUGUR**   Aggregate Uttering Gloomy Unctuous Regrets. Was deemed unnecessary and removed from production in Kovrigin's time.

Andrei left the House of Farewells silently, with lowered head. I caught up with him and asked if there was anything I could do.

"No," he replied. "There's nothing that can help me. I sent her to her death."

"Don't say that, Andrei!" I exclaimed. "It's not your fault."

"I sent her to her death," he repeated. "It's my fault."

He hurried off, and I went over to Nina's mother to express my sympathy.

"This wouldn't have happened if she had married you," her mother said through tears. "She would have lived out her MILS in peace with you."

In the bottom of my heart, I had to agree.

The Final Victory **22**

A day later I contacted Andrei by thought transmission and was rather surprised to see that he was back on the island with my name, at his Main Laboratory. I would have thought that his sorrow would have caused him to interrupt his work for at least a short time.

"What are you busy with?" I asked.

"Today we will be testing NEPTUNA, the tests that were postponed. . . . Come, if you like. It begins at two."

"All right, I'll come," I replied. "Thought transmission over and out."

Arriving at the island with my name, I headed for the Experimental Fields, now familiar to me, and to you, my Reader, and encountered a large crowd looking at NEPTUNA. But this time the crowd was silent. They all knew of the tragedy that had befallen Andrei.

Before the start of the experiment, Andrei seated me between himself and a Lab Assistant in the seat by the control console, and pushed a button. The monster silently moved forward, dragging us on its tail.

Soon I realized that NEPTUNA was going down into the ground. It was going at a small angle, and at first the angle was almost imperceptible. We seemed to be in a ravine, and then the aggregate dragged us into an underground tunnel it had dug. Lights went on on the aggregate, and I saw the round walls of the tunnel. They seemed to be lined with a caked mass that resembled ceramic. They gave off warmth.

Suddenly the steady hum emitted by NEPTUNA turned into a strained roar. The aggregate shuddered, as though it had encountered a difficult obstacle.

"NEPTUNA is entering the water," the Lab Assistant said.

Soon a murky light flickered. The tunnel walls became transparent. Through them we saw water plants. Schools of fish swam overhead. We moved slowly but inexorably over the floor of the bay, separated from the water by a thin layer of transparent aqualide, which NEPTUNA was manufacturing from the water itself. The sensation, I must add, was strange and rather scary.

"Will this tunnel resist the pressure of the water?" I asked the Assistant.

"It can withstand any pressure. It can be laid along the bottom of the Marianas Trench, and nothing would happen to it," he replied.

It was getting darker in the tunnel; we were headed for deeper water. Andrei pushed another button, and NEPTUNA turned slowly to the right, describing a wide semicircle. It got lighter again, and the plants were visible once more. Soon we were back on the Experimental Field, but at its other end. Behind NEPTUNA, which had dragged us out on its tail into daylight, People came out of the tunnel. It turned out that a whole crowd had followed us, making an underground, underwater excursion.

"Well, that's all," Andrei said, leaving the control console.

"What's all?" I asked.

"Everything."

I didn't question him about what "everything" meant. He was surrounded by Scientists, Cosmonauts, and Journalists, and I went off to one side so as not to get in the way of technical discussions. However, Andrei's words seemed significant to me, and I decided not to let him out of my sight. When the crowd of scientific luminaries around Andrei had thinned out, I went over and told him that I would walk home with him, and he agreed gladly.

"Would you like to have my stamp album?" he asked. "I've been going through my things today."

"I don't need your album," I replied. "But if you like, I'll take it for safekeeping. One day you'll be interested in stamps again, and then I'll return it."

We went in the house. It was so empty and lonely now.

"You should move away from here," I told my friend.

Just then we heard someone open the front door without knocking and come in the foyer. Andrei looked up. I thought I saw the reflection of a mad hope in his eyes.

But an aggregate walked it. It was an EROS, it had flown in for orders. Wings folded, it stood in the vestibule and waited.

"From this day on, you go to the Chief Lab Assistant or EDPO," Andrei said. "I don't work here anymore."

"I understand," the EROS said and left, quietly shutting the door.

"I wholeheartedly approve of your decision to leave here," I said. "But are you planning to give up your work completely?"

"My work is finished. Now everything can go on without me."

"Where are you planning to move to?" I asked.

"I'm going to live in the hut. Do you remember that hut, in the forest, by the lake?"

"Of course I do. But I doubt you'll last there for long. It has no conveniences."

Andrei said nothing to that, and I didn't try to change his mind. I knew how stubborn he was. *It's all right,* I thought, *he'll live in the woods for a while, peace and quiet, he'll weep and come to terms with it there.* Of course, I was worried that he was not only grieving for Nina but blamed himself for her death. But time would heal all, I thought.

I came home, put the album in my desk, and told Nadya about my visit to Matvei Island and my conversation with Andrei. Nadya took it more tragically than I had. Holding the stamp album and leafing through it, she suddenly started to cry.

"This is not good, it's not. You'll lose your friend soon."

Unfortunately, she was right.

Andrei soon left the city and moved to the lake. The press announced it briefly, tactfully avoiding excessive detail. The papers were full of praise for Andrei Svetochev, the creator of aqualide. The praise increased after the demonstration of NEPTUNA. For one thing, they reported that the Commission on Life Extension offered Andrei an extra three MILS (just think: 330 years!) and the Naming Commission wanted to name a new city after him. They wrote about projected monuments to Svetochev, medals in his honor. . . . And suddenly the famous Svetochev Letter appeared in print. Even though I'm certain that my readers know the letter by heart, I will quote it for full effect and so as not to disturb the construction of my tale.

Because of reasons known to myself, I do not feel I have the right to live beyond my MILS and I refuse to have my life extended. Besides that, I ask that no monuments be erected to me in my lifetime or after my death. I request that my name not be given to cities, streets, industrial enterprises, ships, or space vehicles. I ask that my name not be mentioned in the press unless there is great need to do so.

With deep respect,
Andrei Svetochev

This letter of Andrei's stunned me. I knew that he was capable of the most bizarre and unexpected behavior, but I certainly hadn't expected anything like this. To refuse three MILS! To refuse 330 years of extra life on Earth!

I couldn't understand, and still don't, his categorical rejection of memorials, of everything that Society wanted to bestow upon him, with good reason. And I still can't comprehend why he took that voluntary exile, why he moved to that old hut on the shore of the lake. I do know that he was grieving deeply. But all sorrow passes . . . .

Joy and Sorrow   23

In the meantime, a joyful event took place in my life. I became a father. I took Nadya to the Maternity House on the corner of the Fourteenth Line and Bolshoi Prospect, and I couldn't sleep the entire night. At dawn there was a knock at the door. I guessed that it was a mechanism of some sort; People entered apartments without knocking.

"Come in!" I called from the room and listened to the Mechanism's approaching footsteps anxiously. The recent sad events had affected me so, I expected almost anything. "What if it's a BAST?" * I thought, horrified.

But a BONUS came in, and my heart leapt. The aggregate bore a bouquet of bluebells. That meant I had a son.

"If I'm not mistaken, you are the famous Literary Historian Matvei Kovrigin?" the aggregate asked in a loud hearty voice.

"Yes, I am the one you seek," I replied. "Sit down."

"It's all right, I'll stand," my kind guest replied with major chords resounding in its voice. "I'm pleased to congratulate you on the birth of a son."

Then it informed me that Nadya was well, gave me the

* **BAST**   Bearer of All Sad Tidings. An ancient mechanism of the 22nd century. Long taken out of production.

child's statistics and the hour of birth, and bowed off. I hurried off to the Maternity House to write a note of congratulation to Nadya.

I wanted to reach Andrei by thought transmission and tell him that I was a father. But then I thought that perhaps this wasn't the time for such news, since my happiness would only deepen his sorrow. So I decided to put off my transmission for a bit.

I sent a transmission in September. Andrei responded immediately.

"I want to come visit you," I said.

"Come any time," Andrei replied. "Is that all?"

"That's all. Thought transmission over and out."

I flew to the preserve that very day. I disembarked from the plane at the same spot where the three of us had landed a little over a year ago. I told the ERP to fly back, and stepped onto the familiar territory. Just think how much had changed since then! We strode along here, a trio. . . .

The weather was different too. Now it was drizzling, and the forest was draped in a fog. My path was strewn with fallen leaves.

Here was the Ranger's house. He spotted me out the window, and the Old Widrinkson came out on the porch and invited me inside. The old man still looked hale—an eagle, not a wet hen, as our ancestors used to say. But, alas, he smelled of home brew again.

"Well, pal, what ill wind blows you here?" he asked, seating me on the old couch near the table with the ancient electrosamovar. "Probably decided to visit your pal? He's not well, your pal. I feel sorry for him. He's doomed."

"Is he sick?" I asked.

"That would be good, if he were sick. He's well. But he's depressed. He won't live long."

"Sadness at the loss of a loved one is natural to all Humans," I countered sensibly. "But People don't die from it."

"Some don't, and some do. Don't use yourself as a yardstick for everyone, you fuddy-duddy."

These words didn't seem completely tactful to me, but I didn't say anything, since he was much older than I and also "under the influence," as they used to say.

"Well, I'll go see Andrei," I said.

"You're a quick bunny, aren't you," the Ranger smiled. "How about something for the road? Look how wet it is, a good master wouldn't send a dog out in weather like this. How can I send you out without fortification! Hey, old woman, bring us three glasses here."

The wife of the Old Widrinkson came in and set three large glasses and a plate with snacks on the table. I greeted her and waited for further instruction.

"Well, let's have a shot, shall we!" the Ranger said, handing me a glass. "Let's drink to my double diamond wedding anniversary. In four months it will be a hundred and fifty years that the old woman and I are together."

I thought that while the occasion was worthy, it was a bit early to start celebrating, four months ahead of time. But his wife added her request to his and, out of deference for the lady, I drank this cup, as they used to say. Munching on a pickle, I bade farewell to the honored spouses and headed toward Andrei's hut.

My ears were buzzing, my head spun lightly, but I didn't feel that devil-may-care lightheadedness that I did the last time I drank. Now I was sad and depressed. Memories of the recent past came to me. Here, by the Old Widrinkson's house, Nina sat on a bench, and the fawn had rubbed its muzzle on her knees and she petted its back . . . And here on the forest path, the three of us walked, and the sun shone for us.

Soon, from the hill I saw the familiar lake, and the river that fell into it, and the memorable bridge without railings. I carefully crossed to the other side of the slippery logs and went to the hut. Fifty feet from the hut, I came across a sign of solitude. It was nailed to a branch of a dry alder. But it didn't apply to me: Andrei had said that he would be happy to see me.

Entering the hut, I saw that Andrei wasn't in. I looked around. The room looked lived in. There was firewood by the stove, the bed was made, books stood on the shelves. I was amazed by the deliberate starkness of the surroundings: not a single aggregate, not a single household aid! Except, on the wall opposite the simple wooden table hung an electronic meteorological map—much like the one, and perhaps the very one, that I had seen on the island with my name in Andrei's study. I started looking at the constantly changing map. A gray spot floated out from the northwest; that meant that the rain would continue for a minimum of two hours. *Why did Andrei hang that map here?* I thought. *It must remind him of that day every day and every minute.*

Suddenly I shuddered at a strange snorting noise. It turned out that it was a hedgehog that had crawled out of some hole and was headed for the stove where there was a plate with food. It ate, showing no fear of me; Andrei had trained it.

I felt even sadder. This forest animal only underlined the solitude in which Andrei now lived.

My sad thoughts were dispersed by Andrei's arrival. He was wearing swamp boots and a raincoat; he had been walking in the woods. He was sincerely happy to see me, and when I told him that I had a son and that Nadya and I decided to name him Andrei—Andrei Nadezhdovich—my friend's face became animated, and he looked like his old self. Alas, this animation was short-lived. Our conversation continued, but I could not help noticing that it interested my friend less and less. He had returned to his sad thoughts, and I sensed that he went on talking only to spare my feelings.

"Andrei," I said. "Why is that map on your wall? Do you want me to take it back to the city?"

"There was a day when I should have looked at it, and I didn't. Now let it be forever before my eyes."

I said nothing: I understood that it was hopeless to change his mind. Soon I said good-bye to Andrei, wishing him health and a speedy return to Leningrad.

Days and months passed, and Andrei still had not returned to the city. I sent him thoughtgrams once in a while. He replied, but his replies were monosyllabic. Summer was upon us. It was almost the anniversary of Nina's death.

A few days before the sad day, I called Andrei by thought transmission. When I asked him how he felt, he said: "Bad." He had never complained of anything before, and I was quite worried by his reply.

"Are you sick?" I asked.

"No, I'm healthy," he replied.

"Would you like me to come visit you?"

"No, don't. I'll fly into town soon and come to see you. Is that all?"

"That's all. Thought transmission over and out."

I guessed that Andrei wanted to stand at the base of the White Tower on that occasion, as was the custom.

But the day came and Andrei didn't come to Leningrad. That evening I decided to find out what was wrong, why he had changed his mind—it was so unlike him. I sent a thought signal, but there was no answer. The living always reply to a call . . .

Later the Old Widrinkson, who often had visited my friend in his solitude, told me that on that July day, when he went into the hut, he saw Andrei lying motionless on the floor. The Ranger immediately called a Doctor on his Personal Apparatus. The Doctor certified the cause of death as an acute incident of heart disease. The Old Widrinkson had his own medical diagnosis of the event: "Love is no potato. He grieved and strained his heart. If he had started drinking maybe he wouldn't have died. The sorrow would have been dissipated." For some reason, People like to quote these words in biographies of Svetochev, finding some deep hidden meaning in the words of the kind but poorly educated and often inebriated Widrinkson.

When the news of the death of Andrei Svetochev was made public, a three-day period of mourning was observed by the entire Planet. At the moment when his ashes fell on the flowers at the base of the White Tower, the sirens of Cosmic Danger wailed across the Earth. I remember that thin, vibrating howl that made my blood turn to ice. Those sirens had never been used before that day. They were turned on then as a sign that the loss suffered by Mankind was immense and had cosmic significance.

Epilogue **24**

Dear Reader!

More than eighty years have passed since the events described in my narrative. The world has changed before my eyes. It is even more unlike the pre-aqualide world I described in my tale. The world has entered the era of the Single Raw Material, the era of the aqualide civilization, which was founded by my friend Andrei Svetochev. Mankind has completely mastered the expanses of its Planet and has bravely moved on into the Cosmos. But it was not my aim to compare the past with the present. After all, you know about the past from history and you see the present with your young eyes, which are sharper than mine. For I am old now, I've lived my MILS and then some, and the day is not far off when my ashes will fall from the top of the White Tower onto the flowers growing at its base.

Before finishing my Notes and placing the final period, I'd like to say a few words about myself.

My life was not fruitless. After the Anthology, I published quite a few books. I won't list them here, for every cultured Person, and particularly Persons interested in the twentieth century, must know them.

My wife Nadya has grown old but, like myself, is in good health. Her phenomenal memory remains and has been of great help in these Notes. Nadya and I have sons, daughters, grandchildren, and great-grandchildren. Almost all of them, continuing family tradition, have become People of the Humanities, and one of my grandsons, Valentin, has followed directly in my footsteps and has chosen the field of Literary History. The major work, *Love in the Novels of the Twenty-First Century in View of Contemporary Morality*, belongs to his pen. Unfortunately, this book was not appreciated and evinced attacks from several hostile critics. They accused my grandson of making a tendentious selection of quotations, of being one-sided, of having a superficial view of literary history, and even of "hereditary narrow-mindedness." Yesterday's youth is not shy with words. But I am calm about Valentin's future; I believe in him and am proud of him.

One of my great-grandchildren worries me. Breaking with family tradition, he became a Physicist and, to make things worse, has joined the group around Belosvetov, a young theoretician who is getting too much attention in today's press. This Belosvetov with his neophytes is developing a so-called Theory of the Great Vacuum, which astounds every right-thinking Person with its impossibility. I won't relate it to you in detail, for unfortunately you all know it—the press has been buzzing about it constantly. I'll be brief as to what I think it's about. This Belosvetov maintains that if an absolute ("Great") vacuum is created in a vessel of absolutely durable material (that is, aqualide) and then something is done to that vacuum, the result will be a Something. This Something, according to the whims of the Experimenter, can be turned either into a universal material or into energy. This is the Herculean level of silliness that some hotheads achieve! Our world stands on aqualide, but that's not enough for them, they want Nothing transformed into Something!

Forgive me, indulgent Reader, for this lyric and scientific digression. But I feel embittered for my friend Andrei, the creator of aqualide, when I hear talk about the "Great Vacuum." And from whom? My own great-grandson! I've told him more than once that he's a fool to believe that Belosvetov, that do what you will, nothing will appear in an empty vessel.

But speaking of vessels and contents, I will throw false modesty to the winds and remind my indulgent Reader of my DOWUBA, which is not empty and continues to fill up. Of course, I add to it more and more slowly, for there are no People left on Earth who remember swear words. The Old Widrinkson, from whom I plucked quite a few strong words and good curses for my dictionary, is now, alas, silent for the ages. Despite his use of strong drink, he lived two MILS plus and died not from disease but as a result of an accident. Flying to a conference of Rangers while intoxicated, he tried to get the ERP drunk, forgetting that it was an aggregate and not a Person. The ERP lost control and crashed. Now the Ranger at the Preserve is the Old Widrinkson's son. He is a Teetotaller. But on the other hand, he does not possess the folkloric wealth that his father could have been proud of.

From time to time I visit the preserve and go to the lake where Andrei's hut stands. It looks just as it did when my friend was alive, both inside and out, but it is all made of aqualide, the exterior and the furnishings. Wood, stone, and metal deteriorate, but aqualide is permanent. On the shore of the lake, by the cliff, there is a statue of Nina. The statue is beautiful. It was done by the best Sculptor on the Planet. Depictions of Nina are everywhere, in every city, in every park. As you know, Andrei requested that no memorials be raised to him, and this request is religiously observed. But in erecting statues to Nina, People obliquely honor the memory of Andrei as well. Sculptors wishing to depict Nina often come to me for advice. But despite the consultation, they all depict her in their own way and usually make her prettier than she was in life.

Not so long ago, I was invited to one of the new underwater cities, named Niniapolis. I liked the city. Everything in it is made of aqualide, and it is separated from the ocean by a translucent pink aqualide dome. And I traveled to the city by transparent aqualide tunnel, laid on the ocean floor.

Aqualide is so much a part of life that many can't even imagine how Mankind existed without it. Once, one of my great-grandchildren, the youngest, ran up to me and asked:

"Grandpa, is it true that you lived back when they made things out of all different things? Houses from one thing, cars from another, ships from another, furniture from another, books from another?"

"Yes, it's true," I replied, "and my first book was printed not on aqualide plates, but on paper."

"What's paper?" my great-grandson asked.

I took a copy of the Anthology from the cupboard and showed it to him. It was the inscribed copy that I never did get to give to its intended recipients. The time spent in the water had obliterated the writing on its title page, but the words "To Nina and Andrei" were still visible. I felt sad.

"What are you thinking about, Grandpa?" my great-grandson asked.

"I was remembering my youth," I said.

"Then tell me what it was like when you were young," he asked.

"That would take a long time to tell," I replied. "And then you wouldn't understand a lot of it, and you wouldn't believe a lot of it."

"Then write a story about it," he suggested.

"I'll think about it," I said. "Perhaps I will write about it. But I won't write a story, I'll write the truth. But the truth will be like a story."